Becoming Lola

By Harriet Steel

Published in 2010 by YouWriteOn Publishing

Copyright © Harriet Steel

First Edition

British Library C.I.P.

A CIP catalogue record for this title is
available from the British Library.

Author's Note and Acknowledgments

The events and characters described in this novel are broadly based on historical facts, the primary exceptions being the scenes in Spain, since apart from Lola's almost certainly false claim that she was a principal dancer at Seville's Teatro Real, there are no records of her time there.

In the nineteenth century, hundreds of books and plays were written about her extraordinary career. The few still available are entertaining but not entirely reliable. There were many apocryphal stories in circulation when they were written and Lola allowed herself considerable dramatic licence in her autobiography.

Little work was done on her life in the twentieth century and she was almost forgotten until the American author, Bruce Seymour, published his excellent biography. (*Lola Montez: A Life. Yale University Press, 1996).* This has been invaluable to me in the writing of my novel. He has also most generously allowed me access to his research. Any errors or misinterpretations of fact are my own.

My gratitude goes to my family, friends and fellow writers at YWO for their constructive criticism and encouragement. Above all, my heartfelt thanks are due to Roger, for his patient advice and support. Without it, I know that this book would never have been finished.

3

Prologue

New York
1851

The dressing room was the grandest that the Broadway Theatre had to offer, lit by an eight-branched, crystal chandelier and expensively furnished.

A screen painted with nymphs and shepherds frolicking in an Elysian landscape groaned under a cascade of taffeta and silk dresses. Hats, petticoats, stockings, necklaces, fans and satin dance shoes overflowed from monogrammed trunks. Lavish arrangements of roses and lilies perfumed the air.

At the creak of footsteps in the corridor, Lola left off studying her appearance in the dressing table's gilt-framed mirror. There was a knock at the door.

'On in five minutes,' she heard the manager, Thomas Barry, call out.

She turned back to the mirror and picked up a squirrel brush to apply a little more colour to her cheeks before she answered. 'I'm ready now. You may come in.'

As she stood up, a swirl of black lace and crimson taffeta flashed across the mirror, fragmenting her reflection. The door opened and Barry stepped into the room. He wore evening dress, the black jacket snug across his broad shoulders. A gold and ruby stick pin sparkled against the starched white of his wing-collared shirt.

'You look very fine, Lola,' he smiled, offering her his arm. 'I hope you're ready for this?'

'Why do you doubt it?'

'Three thousand people out there to see you? Some performers might find that daunting.'

She laughed. 'Not me.'

Outside in the corridor, the air hummed with activity. A gaggle of chorus girls, dressed in Tyrolean skirts and white peasant blouses, chattered and giggled, then fell silent as Lola and Barry approached, squeezing up against the wall to let them pass. Lola's nose wrinkled at the stench of the greasepaint that caked their glowing faces.

Further along, a juggler in cream breeches and an emerald jacket set off by a billowing primrose cravat deftly caught his clubs in one hand when he saw her. She nodded to acknowledge his low bow.

Her fingertips tapped a rhythm on Barry's sleeve as they passed another dressing room and heard a rich baritone voice sing a catchy popular song. A moment later, with whispered words of good luck, Barry left her alone in the wings.

The Master of Ceremonies was onstage, reeling off his patter. A stout man in a scarlet cutaway coat, the glare of the footlights bounced off his top hat and polished boots.

The blood raced through her veins and her heart thudded. In the dimmed gaslight, a sea of opera hats filled the auditorium. She recognised some of the critics in the front row. Gripping the edge of the stage curtain, she wished it was their throats.

'Damn them all,' she muttered. 'Insects not fit to be crushed under my heel.'

6

Her chin jutted. She didn't care about their opinions anyway. She could work her magic on any audience she chose to; particularly when, as tonight, it was a 'black house' with no women present. She smiled. It was rarely difficult to make men love her.

To uproarious laughter, the M C delivered his final punch line and then paused for the noise to die away before he spoke again.

'And now the bright star you've all been waiting for. As a bonus, after she's delighted us with a performance of her famous *Spider Dance*, she has graciously agreed to answer any questions you care to put to her,' he winked and tweaked his handlebar moustache, 'provided they won't set my delicate ears on fire.'

A ripple of anticipation spread through the audience.

'Gentlemen, pray silence. Without any more ado, I give you the one, the only, Lola Montez!'

Part One

1823 - 1843

Eliza

Chapter 1

The Ganges
Two days upstream from Calcutta.

A scream split the fetid air of the cabin.

Eliza woke and sat up.

In the watery dawn light filtering through the porthole, she saw the ayah, her Indian nurse, crouched in one corner, her eyes wide with terror. Sweat beaded her forehead and smudged the scarlet bindi mark between her brows. She screamed again and pointed with a trembling hand to the end of the bed. Eliza just had time to glimpse the scaly, grey-brown shape coiled there before her father burst in, his nightshirt flapping around his bare legs and his service revolver in his hand.

The hooded snake reared. With a swift blow to the back of its head from the butt of the revolver, Edward Gilbert knocked it to the floor. It writhed on the bare planks, hissing and flicking its forked tongue. Before it could attack again, he pointed the gun at its head and fired.

The stench of cordite filled the cabin as he dropped the revolver and went to Eliza. She clung to him, burying her face in his shoulder.

'It's all right, my darling,' he soothed. 'You're safe.'

After a few moments, she peeked out, wiping away her tears with the back of her hand.

'What is it, Papa?'

'A snake. It's dead now. Do you want to see it?'

Taking his hand, she scrambled off the bed and looked down at the snake's remains.

Edward turned to the ayah. 'No need to be afraid. Fetch some water and cloths to clear up this mess.'

A moment after the ayah had left, a young woman hurried into the cabin. She wore a loose, sea-green silk wrap over her nightgown and a lace-trimmed nightcap that hid the curling papers in her auburn hair.

'What on earth is happening?' she asked then stopped, seeing the pool of scales and slime on the floor. Her pretty face blanched and she put her hand to her mouth. 'Oh,' she gasped, 'how revolting.'

'A cobra,' Edward said. 'A young one, I think. It must have come on board hidden in one of those crates of mangoes we took on yesterday evening. Thank God Eliza is unharmed.'

He stroked her dark hair. 'She was a very brave girl.'

Her fright forgotten, Eliza beamed. He picked her up and put her back into bed where she snuggled against him, one hand gripping the linen collar of his nightshirt.

'Want a story, Papa,' she demanded.

Her mother raised an eyebrow. 'She seems none the worse for her ordeal. Don't overexcite her, Edward. She won't settle again.'

'I'll stay with her until ayah comes back. You go to bed if you want, Elizabeth.'

Elizabeth hesitated. 'Do you suppose there are any more snakes?'

He shook his head. 'I doubt very much that there will be, but I'll check the room just in case.'

'Very well, I think I shall go then. This dreadful heat exhausts me. I hope it will be cooler when we reach Dinapore.'

'I doubt it, I'm afraid.'

She scowled. 'I wish we could have stayed in Calcutta. It would have been a far better posting. I still don't know why you accepted this one.'

Edward sighed. 'Please my love; let's not argue about it again. You know perfectly well that I had no choice. I have to follow the regiment. Now go and get some sleep.'

She sniffed and bent gingerly over Eliza to pat her shoulder.

'Goodnight, child.'

'Goodnight, Mama.'

The next morning, Elizabeth Gilbert rested in her cabin. After the ayah's fright, Edward allowed her time to herself and took charge of Eliza. She chattered away gaily as they went up on deck after breakfast and found a quiet spot shaded by a small awning.

They had left behind the flat, fertile land of the delta. Now lush trees crowded up to the banks of the river. As the day went on and the sun grew hotter, Eliza and Edward sat and watched the scenery pass by. Sometimes he read aloud to her. The small library he had packed included a few children's stories as well as the works of Alexander Pope, ten volumes of *New British Theatre*, *Essays on Physiognomy* and a popular French Grammar. Eliza understood very little of what she heard, but she loved having her father to herself.

When she was bored of books, they played a guessing game and later, he brought out his box of watercolours and pencils and helped her to make drawings of the landscape. Eliza beamed when he praised her efforts, until eventually she tired of that game also.

'Papa?' she asked as, late in the afternoon, he tidied everything away.

'Yes, my love?'

'What are t – t - tigers?'

'Do you remember the old tabby cat that caught mice on the ship from England?'

'Horatio?'

'Yes. A tiger is another kind of cat: much, much bigger with orange and black stripes.'

'Don't like tigers. Ayah says they eat you.'

She pointed at a white cross on the riverbank. Edward remembered hearing that these crosses marked the places where tigers had killed unwary travellers. The native crew refused to go on shore anywhere near them.

He looked down at Eliza's anxious face and frowned.

'Ayah should not be frightening you with her stories. You must take no notice.' He patted her shoulder. 'I shall always keep you safe, I promise.'

Happy again, she settled in the crook of his arm.

'I'm not afraid.'

Edward laughed and rumpled her hair. 'Good girl.'

A flock of egrets, disturbed by their approach, rose from the water and wheeled away. Landing further off like a scattering of confetti, they began to feed again.

Eliza clapped her hands. 'Pretty.'

Her father smiled. 'Like you, Eliza.'

He picked up the ebony flute with silver fittings that he had brought with him.

'Shall we have some music?'

She nodded and snuggled against him.

The tune he played was an old Irish ballad that he remembered hearing in the taverns in County Cork, on the tour of duty when he had first met Elizabeth.

When the last notes drifted away on the river's smooth, brown swell, he laid the flute in his lap. What a pair we were, he thought: me with no money to my name except my army pay and she the by-blow of a Protestant grandee. Still, we have something good to show for it. He smiled down at Eliza and saw that her eyelids drooped. He put an arm around her shoulders and let her doze.

As twilight approached, the sun changed from gold to orange. It seemed to swell and shimmer, sweeping great waves of apricot and lavender light across the sky. Edward shook Eliza gently and she stirred. They watched together as the colours deepened and then faded to indigo. Clouds of mosquitoes danced on the dark surface of the river.

'We'll go below now and find you some supper,' Edward said. 'Then it's time for bed.'

Picking her up in his arms, he carried her down the wooden stairs to the cabins. Behind them, the encroaching night ate up the banks of the river and the jungle that lurked beyond.

The boats idled up the river, covering only a few miles each day. Sometimes the main channel was three miles wide and it was impossible to see across it. On other days, the boats had to ease through narrow tributaries where the banks were so close that the tree roots standing proud of them scraped the hulls.

In spite of the heat, Eliza was entranced. She watched for half-submerged logs that might turn out to be crocodiles cooling themselves in the brackish shallows. She saw howling monkeys leap through the tree canopy and iridescent birds dart along the banks. Once, a spotted deer drinking from the river raised its dripping muzzle to eye the boats as they chugged by.

The landscape changed once again, this time opening out to vast plains where crops of wheat, rice and sugar cane flourished in the rich alluvial soil. Huts made of mud and palm fronds dotted the fields. She saw women in jewel-coloured saris working among the crops or swaying along dusty tracks, huge bowls or baskets full of produce balanced on their heads.

After many days, they came to Patna. 'It is a very ancient city,' Edward said to Eliza, 'and important too.'

She looked curiously at the crumbling buildings and the mass of hovels, some of them made of nothing but grimy cloth propped up with a few stout branches to make a roof. How could this place be important?

But the crowds along the banks fascinated her. When the boat came level with a half-ruined temple, she stood between her father and mother with her chin pressed against the boat's rail and watched the crowds jostling to throw garlands of marigolds onto the water. A little higher up on the riverbank, a large group of men with shaven heads and dressed in saffron robes chanted words she could not understand. Beyond them, plumes of black smoke snaked up into the sky from a multitude of fires.

A gaggle of small boys dived into the churning water and swam towards the boats. The leader reached the rail where the Gilberts stood and hauled his body up, shaking like a wet dog. A flurry of droplets flew from his gleaming, black head. Eyes wide with curiosity, he looked up at Edward's fair hair and moustache.

Edward laughed. 'It seems that I am rather a novelty.'

He fished in his pocket, then put his hand through the rail and dropped a small coin into the boy's outstretched hand.

The boy grinned and put the coin between his white teeth. With one hand, he stayed clinging to the boat and with the other, scooped up a handful of water and poured it gently over Edward's palm. As his blue eyes met the boy's brown ones, Edward felt that some kind of blessing had been bestowed on him.

Elizabeth gave a snort of anger. 'You are too soft hearted,' she hissed. 'They won't leave us alone now, and that water is filthy: the whole river is no better than a latrine.'

The rest of the band of swimmers caught up with the boy, clamouring for more money, but as they grinned and pleaded, the boat veered away once more into mid-stream. Soon their heads were mere specks in the water. The convoy steamed on to the place where they would tie up for the night.

Eliza spent the next day with her father but on the following morning, he did not come out of his cabin. Elizabeth remained inside with him and Eliza was left to trail about the boat with her ayah.

It was a scorching day, made worse by the fact that the boats had to creep through narrow channels obstructed by floating logs and fallen trees. Often, they had to stop to allow the crew to get out and clear the way. The ayah had begged a dish of sticky, brightly-coloured sweets from the cooks and with these and the stories she recounted in her imperfect English, she tried to amuse Eliza, but it was no use. Sweets and stories were no substitute for Edward's company.

'Want Papa,' she said for the hundredth time that morning. The ayah spread out her thin, brown fingers in a hopeless gesture. 'The memsahib say no come.'

Eliza scowled then jumped up. Before the ayah could catch hold of her, she ran to the stairs leading to the cabins and hurtled down them. Bursting into her parents' cabin, she saw her father lying on the bed. Her mother sat beside him, a handkerchief in one hand and a glass of water in the other. The stale smell of sickness in the room made Eliza gag.

Elizabeth blenched and turned on the ayah.

'Take the child away at once,' she spat.

Mumbling apologies, the ayah reached for Eliza but was too slow to catch her. She flung herself on the bed and buried her head in the covers. She felt her father stroke her hair, but his hand was not steady and cool as it usually was.

'Do as you are told, Eliza,' he croaked. 'I shall be well enough to play with you again soon, but you must go with ayah now.'

Eliza grasped a handful of the sheet and did not move. She had never seen her father like this. It frightened her.

Elizabeth shook her roughly by the shoulder. 'Stop being so disobedient, child,' she snapped.

Edward moistened his cracked lips with his tongue. 'Don't be angry with her, Elizabeth,' he croaked. 'Eliza, if you are good, you can help me paint a picture when I am better.'

She looked up. 'Can we paint a tiger?'

He smiled but his eyes were full of pain. 'Whatever you want.'

'When?'

'Soon, I promise.'

A spasm of coughing silenced him; a few moments passed before he recovered sufficiently to speak again. When he did, his voice was barely audible. 'Soon.'

Elizabeth mopped his forehead and straightened up. 'Ayah will look after you now, Eliza,' she said firmly. 'Say goodbye to your papa.'

When they reached Dinapore late the following afternoon, Eliza and her ayah were forgotten in the confusion of unloading the boats. Forlorn on the dusty quayside, Eliza balled her small fists and dug her knuckles into her eye sockets to keep out the sun. Pinpricks of red light danced in the darkness. The ayah hovered at her side, not daring to follow Elizabeth Gilbert and the small group of native bearers who, under the supervision of the garrison doctor, had carried Edward off in the direction of the bungalow that served as a hospital.

'Eliza?'

A voice behind them made the ayah jump. Eliza took her knuckles out of her eyes and looked around. She saw a tall, spare woman with grey hair knotted at the nape of her neck. The woman wore a high-necked dress that was little different in colour from the parched ground. A black lace parasol shaded her face.

'I am the Resident's wife. You are to come with me, child. Your mama is busy and cannot look after you just now.'

She held out her hand. Eliza stared at her without speaking.

'I hope I shall not have to tell you everything twice,' the Resident's wife snapped.

Eliza shook her head.

'Then come along.'

A palanquin carried by four Indian servants conveyed them towards the Residency. Peeking through the curtains, Eliza saw neat, straight lines of bungalows, all identical with their low roofs and wooden verandahs. As they neared the Residence, the bungalows grew larger and the Residence itself boasted an upper floor and a shallow portico flanked by stone columns.

That night, Eliza slept in a small spare room overlooking a patch of withered grass at the back of the house. Apart from a rush-seated chair and a four-poster bed made of bamboo and draped with a mosquito net, the room contained no furniture. The next day, she played with the dolls that the Resident's wife found for her. There was still no sign of her parents.

A little before four o'clock, her ayah put the dolls away. Eliza squirmed as her hair was brushed.

'Want to play,' she complained and tried to break away. She grabbed the hairbrush and threw it across the floor.

'Should look pretty to go to the drawing room,' her ayah wheedled.

'Don't want to.'

'Resident Memsahib is waiting.'

Eliza's lower lip quivered.

'Papa?'

The ayah looked troubled. 'Please, little memsahib, be good girl.'

Eliza folded her arms across her chest and pouted, but she ceased to resist as her ayah finished tidying her hair and washing her face. The woman stood back.

'Finish. We go now.'

In the drawing room, The Resident's wife sat on the best chair in a circle of other ladies. Eliza noticed that most of their dresses were dowdy in comparison with her mother's. They all looked up when she came in and the Resident's wife gave her an encouraging smile.

'Ah, here is Eliza. You may come and sit with us, child.'

Eliza crossed to the footstool that the Resident's wife indicated and sat down. Tea was brought in and the ladies talked as they sipped from bone china cups.

Eliza nibbled at the macaroon that she had been given. It was dry but sweet. None of the ladies addressed a remark to her, but she noticed how, from time to time, their eyes swivelled to observe her. She fidgeted on her stool; the best dress that her ayah had made her put on felt itchy and hot compared with the loose, cotton shifts that she was usually allowed to wear. When she had licked the last crumbs of macaroon off her fingers, she got up and went over to where the Resident's wife sat.

'Want to go now' she said in a high, clear voice.

A collective intake of breath ruffled the polite surface of the gathering and all the ladies put down their cups and stared at her. In the silence that ensued, Eliza felt the blood rush to her cheeks.

'Please,' she faltered.

The Resident's wife frowned. 'Very well, you may go child, but I do not wish to hear such rudeness again.'

The visit was not repeated and for the next two days, the ayah and Eliza remained alone. Hardly an hour passed without her asking when her father would come to play with her. But each time, her ayah spread out the long fingers of her bony hands in the helpless gesture that was becoming all too frequent. Misery hollowed a pit in Eliza's stomach. No amount of treats and songs consoled her.

On the third morning, as her ayah was dressing her, the door of the bedroom opened. The Resident's wife came in with a black dress over one arm. Her expression was solemn.

'This belonged to one of my own girls,' Eliza heard her murmur to the ayah. 'It will be too large: my daughter was several years older than Eliza when she wore it, but you must do the best you can. I have told the servants to provide you with pins and a needle and thread.'

Eliza felt a stab of alarm. She noticed how the ayah's hands trembled as she took the dress.

'Why must I wear that?' she asked sharply.

The Resident's wife came to stand beside her and put a bony hand on her head. Eliza peered up at her. The expression on her face was softer than she remembered.

'I am sorry, my dear, it is because of your papa.'

Eliza looked at her blankly.

'When will Papa come back?'

'He will not come back, my child. His suffering is over: He is dead.'

Eliza's face crumpled. She remembered that word. The snake had been dead. Tears welled up in her eyes. Papa must not go away when she needed him.

The Resident's wife cleared her throat. 'I think it will be best if I leave you now,' she said. 'Your mother will come to see you soon, I'm sure, and in the meantime, you have your ayah.'

She walked to the door and then turned back to look at Eliza. 'You must be very brave, child.'

When she was gone, the ayah opened her arms and drew Eliza into them. She buried her head in the folds of the woman's ochre sari and, convulsed with tears,

22

clung to her familiar, warm body. Nothing would ever be right again, she knew it.

In spite of the Resident's wife's words, Elizabeth did not come for several days. It was the ayah who comforted Eliza when she woke crying in the night. When her mother visited her at last, she looked different. A plain black dress had replaced the pretty silks and lace and ribbon trimmings that she usually wore. Her face seemed more lined than it had been and her eyes were red-rimmed.

'You must be a good girl,' she said, resting her hand on Eliza's shoulder.

She turned to the ayah. 'We shall be returning to Calcutta as soon as the next supply convoy comes downriver. Until then, you and Miss Eliza will stay at the Residence. If you need anything, the memsahib will help you. I shall have no time. I have great deal to do.'

It was a Sunday morning when the garrison turned out to welcome the convoy. Surrounded by the stacks of crates, boxes and lumpy, grey bundles secured with hemp rope that lay waiting for the crew to load them, Eliza stood on the quayside with her mother and the Resident's wife as the boats came in. The lead boat bumped the dock and some of the crew jumped off to secure the ropes fore and aft. With a scraping sound, the gangplank was lowered and passengers began to disembark.

Amongst them, Eliza saw a tall man walk in their direction. He looked older than her papa and he was not as handsome but he wore the same red coat. Instead of fair hair, his was dark and wispy, so that the top of his head gleamed in the sunshine. It reminded Eliza of an egg.

'Why Lieutenant Craigie, what a pleasure to see you again,' the Resident's wife beamed. 'Your sojourn in Jaipur was not too uncongenial, I hope?'

He took her hand and raised it to his lips. 'A great pleasure to see you also, ma'am.' He smiled ruefully. 'Politics and treachery have been my lot, I fear. I was greatly relieved to depart.'

The Resident's wife turned to Elizabeth. 'May I introduce Lieutenant Patrick Craigie, who has been Her Majesty's Representative to the Maharajah of Jaipur these past two years? Lieutenant Craigie, this is Mrs Gilbert.'

Craigie bowed. 'At your service, ma'am.'

'Mrs Gilbert and her daughter are to travel to Calcutta with you, Lieutenant Craigie. Perhaps you would be so kind as to look after them? They are recently bereaved.'

'I am very sorry to hear that.' He gave Elizabeth a solicitous look. 'Please accept my deepest condolences, ma'am.'

'You are very kind, Lieutenant Craigie. We shall do our best to be no trouble to you.'

'I'm sure you could never be that,' he said gallantly.

He looked down at Eliza. 'And what is your name, child?' Eliza stared at him but did not reply.

'Don't be rude, Eliza,' Elizabeth snapped. 'Answer when you are spoken to.'

'It is no matter. Perhaps she is a little shy. I'm sure we shall get to know each other better on the journey.' His smile was kind and Eliza gave him a shy one in return.

'There, that's better,' he said. 'I'm sure you and I shall be great friends. Now ladies, I fear I must excuse myself and make my report.'

He bowed again. 'As we are to travel together, may I take the liberty of calling on you later, Mrs Gilbert.?'

Elizabeth inclined her head. 'I should be delighted.'

Chapter 2

In her darkened bedroom, Eliza woke to the swish of a punkah fan. She curled her arms behind her head and stretched like a cat, listening to the bluebottle that buzzed fatly against one of the window panes. Three years had passed since her mother had married Patrick Craigie and set up home with him in Calcutta.

'Eliza baba waking?' The ayah let go the cord of the fan and came over to the bed.

Eliza wriggled across and wound her fingers around a lock of the woman's gleaming black hair. She tugged on it as if it was a bell pull.

'Want drink, want sherbet!'

The ayah disentangled herself.

'The memsahib will be angry if she hears you talk baba talk.'

Eliza giggled and stuck out her tongue. The ayah wagged her finger. 'Naughty girl,' but her chuckle robbed the words of meaning.

Eliza jumped up and bounced onto her lap, her small fingers tickling and jabbing at the ayah's ribs.

'I go, I go,' the ayah gasped, slipping out of her clutches. The hem of her purple sari skimmed the waxed floor as she disappeared in the direction of the kitchens. She returned a few minutes later with a frothy drink that smelled of mangoes and cardamom. A delicate china bowl, decorated with gold and blue birds, held soft pink and acid green jellies, liberally dusted with powdered sugar, and fragrant with the odour of rosewater.

Eliza crammed a handful of the sweets into her mouth and drank some of the sherbet. Sugar stuck to her hands and licks of froth smeared her mouth. The ayah waited until she had eaten and drunk all she wanted before bringing a cloth and a bowl of warm water to wipe her clean.

They spent the rest of the afternoon in the shade of the verandah. Only the drone of insects in the bushes disturbed the silence. The porter slept at the gate; the mali snored under the great peepal tree growing in the centre of the courtyard, his head slumped on his chest. The rake that he had been using that morning lay idle at his feet.

A light breeze arose and Eliza watched it spin the leaves of the peepal, making the sunlight dance in the crown of the tree. She snuggled up to her ayah, smelling the familiar, comforting scents of her warm brown skin and the nut oil that she used to make her hair shine.

'Tell me who lives in the peepal tree,' she demanded through the peppery wad of betel her ayah had given her to chew. She had heard the tale a hundred times before but she loved the ayah's stories.

'Memsahib will be cross.'

Eliza pouted. 'Tell me.'

The ayah lowered her voice. 'You will not be afraid?' Eliza shook her head; her dark curls bounced.

'It is the Munjia, but he only lives in lonely peepal trees, not in this one; when people come by on their tongas and bullock carts, he rushes out and tries to frighten them.' The ayah lowered her voice. 'You must never yawn under a peepal tree and if by mistake you do, you should cover your mouth with your hand or snap your fingers in front of it in case the Munjia rushes down your throat and gives you a bad pain in your tummy.'

Eliza pursed her lips. 'I wouldn't be scared of the old Munjia,' she said resolutely. Her attention wandered to a squirrel monkey near the verandah. It held a blackened husk of corn that it must have stolen from the kitchen refuse and was gnawing at the few remaining kernels.

The ayah heard the tap of footsteps coming from inside the house. She scrambled to her feet and a moment later, Eliza's mother stood at the french windows that opened out from the drawing room. Frowning, she held Eliza's copy book in her hand.

'What is that in your mouth, Eliza?'

Eliza put her hand up and palmed the wad of betel but a tell-tale stain of red remained on her lips.

Her mother darted forward and prised her fingers apart. 'Betel!' She flashed a venomous look at the ayah. 'How many times have I told you that Eliza is not to chew it? Go and get a cloth to scrub out her mouth.'

The ayah scuttled away.

'So you are disobedient as well as lazy and stupid, Eliza. Your tutor has complained to me again that you will not copy your alphabet properly; how do you expect to learn anything if you will not do as he tells you?'

'I hate Mr McAllan. He smells.'

'I will not tolerate such rudeness, Eliza.'

Eliza pouted. 'He does.'

Her mother's slap took her by surprise. She felt her throat tighten and her chest heave. Screwing up her eyes, she threw herself onto the wooden floor, flailing it with her fists. A long scream burst from her mouth. When she had no more breath left, she snatched another gulp of air then screamed again. In the commotion that swelled around her, she was dimly aware of an angry voice and sharp fingers that dug into her shoulders and shook her violently.

She could not tell how much time passed before the voice and the shaking stopped but eventually, she was too exhausted to scream any more. In the silence that ensued, she felt a gentle hand rubbing her back and heard a low voice murmur soothing words in her ear. She opened her eyes to see her ayah kneeling by her side. Her mother had gone.

She did not come again that day or the next. Eliza felt uneasy; her mother was often angry but her anger had never lasted so long before. That night, after her ayah had settled her down to sleep, she crept out from under the mosquito net that draped her bed and tiptoed from her room, her bare feet soundless on the teak floor.

In the drawing room, the french windows leading to the verandah stood open and she heard her mother and stepfather talking outside. She slipped into the shadow of the muslin curtains and listened. Elizabeth's voice sounded shrill and indignant in comparison with Patrick Craigie's calm, Scottish burr. Eliza could not pick out every word of the conversation but she understood enough to chill her. Her mother wanted to send her away. Numb and cold, she crept back to bed. There, cocooned once more under the milky canopy of the mosquito net, she lay listening to the familiar creaks of the old house and the cries of the night outside. Surely, she tried to reassure herself, her stepfather would speak up for her? He would not make her go.

The next day, she was with her ayah in the garden feeding slices of mango to her green parrot when Patrick came to find her. His serious expression made her heart lurch. Perhaps he agreed with her mother after all.

He smiled awkwardly and scratched the parrot's head. 'Let ayah put Polly back in her cage now, Eliza. I want you to take a walk with me. There is something I need to talk to you about.'

For some time, they walked in silence then at last, he spoke.

'Your mother and I have decided that the time has come for you to go to school, Eliza.'

'Here in Calcutta?' she asked, feeling a rush of hope.

He shook his head. 'We are not staying in Calcutta. I have been posted up country. I had hoped that you might stay with us for a little while longer, but my new posting changes everything. It would be impossible to make arrangements from Meerut; it is more than a thousand miles away.'

'So where will I go?'

He heard the note of dismay in her voice and had to stifle his own doubts. 'I have asked my family in Scotland to take you in and see to your education. I know that they will make you very welcome.' He cleared his throat. 'There there child, you will be happy in Montrose, I'm sure of it.'

'Can I take Polly?'

'It is a long way to Scotland, Eliza, and very different there. It would not be a good place for poor old Polly, much better to leave her here. I promise she will be well looked after. Now, let us go and find your ayah again. She will know how to cheer you up.'

The ayah looked anxiously at Eliza when they returned. She had never seen her so subdued. With a muttered goodbye, Patrick Craigie left them together.

Silently, Eliza went to the parrot's cage and opened it. The bird cocked its head to one side and shuffled up and down the perch, ruffling its feathers. Eliza put her hand into the cage. In a few moments, the bird calmed and let her take it out and hold it close. She bent her head, breathing in its musty scent. The tears that swam in her eyes brimmed over and fell in scalding rivulets down her cheeks. If Polly would not be happy in Scotland, why ever should she?

Holding fast to Patrick Craigie's hand, Eliza trotted beside him, keeping up with his long stride as they drew close to the ship. She had cried when her ayah said goodbye, but for the moment, the bustle of the docks distracted her.

The quayside was a kaleidoscope of colour. Here a Brahmin stepped from his gold-curtained palanquin and, with haughty disdain for the crowd around him, strode towards the gangplank. There a massive white bull, painted with bright arabesques and flowers and garlanded with marigolds, helped itself undisturbed to mangoes and cabbages off a vegetable stall. Skinny urchins snaked through the crowd offering to run errands in return for a few annas. A water seller shouting his wares cursed when one of them cannoned into him, splashing water from his goatskin bag onto the dusty ground.

At the bottom of the SS Malcolm's gangplank, Eliza dragged her feet once more.

Patrick looked down at her with a solicitous expression. 'Come along, Eliza.'

She did not move. With the toe of her right shoe, she drew little circles in the dusty ground.

Elizabeth Craigie stifled her annoyance. 'Be a good girl now, Eliza. We shall come and see you as soon as we can.' She held out her hand and hesitantly, Eliza took it.

'There, that's better,' Patrick smiled. 'Now shall we go on board and find Lieutenant-Colonel Innes and his wife?'

The Innes' suite was on the starboard side of the ship; Patrick knocked at the door. When it opened, Eliza saw a tall man dressed, like her stepfather, in army uniform.

Patrick saluted. 'Good morning, sir. May I introduce my wife, Elizabeth, and my step-daughter, Eliza?'

Innes peered down at Eliza. 'So you are the child who is to sail with us?' he asked in a gruff voice. His stern expression and ramrod-straight figure looked very intimidating. Eliza hung back, but Elizabeth pushed her forward.

'Speak when you are spoken to, Eliza.'

A small, plump woman wearing a voluminous blue dress and with her white hair drawn back from her face in a tight knot bustled in from the next door room.

'At least the bedding seems clean,' she was saying. 'Have you spoken to the captain yet about … Why, Lieutenant Craigie, do forgive me. I did not know you were here.'

'We have only just arrived, ma'am. Elizabeth and I are so grateful to you for agreeing to look after Eliza.'

'I'm sure she will be no trouble.'

At that moment, a loud blast of the ship's siren sounded.

Mrs Innes smiled kindly and reached out her hand. 'Come, my dear, say goodbye to your mama and Lieutenant Craigie.'

Eliza felt dismay overwhelm her. She turned her face so that it was half-hidden by her hunched shoulder. Mrs Innes took a step forward, a subtle scent of violets wafted with her. 'We shall have such a lovely time,' she said. 'Once we leave harbour there will be dolphins to watch and perhaps even whales. You will like that won't you?'

Eliza peeped under her eyelashes as Mrs Innes turned the handle of a small door in the wood-panelled wall of the cabin to reveal a tiny room, little bigger than a cupboard. In it was a narrow bunk covered in a pink quilt. 'See you even have your own special bed to sleep in.'

'How cosy it looks, Eliza,' Elizabeth said. 'What a lucky girl you are, to be sure.'

Mrs Innes smiled. 'I expect you know lots of games. I should like it very much if you would show me some new ones.'

Eliza took a hesitant step towards the outstretched hand. 'I play games with my ayah: we play hide and seek. That's my favourite.'

'Mine too.'

Two blasts of the ship's siren rattled the cabin door. Eliza felt her stepfather's strong, sinewy hand on her head.

His voice sounded hoarse. 'Goodbye, my dear.'

'Will you give me a kiss, Eliza?' Elizabeth asked.

Eliza tilted her head and stood on tiptoe. The shovel brim of her mother's bonnet hid her eyes; the lips that brushed Eliza's cheek felt cool.

Elizabeth straightened up again. 'Be a good girl for Lieutenant-Colonel and Mrs Innes,' she said briskly.

Back on deck, Eliza watched her mother and stepfather wave from the quayside. Then the ship's siren boomed three times. She felt the deck judder as they moved away from the shore. Tears pricked her eyes. Scotland seemed a very long way off.

That first night, in spite of Mrs Innes' kindness, Eliza cried herself to sleep. The next day, she trailed disconsolately about in her wake.

It was only after a few days had passed that the novelty of shipboard life proved a sufficient distraction to dispel her homesickness. As Mrs Innes had promised, they saw dolphins leaping in the warm waters of the Indian Ocean, and once in the distance, a whale spouting.

Eliza liked the romantic names of the places they passed: the Eastern Ghats and the Coromandel Coast. Even Lieutenant-Colonel Innes unbent a little. In spite of his wife's concern that Eliza might be frightened by them, he regaled her with bloodcurdling stories of pirates and shipwrecks that she begged to hear over and over again. At Madras, when they docked to take on rice, coconuts and sugarcane, one of the crew threw a coconut in the air and sliced it in half with one blow of his knife to amuse her. She laughed as the blade flashed and watery milk sprayed out.

As the weeks wore on, however, the ship's course took them out of sight of land. The endless expanse of ocean, now the grey, cold waters of the South Atlantic, lowered everyone's spirits. Eliza missed her ayah and her old home. The ship's meals dwindled to watery stews and gruels, served with hard bread. Water was rationed to five pints a day for each person, little more than the amount needed for drinking and cooking.

Instead of the lovely, leisurely baths her ayah had given her, Eliza had to shiver through a cold strip wash once a week.

It was Mrs Innes' kindness that cheered Eliza, and a real affection grew up between them. Mrs Innes was a born teacher and under her patient tutelage, Eliza's reading and writing improved by leaps and bounds.

Mrs Innes was shocked that she had been used to doing so little for herself. 'You are not too young to know how to brush your own hair and lace your shoes,' she said firmly. 'And it is time that you learned how to cut up your food and use a knife and fork to eat it. No more feeding you as if you were a little bird.'

One of Eliza's favourite lessons was embroidery. Amidst so much grey, the rich shades of the wools that Mrs Innes gave her to work with delighted her, for they reminded her of the vibrant colours of India. By the time the *Malcolm* steamed up the busy Thames estuary one fine morning in the middle of May, she had sewn a neat, cross-stitch picture of a thatched house, with a country garden crammed with lavender, hollyhocks and roses. She hoped that her new home would look like it.

Where the ship came to rest at Blackwall docks, Patrick Craigie's sister Catherine Rae and her husband William waited to meet them. Eliza felt full of misgivings. Here was another new life that she must follow. When the time came to disembark, Mrs Innes hugged her and said goodbye with a tremor in her voice.

'Be a good girl, Eliza. I hope that one day we shall meet again.'

Chapter 3

The first thing that Eliza noticed about Montrose was its smell. Later she learned that it came from the markets by the harbour where herrings were cleaned and gutted for sale. The fishy stench mingled with the salt tang of the wind blowing up the estuary that sheltered the town from the North Sea.

They arrived on a cool, damp evening as a fine rain fell over the town, making the streets and pavements gleam like polished pewter. Tired after the long journey from London, Eliza's spirits sank at the sight of the sober, grey stone houses and drab shops. No pretty cottages and flower gardens here.

It was eight o'clock by the time the coach deposited them at the house. Patrick Craigie's father, another Patrick, and his wife Mary had dined early as usual but supper was set out for the travellers at a table in the window of the parlour that overlooked the garden at the back of the house. Whilst the adults talked of the journey and the news from London, Eliza ate her bowl of thick soup in silence, hungry enough to finish every drop, although she found the bland mixture of barley and vegetables tasteless compared with the spicy food of India.

As she ate, her eyes darted around the room. Dark green paper embossed with lozenges picked out in drab brown covered the walls. The button-backed chairs arranged around the fireplace had their legs concealed by ruffled skirts.

A large oil lamp with a globular, etched glass shade stood on a side table. The rest of the light in the room came from a heavy, brass chandelier hanging from the middle of the ceiling.

There were many ornaments: a brass clock on the mantelpiece; domed glass cases containing stuffed birds and small animals that she did not recognise; a pair of tawny and white china dogs sitting on their haunches and numerous pots containing spiky, flowerless plants. Beside Mary Craigie's chair stood a basket full of wool from which a skein of grey stretched to the sock that she knitted as she talked.

The crackle of the fire and the click of needles began to make Eliza feel sleepy. She cupped her chin in her hands and yawned.

'I expect you are ready for bed, Eliza,' Catherine Rae said. She got to her feet. 'I will take you up and show you your room.'

Together they mounted the stairs. The treads were of dark, well-polished wood that creaked beneath their feet. Mezzotints framed in black depicting highland scenes and ruined castles lined the wall opposite the banisters.

'Here we are,' Catherine said walking into a small room and holding the door open for Eliza to follow her. The lamp on the table by the iron-framed bed cast a yellowish glow over off-white walls and a bare floor relieved only by a faded rag rug. Thin curtains hung at the single window and in one corner, a washstand held a plain white basin and jug.

Catherine pointed to a chest at the end of the bed. 'Your clean clothes will be kept in there and there are hooks on the back of the door.'

Eliza went to the half-open window and looked out into the darkness. The rain had stopped but fog, grey as an elephant's hide, enveloped the street. Behind her, she heard Catherine snap open the locks of the trunk that the manservant had brought upstairs earlier.

'Most of these clothes will be unsuitable for the Scottish climate,' she remarked, 'but I suppose they will have to serve for the time being. Now let me see, here is a nightdress that will do for tonight.' She pulled out a cotton shift with long sleeves and a smocked bodice trimmed with lace.

Eliza shivered. She did not want to undress in this chilly room but her Aunt Catherine was adamant. Soon, her clothes had been hung up and, wearing the nightdress, she wriggled into the tightly-made bed and pulled the covers up to her chin. The sheets felt like ice and her teeth chattered. 'It's so cold,' she complained.

Catherine frowned. 'The fresh air is good for you,' she said, but she went across to the window and pulled it shut a little. Picking up the oil lamp, she took it to the door and stood there for a moment. The lamp flame cast a warm light over her strong jaw and Roman nose, softening the appearance of her face. 'Sleep well, Eliza.'

The door closed behind her with a click. Eliza lay in the darkness listening for a sound. A feeling of unease oppressed her. Montrose seemed so quiet and alien. She felt the cold air blowing through the window, stinging her cheeks. With difficulty, she turned over and buried her face in the pillow. As the rain hissed down once more, she slept.

After breakfast the next morning, Catherine completed the unpacking of the trunk, watched by Eliza who sat on the bed swinging her legs in time to a private tune going on in her head.

'There, all done,' she said at last. 'Now we shall go to the nursery. I think there are some old toys that you can play with.'

The nursery had not been used for years but it still contained several china dolls, a teddy bear whose fur was almost worn away with age, and a box of dominos. Eliza passed the day happily enough.

Later that afternoon, she sat in the parlour with Catherine and Mary Craigie as they knitted and talked.

Catherine looked up at the brass clock on the wall. 'I think that you should have a bath tonight, Eliza. There is time before tea.'

She stood up and tugged the bell pull beside the mantelpiece. Somewhere in the house, a distant clanging sounded. A few minutes later, a maid dressed in smart black covered with a spotless white apron entered the room.

'Ah, Betsy, take the tin bath up to the nursery and fill it with water. Ask Sarah to help you.'

The maid bobbed a curtsey and hurried away.

Half an hour later, Eliza eyed the tub.

'What's the matter child?' Catherine asked. 'Did you never have baths in India?'

'Oh yes, my ayah bathed me twice a day,' Eliza replied. 'She washed me in the waters of the Holy Ganges.'

Her aunt raised a disapproving eyebrow. 'You must learn not to tell tall stories, Eliza.'

Eliza tossed her head. 'It's true.'

Catherine pursed her lips. 'It is rude to argue, Eliza. Apologise at once.'

'I'm sorry,' Eliza muttered.

'That's better. Now take off your dress and undergarments and jump in before the water grows cold.'

Eliza dipped her hand into the tub then snatched it away. Clasping her arms around her chest, she shivered, but then seeing her aunt's stern expression, she began to peel off her clothes. Standing in the shallow water in the tub, she was a sorry sight: thin and small for her age, her thick, dark hair and large eyes, of such a deep blue that they were almost black, making her skin look pale as paper.

Catherine took up the large bar of carbolic soap that stood on the little table beside the tub and dunked it into the water. She picked up a flannel then lathered it briskly. Beginning at the neck, she soaped Eliza all the way down to her ankles.

'Now we must wash your feet.'

Eliza held up each foot in turn. 'My ayah said I have very pretty ones.'

'God gives us our bodies, Eliza; there is no cause for vanity.' Catherine straightened up. 'There we are; that's better. In future you will have a bath once a week.'

Eliza looked doubtful.

'Once a week is quite enough,' Catherine said. 'Hot water and soap do not grow on trees. Now duck under and rinse off the soap.'

Eliza looked at the water, now slicked with a pungent, yellow film. She hesitated.

'What a fuss,' Catherine snorted. She scooped up a handful of water and tipped it over Eliza's shoulders. Quickly, Eliza ducked under the water and emerged as fast. Catherine stepped back in alarm as she jumped out of the bath and stood dripping on the mat like a bedraggled kitten rescued from a water butt.

'Really Eliza, there is no need for that. Look at the floor; there is water everywhere.'

'I'm sorry.'

Catherine sighed and held out a small blue towel. Eliza didn't move.

'Surely you know how to dry yourself?'

'Ayah always dried me.'

'Here you shall learn how to dry yourself.'

She draped the towel around Eliza's bird-thin shoulders. Suddenly Eliza's face lit up with a smile of such mischievous charm that her aunt's heart softened. 'Oh very well; I shall help you, but just this once, mind.'

Eliza perched on the side of the bath as her aunt rubbed her down and dried her feet carefully between each toe.

'Ayah always said we must dry my bottom very well too,' she giggled.

Catherine emitted an involuntary gasp. 'Eliza I do not want to hear you use that word again. It is most improper.'

Eliza drew down the corners of her mouth and tried to look repentant. Mama had not liked her to say that word either and she had been cross with ayah for allowing it but it was fun to tease her aunt.

She hid a smile. 'Sorry, Aunt Catherine.'

The following Sunday, as was their custom, the family walked from the house to the red-sandstone church in the centre of the town. The weather had cleared and tulips and forget-me-nots brightened the front gardens

41

of the houses along the way. Church bells pealed in the clear air and Eliza skipped along beside Catherine clutching the small bunch of flowers she had been allowed to pick to bring with her.

'Good morning, Mrs Rae, I trust you are well?'

Eliza felt her aunt stiffen as they were accosted by a woman dressed in a plain black cloak and bonnet. She had a pinched, disapproving face.

'Very well thank you, Mrs McDonald and looking forward to your husband's sermon.'

'I take it that this is your niece?' Mrs McDonald stared at Eliza who returned the look. The Minister's wife coloured.

'Why are you carrying those flowers, child?'

'In India people always bring flowers to the gods.'

'We must go in Eliza,' Catherine said hastily. 'If you will excuse us, Mrs McDonald?'

'What's the matter, Aunt Catherine?' Eliza asked as her aunt hurried her away.

'You must not say such a thing, Eliza.'

'Why?'

'Because it is naughty.'

Eliza sat down beside her aunt in the family pew and laid the flowers in her lap. She felt bewildered. So many things seemed to be different in Scotland. She was not sure that she liked it.

A hush fell when the Minister appeared; he announced the opening hymn and the organ wheezed into life. Eliza felt a hand on her shoulder. 'Now remember, don't fidget,' Catherine whispered.

Eliza liked to sing and she joined in lustily as the congregation followed the laborious strains of the organ. But a few minutes into the sermon that followed, her attention wandered from the Minister's stentorian admonishments. Checking to see that her aunt was not looking, she undid her small bouquet of flowers then leant forward to put a sprig of stitchwort into the powdered wig of the elderly gentleman dozing in the pew in front of them. A puff of powder from the tight, horsehair rolls dusted her hands. Lips pursed in concentration, she added two harebells, a daisy and a sprig of heather.

'Stop that at once.'

Eliza jumped at the intensity of her aunt's voice beside her. 'Take those out immediately,' Catherine hissed.

Eliza stifled a giggle and removed the wilting flowers but their pollen left a rusty stain on the wig. Red-faced, Catherine glanced surreptitiously at the rest of the congregation.

'You must never be so wicked again,' she scolded Eliza on the way home. 'You will spend the rest of the day in your room to give you the opportunity to repent.'

Eliza opened her mouth to protest then closed it again; perhaps she had gone too far. A little shiver went through her. If Aunt Catherine turned against her, who would be left?

'Yes, Aunt Catherine,' she said meekly.

Slowly, Eliza grew accustomed to living under sombre, northern skies but she missed the light and colour of India. She often wondered when her mother and stepfather would send for her, but as the years passed and they did not, she found comfort in her Aunt Catherine's kindness. On winter days, they baked scones and bannocks together in the warm, floury kitchen. In summer, they walked in the country lanes or worked in the garden.

She had few companions of her own age. The families of Montrose were suspicious of outsiders and most of her Craigie cousins were grown up. But when her cousin Mary, the youngest of the seven, returned for the holidays from boarding school, they became good friends.

'You have such lovely things,' Mary said one afternoon as they sat in Eliza's room. She looked enviously at a gauzy pink scarf decorated with shiny sequins and beads.

Eliza picked it up. 'My ayah made it for me when I was in India. She taught me how to use it when I danced.' She pointed her toes and took a few steps, letting the scarf shimmy through her fingers and swish along the floor.

Mary clapped her hands. 'Can I try?'

'Of course.'

After a few moments, Mary sat down laughing. 'I am not as good at it as you.'

'My ayah said I was born to dance.'

She took back the scarf and stroked it. 'Do you like being away at school, Mary?'

Her cousin shrugged. 'I missed home badly at first but I am used to it now. I suppose you will go one day.'

'Are the teachers very strict?'

'Some of them.'

'I don't think I should like it.'

'You won't have a choice, Eliza. Mother says that we are gentry and must be properly educated so that we can find a good husband. That is the purpose of our lives. Oh don't scowl, Eliza. By the time you are sixteen like me, you may be glad of a husband and a home of your own.'

44

Shortly before Eliza's eleventh birthday, letters were exchanged between India and Scotland and it was decided that it was time for her to go south to attend Camden Place, an academy for young ladies in the fashionable spa of Bath. She viewed the prospect with a mixture of excitement and trepidation.

The school was run by two elderly spinsters, Miss Aldridge and her younger sister, Miss Mary Aldridge. It was situated at Camden Crescent, a terrace of tall, stone houses originally conceived as a grand architectural scheme to rival the more famous Royal Crescent. Unfortunately, soon after the work commenced, it became clear that not all the steep hillside was suitable for building, so the crescent remained truncated on one side. Nevertheless, the general effect of the honey-coloured stone façades, with their Corinthian pilasters, was pleasant and imposing.

On arrival, Eliza noticed that a plaque above the stout oak door displayed a carved Indian elephant. Perhaps, she thought, it was a good omen.

Inside, she found a warren of schoolrooms and dormitories. The one where she was to sleep was a narrow, attic room with six iron bedsteads on each side. In the dining hall that first evening, she looked around at the other girls and counted a hundred in all. It felt strange but exciting to be amongst so many: some short, some tall, some pretty, some plain. She wondered which of them would be her friends.

The low chatter stilled then Miss Aldridge said grace. With a scraping of chairs, they sat down to a meal of mutton broth and stewed prunes: the first of many school dinners.

Every moment of the day was accounted for at Camden Place and each change of activity was signalled by the clang of the big school bell. There were many rules to be observed too. Eliza often found them irksome; but the subjects the girls studied came easily to her. Well-taught by Aunt Catherine, she knew the kings and queens of England back to the time of William the Conqueror. She could point to all the major countries on a map and recite her tables. Her writing was neat and she had far less trouble than most of her schoolmates in following the rule that only French must be spoken on one day each week.

A natural ringleader, she was popular with the other girls. Miss Aldridge and Miss Mary soon discovered that if there was a midnight raid on the kitchens or someone had put glue on the blackboard rubber, Eliza was likely to be at the bottom of it. The detentions they imposed did little to curb her mischievous spirit. But they were good women and when she remained in Bath during the holidays and came to know them better, she responded well to the kindness they showed her.

One day just before her sixteenth birthday, she was called to their private parlour.

'How odd,' she remarked to her best friend, Fanny Nichols. 'I'm sure I've done nothing wrong this week. Oh well, I suppose I shall have to go.'

But Miss Aldridge and Miss Mary were smiling.

'We have received a letter from your mother, Eliza,' Miss Aldridge said. 'She is coming from India to visit you. Isn't that exciting?'

Eliza frowned. Ten years had gone by since she had last seen her mother. She could hardly remember what she looked like.

'Is my stepfather coming too?' she asked.

'No, he cannot leave India. But then I'm sure it is your mother that you really want to see, isn't it my dear? The letter was sent only a few weeks before she sailed so not long until she comes now.'

'What happened?' Fanny asked when she returned. 'Are you in trouble for something?'

'No, they wanted to tell me that my mother is coming.'

'But that's wonderful.'

Eliza gave her a sideways look. 'I hope so.'

On the day that Elizabeth was due to arrive, Eliza and Fanny were given permission to miss their usual afternoon reading and piano practice. Fanny squeezed her arm as they walked down the corridor to the bedroom that they shared.

'You mustn't fret, Eliza, your mother will love you, I know she will.'

Eliza frowned. 'I wish I could be as sure as you are, Fanny.'

Fanny smiled. 'Let me arrange your hair. You must look your best for her.'

Eliza sat down at the little dressing table and looked in the mirror that hung on the wall above it. Fanny picked up a brush and loosened the pins that held the soft, black waves back from Eliza's pale, oval face.

'You are so lucky to have such lovely skin. Mine is all freckles. And your figure is much nicer than mine too.' She looked down at the flat expanse of brown, school pinafore over her chest. 'Mama says it will be better when I wear a corset but I'm not so sure.'

She put down the brush and stood back. 'I think a centre parting with the hair drawn back over your ears and fastened at the nape of your neck would look very grown-up.'

Eliza watched as Fanny worked. When she had applied the finishing touch of her own favourite tortoiseshell clip, Eliza twirled her head and surveyed the effect. 'How lovely, thank you.'

'I'm sure your mother will approve,' Fanny beamed.

An hour later, Eliza stood at the door of the Aldridges' parlour. The tinkle of tea cups and a low murmur of conversation drifted through the polished wood, the familiar voices mingled with a strange one that must be her mother's. Her hand shook as she raised it to knock. She felt sure that the whole school must be able to hear her heart thudding.

'Ah, here you are, Eliza,' Miss Aldridge smiled. 'See, your mama has arrived. Say hello to her, dear, there's no need to hang back.'

Elizabeth Craigie remained in her chair. A few strands of grey silvered her auburn hair and her face was more lined than Eliza remembered, but she was still a very attractive woman. Eliza looked into the dark eyes with their appraising expression and felt a wave of disappointment at the lack of warmth she saw there.

'Eliza! How you've grown,' Elizabeth tilted her head a little to one side; 'but how very ill your hair is dressed. We must do something about that at the first opportunity.'

Miss Aldridge and Miss Mary exchanged covert glances of dismay.

'Well, give me a kiss.' Her mother proffered a scented cheek. 'Are you not glad to see me?'

'Your mama tells us that she has found a house in Bath, Eliza,' Miss Aldridge interposed. 'Won't that be lovely? You will continue to come to school in the day, but now you will have a home where you can spend your leisure hours.'

Eliza bit her lip. 'I do not need a new home, I am happy here.'

Elizabeth Craigie gave a tight smile. 'You are not yet old enough to know what is good for you, Eliza. Where you live is my decision.'

'I'm sure Eliza did not mean any harm, Mrs Craigie,' Miss Aldridge said hastily. 'I expect she is just a little overwhelmed by these sudden plans. That is it, isn't it, Eliza? I'm sure that when you have had time to get used to the idea, you will be very happy to be going with your mama.'

Eliza did not reply.

'Perhaps you would like another piece of seed cake or some more tea, Mrs Craigie?' Miss Mary asked in a flustered voice. She lifted the lid from the pot. 'It looks a little strong I'm afraid; I'll ring for some hot water, shall I?'

Elizabeth cleared her throat. 'You are very kind, but please do not trouble yourself for my sake. I really should be getting on. I have an appointment to discuss the furnishing of the house in an hour.'

She stood up, rearranged the skirt of her midnight-blue costume and picked up her parasol. 'Thank you for your hospitality. I shall let you know when the house is ready for Eliza to come.'

Without another word, she swept from the room. The swish of her skirts gave way to silence. It was Eliza who broke it. 'May I go back to my room now?' she asked in flat tone.

'Of course, my dear,' Miss Aldridge said awkwardly.

Alone with Fanny, Eliza gave way to angry tears.

Fanny put her arms around her.

'Oh Eliza, did it go badly?'

'It was horrible; she is horrible. She said my hair was ugly. And I have to go and live with her.'

Tears sprang into Fanny's own eyes.

'You aren't leaving school? We can still be friends, can't we?'

Eliza took the handkerchief that Fanny offered and blew her nose then nodded.

'I am to come every day for my lessons. But oh, Fanny, I wish she had never come back. I don't think she loves me at all.'

Chapter 4

Eliza sat opposite her mother in the drawing room of the rented house in Walcott Street where they had set up home. Her eyes smouldered.

'I won't do it! I won't marry an old man. If Papa was still alive he would not try to make me.'

Her mother bit her lip. Her visit to Bath was not going as she had planned. The city was not particularly amusing. Clearly it had lost the cachet it enjoyed when it was patronised by royalty. To make matters worse, Eliza had become even more wilful as a young girl than she had been a child.

'I am tired of telling you, Eliza,' she snapped. 'How many times must we go over this before you understand? You are extremely fortunate that a wealthy gentleman like Sir Abraham Lumley is willing to marry you. You have practically nothing to offer in the way of a dowry, but you can look forward to a comfortable, secure life. You should be grateful that your stepfather and I have been able to make such a good match for you.'

Eliza scowled. 'I don't care if Sir Abraham is rich; I shall never love him.'

'Love? Love is a luxury not everyone can afford, Eliza. One day you will learn that. Fortunately, it is perfectly possible to live without it. Many people do.'

'You of all people would think so; you have certainly never loved me. You only came back to England to sell me to the first man who offered so that you could be rid of me for good.'

Elizabeth drew a sharp breath. 'Eliza, you know perfectly well that your stepfather's military duties kept him in India; my place was at his side. It was impossible for you to remain with us and be properly educated. That is the reason we sent you away.'

'The only reason?'

Elizabeth Craigie pursed her lips. 'I can't think what you mean. You had better spend the rest of the afternoon in your room. Perhaps a few hours on your own will bring you to your senses.'

'Perhaps it will not,' Eliza muttered.

'Insolence! When I have done my best for you! You will have a far better start than I did. Your father had nothing to...'

She saw the surprised look on Eliza's face and stopped. Her next words slipped out through tight lips. 'Go to your room, Eliza. I do not wish to discuss this again. The decision is made.'

For a long moment, they faced each other. Eliza felt her heart pound, the blood rushing to her face as anger fought with tears. When she could endure the tension no longer, she jumped up and ran out of the room, slamming the door behind her.

Upstairs, she threw herself onto her bed, her knuckles white as she clenched the pillow. When she and Fanny had giggled about who they would marry, she had never anticipated a marriage without love or romance. Her eyes narrowed. Whatever it cost her, she would not marry Sir Abraham. She would not.

One morning a few days later she and her mother sat sewing in the drawing room. It was a Wednesday. Usually she would have been at school, but the maid had a bad cold and had begged to be let off the duty of walking her to Camden Place.

Apart from the rumble of carriages driving up and down Walcott Street nothing disturbed the silence. Since their quarrel, the subject of Eliza's marriage had not been raised again.

Elizabeth Craigie took her scissors from the workbox on the table beside her and snipped a stray thread from the collar that she was mending.

'I believe that Lieutenant James will be back from London by now,' she remarked. 'Perhaps he will come today.'

Eliza grimaced; she could not understand why her mother was so taken with Thomas James. She often talked of how charming he had been on the voyage back from India where they had met, but he seemed so old, thirty at least and not handsome. Still, he was more congenial than most of the decrepit Indian army officers who came to call with their faded wives.

Elizabeth dropped the scissors back into her workbox. They fell with a clatter.

'I hope that you will be civil if he comes, Eliza. Goodness knows we have few enough visitors. Bath is really very tiresome. In India I was constantly being called upon.'

Eliza made another stitch in her embroidery.

Her mother rapped on the arm of her chair. 'Are you listening to me, Eliza?'

'Yes, Mama, but I'm sure that Lieutenant James has as little interest in my company as I have in his.'

Elizabeth coloured. 'I've told you before, Eliza, I will not tolerate this insolence.'

A knock on the door halted the argument before it could brew any further.

'Lieutenant James is here to see you, ma'am,' the maid snuffled, her eyes rimmed pink with her cold.

'Mrs Craigie, Eliza, good morning!' Thomas James stood beaming in the doorway. 'What a charming picture you make together.'

If he thinks that, Eliza mused, he does not notice very much.

Elizabeth Craigie patted her hair and brightened.

'Oh, Lieutenant James: what a pleasure! We have just been talking of you. We have been very dull today with no visitors; I count on you to raise our spirits.'

Thomas James bent to kiss her hand. 'I shall do my best to make up for the deficiencies of the ungrateful inhabitants of Bath who should be wearing out the cobbles on the path to your door.'

He turned to Eliza.

'And how is dear Eliza this morning? No lessons to go to?'

She threw a triumphant glance in her mother's direction. It was pleasant to be able to draw attention to the fact that they had so few servants; she knew it rankled with Elizabeth.

'I am very well, thank you, Lieutenant James,' she smiled. 'I could not go to school this morning as our maid has a bad cold. She usually walks with me, and we have no one else to take her place.'

With satisfaction, she saw her mother flush.

'Do tell us the news from town,' she said quickly. 'Is King William still unwell?'

'I fear so, madam, but the papers report that he is determined to see in another anniversary of Waterloo. If his will is stronger than his constitution, I suppose he may live until the eighteenth.'

'And then we shall have the young princess. They say she is very wilful.' Elizabeth directed a sideways glance at her daughter. 'It is most unseemly in a young girl.'

Eliza did not speak and sensing the antipathy between mother and daughter, although he did not understand the reason for it, Thomas changed the subject.

When he got up to leave a quarter of an hour later, he kissed Elizabeth's hand then smiled at Eliza. 'Should the maid be indisposed tomorrow, I should be glad to offer any help you may need. If your mama agrees, I should be honoured to escort you to school.'

'How kind of you Lieutenant James; I do hate to miss my lessons.'

'I'm sure you are an excellent pupil.'

Eliza rewarded him with a dazzling smile.

'We would not dream of troubling you, Lieutenant James,' Elizabeth said.

'Oh, but I insist. It will be no trouble at all, and perhaps on my return, I might have the honour of escorting you to the Pump Room, Mrs Craigie?'

She sighed. 'Thank you. Perhaps it will do me some good. I fear that the damp climate of England does not suit my constitution.'

Thomas bowed. 'No one would know it, ma'am. You are, as always, the picture of beauty and health.'

'Until tomorrow, Eliza,' he smiled. 'I promise to be punctual.'

In fact, he arrived early the next morning. Watching for him from the window, Eliza thought that he looked particularly smart. It had rained heavily in the night and the pavements gleamed. As they turned the corner into the Royal Crescent, a brisk wind tugged at the strings of her bonnet.

'I hope you are not cold?' he asked.

'Not at all; I love windy days.'

'And if I may say so, they impart a most charming colour to your cheeks.'

Eliza stifled a laugh. Lieutenant James was flirting with her. How cross that would make Mama.

'You are teasing me, sir.'

'I would not dream of taking such a liberty,' he chuckled. 'It is the truth.'

They walked on in silence.

'I wish you would tell me about Princess Victoria;' Eliza said after a few moments. 'I don't think Mama approves of her behaviour, but surely, if she is to be queen, she will need to know her own mind?'

'I have often thought so, although naturally, a child should respect their parents.'

He puffed out his chest, her interest encouraging him to go on.

'Of course the princess's mother, the Duchess of Kent, is much influenced by her favourite, Sir John Conroy. It is at his urging that the princess has been forced to live a life full of rules and restrictions – they call it the Kensington system. It does seem undesirable for a girl who will need to know and understand a great deal about her country, and her people, if they are to love her. It will be a hard enough task to win their hearts. The monarchy has lost so much respect thanks to the dissipations of King George and King William.'

'Is the princess beautiful?'

'I doubt that she could match you, my dear.'

By now they had reached Camden Place and stood at the school porch. Thomas looked downcast.

'Ah, we have arrived already,' he said.

'Thank you so much, Lieutenant James.'

'Surely we do not need to be so formal, Eliza? I should like it very much if you would call me Thomas.'

She gave him a sweet smile. 'Then thank you, Thomas.'

In the hallway, she glanced back and saw him standing on the pavement watching her as she went into the hallway and joined her school friends.

'I think I shall steal Mama's cavalier,' she joked to Fanny as they ate dumplings and mutton stew at dinner time. 'That would be great fun.'

Fanny's eyes widened. 'Eliza, you are wicked. You wouldn't would you?'

Eliza laughed. 'Of course not, he is far too old and dull.'

Fanny hesitated.

'What is it?'

'I just wondered if your mama had said anything more about your marriage.'

Eliza shrugged. 'She mentioned it again yesterday evening but I refused to talk about it.'

'Did she tell you any more about the man she has chosen for you?'

'Sir Abraham Lumley? Oh, he's old and he has lived in India for most of his life. I expect he is as wrinkled as a tortoise and just as tedious.'

Fanny frowned. 'If he is so old, has he never been married?'

'I think Mama said he was, but his wife died. I expect that he bored her to death.'

Fanny giggled, then sobered. 'Oh Eliza, be serious, you will have to do as your parents say you know: in the end, we all do.'

Eliza shook her head. 'I want more from my life than that, Fanny, and I mean to have it.'

The maid recovered and the following day, she and Eliza left the house for the walk to school. It was a warm morning and the gardens outside the houses they passed were gay with geraniums and roses. As they turned the corner out of Walcott Street, they met Thomas coming the other way.

He raised his hat. 'Good day to you, Eliza.'

'Oh! You startled me.'

'I wondered if I might keep you company again? It is such a fine morning for a walk.'

Without waiting for her answer, he turned to the maid and handed her a penny. 'I'll go the rest of the way with Miss Eliza. I'm sure you can amuse yourself for an hour?'

A flicker of uncertainty crossed the girl's face.

He scowled. 'What are you waiting for?'

'Should I go back and tell the mistress?'

'No need for that. She will not mind.'

The maid bobbed a curtsey and trotted away.

After that, Thomas walked with Eliza every day and the maid amassed enough pennies to ensure her continued silence. They talked of many things and Eliza revelled in the attention he paid to her opinions and the patience with which he answered her questions.

In London, King William fulfilled his ambition to see in another anniversary of Waterloo then died the following day. Eliza often thought of the young Victoria. Only two years older than me, she mused, and her own mistress. In some ways, our history is similar. We both lost a father when we were very young and we both have mothers who are too selfish to care for our happiness.

She felt a surge of hope at the stories of how Victoria had refused to continue sharing a bedroom with her mother as she had done at Kensington Palace, and how she had thwarted the duchess's ambitions for her favourite, Sir John Conroy. That would pay him back for bullying his future queen.

The man Victoria had turned to was her first minister, Lord Melbourne. Eliza thought he sounded entrancing. Who could be more delightful than a charming man of the world with a rakish past?

'They say that the queen puts complete trust in him. He has become like a father to her,' Thomas remarked one day when Eliza had raised her favourite subject. He gave her a sideways glance. 'With her own father snatched away too soon, a young girl needs a man like that, would you not agree?'

He tucked her arm more firmly into his own, and she did not resist.

When he was not escorting her to school, Thomas paid frequent calls at Walcott Street. He often brought her books and they read the poetry of Tennyson and Wordsworth together.

She listened to his stories of his military service in India with rapt attention and laughed at his jokes. When she tried to teach him the steps of a Russian folkdance that she had learnt at Camden Place and his long legs refused to keep up with her deft movements, they both ended up convulsed with breathless laughter. Sneaking a glance at her mother, the sour expression she saw on her face filled Eliza with glee.

'I have been learning a new piano piece,' she remarked one evening when he was with them. 'Would you turn the pages for me?'

He stepped briskly to her side and, as she played the opening bars, she leaned towards him a little. When he turned the page for her, she felt his arm brush hers. She smiled at him under her lashes and saw an answering flash of his very white teeth. He was not handsome, but he was tall and his regimentals gave him presence. She liked it too that he smelled of tobacco and leather. The menservants at Walcott Street and Camden Place just smelled of coal or boot blacking. Unless it was a bath day; then they smelled of carbolic soap.

'I have never heard Chopin sound so delightful,' Thomas murmured when she had finished.

Elizabeth shivered. 'Very nice, Eliza; but how cold it is in here; fetch my shawl from upstairs, please.'

Eliza stood up from the piano stool and walked slowly to the door. She felt Thomas's eyes on her. Outside in the passage, she leant against the wall and caught her breath. Her heart thudded. Mama was annoyed and that was good, but something about Thomas's touch made her feel confused. She closed her eyes. I won't think of it now, she resolved. It is far too hard to make out.

On her return from school the following afternoon, Eliza found her mother alone in the drawing room. Something in her manner – the too-friendly smile, the

60

forced brightness in her voice – made Eliza's heart hammer against her ribs. She felt light-headed.

'Good afternoon, Mama,' she said warily. 'I hope you had a pleasant day.'

'A busy one,' Elizabeth said briskly. 'Now go and tidy yourself. I have already rung the bell for tea.'

Upstairs, Eliza took off her cloak and bonnet and smoothed her hair. The feeling of foreboding that had started in the drawing room grew stronger. As she walked back downstairs, her hand shook on the banister. In the hall, she heard her mother telling the maid off for something. When she opened the door, the girl scuttled past her and disappeared in the direction of the kitchen.

Elizabeth looked up. 'Ah, here you are, Eliza. Sit down, dear, while I pour the tea.'

Eliza perched on the hard, uncomfortable chair by the fire and waited.

'I received a letter from your stepfather this morning,' Elizabeth remarked, handing her a cup and saucer.

The astringent scent of her mother's favourite Earl Grey rose to Eliza's nostrils. She felt her stomach curdle. Elizabeth ploughed on.

'We shall be leaving Bath soon. He has arranged our passage back to India.'

Eliza set down her teacup with a clatter. 'But am I not to finish school?'

'No. Your stepfather and I have to come to a decision. Sir Abraham Lumley may not wait for much longer. It's time that we gave him an answer.'

'Then it must be no.'

'On the contrary, it must be yes. It is time that you got this nonsense out of your head, Eliza. You may count yourself lucky. Some parents would beat it out of you.'

Eliza was on her feet, striding to the door.

'Come back here. Don't you dare leave the room whilst I am talking! Do you hear me, Eliza? Eliza!'

Eliza ran upstairs, locked the bedroom door behind her and threw herself down on her bed. She clenched a handful of the pillow in her fist. Her thoughts raced but one was clear and constant: somehow she must escape.

Later, when she slept, dreams tormented her. An ancient man with an ugly face loomed in the doorway to her bedroom.

'Sir Adrian Lumley! Make way, make way,' a voice boomed.

Then she was being prepared for her wedding; laced into a dress that made it hard to breathe. Her mother was decorating her hair with feathers, but the quills dug into her scalp and she screamed. Trying to run, the heavy dress tangled around her feet and pulled her down. As she fell, a man's hand reached out to her but her fingertips only grazed it before it slipped away.

She woke shaking, to find that she was trapped in a tangle of twisted sheets. Outside the window, it was already light. Getting up, she went to the mirror. Her eyes were puffy and her head throbbed. The dream was still vivid. She wondered who the man had been. Could he have been Papa or was he Thomas James?

She heard footsteps in the corridor then a rap at the door. 'Come out now, Eliza,' her mother's voice called.

'No, I won't.'

Eliza stuffed her fingers in her ears to blot out her mother's angry tirade. It seemed a long time before Elizabeth Craigie stomped away.

'I hope that you have decided to be sensible,' she said sharply, when hungry and thirsty, Eliza came down to dinner that evening. The maid had already served the soup and left them alone.

'Your stepfather and I only want the best for you. You will never find a more eligible husband than Sir Abraham. I am surprised that you are not grateful that we have done so well for you.'

Eliza didn't answer and her mother frowned. 'I suppose I cannot expect thanks from such an ungrateful daughter. Well, I won't dwell on that, there is a lot to be done before we sail. You will need a trousseau of course. There are plenty of good dressmakers in Bath and your stepfather has been very generous with your allowance. You may as well leave Camden Place at the end of the week.'

A knot of panic tightened in Eliza's stomach. Her mother really meant to marry her off. There was to be no escape.

'I have heard from my husband,' Elizabeth remarked on Thomas's next visit. 'Eliza and I sail for Calcutta in a few weeks.'

'So soon?'

'Yes, it is a little sooner than I anticipated,' she smiled, 'but Eliza is to be married.'

'Married?'

'To Sir Abraham Lumley. It is an excellent match: Eliza is extremely fortunate.'

Eliza saw Thomas give her an oblique glance. She lowered her eyes.

'May I congratulate you, Eliza?' he asked.

She heard the unease in his voice. 'Thank you,' she murmured, her own so quiet that the words were almost inaudible.

'Eliza is a little overwhelmed, as you can see.'

Thomas cleared his throat and laughed awkwardly.

'As any young lady would be.' He looked at Eliza earnestly. 'Bath will be the poorer without her; without both of you, I mean to say.'

The next morning, as they walked to school, a few minutes passed before Thomas broke the silence.

'I cannot deny that your mother's news alarmed me.'

Eliza bit her lip. 'I am so unhappy.' A tear rolled down her cheek.

He found a handkerchief in his pocket and gave it to her.

'You do not like the man?'

She dabbed at her eyes. 'I have never met him. He is very old, at least sixty. Mama says that his age will not matter, but I know it will.'

'Have you told your mother how you feel?'

With a mute nod, Eliza began to cry again. 'It makes no difference to her,' she sobbed. 'Oh Thomas, what shall I do? If Papa was still alive, he would never have made me marry a man I could not love.'

She heard his sharp intake of breath. 'Then let me take his place, Eliza. I can be like a father to you.'

'What do you mean?'

'Come away with me. You shall not marry Lumley. I'll keep you safe.'

'Oh Thomas, would you really do that?'

He squeezed her arm. 'For you, my dear, I would do anything.'

'And Mama?'

'She will soon forgive you, I'm sure. We could come back to Bath then.'

Eliza looked down at the ground. Was this the way out she had longed for? Surely it must be? She felt the pressure of his fingers on her arm.

'You can trust me, Eliza. What do you say?'

She hesitated.

'I swear it on my honour, Eliza: you will be safe with me. I would do anything rather than see you unhappy.'

She raised her eyes to his. The expression in them looked so earnest: it convinced her. She took his outstretched hand.

'Yes, Thomas,' she said. 'Yes, I will come with you.'

Chapter 5

The hired horses strained in the shafts as they pulled the carriage up the steep Bristol road and away from Bath. When they crested the hill, Eliza looked back at the old city, asleep under a starlit sky.

'What an adventure,' she laughed. 'Mama will be furious when she finds out.'

Thomas chuckled and squeezed her arm. 'She will soon get over it and tell Sir Abraham to find someone else to marry.' He rolled down the window and leaned out. 'Hurry along, my good fellow. I'll make it worth your while.'

The moon was high in the sky and the night half over by the time they reached a small village. 'We'll stop here for a rest,' he said as they drew up at the only inn. He climbed down and rapped with his cane on the door. In the yard at the side of the building, a chained dog jumped to its feet and started to bark. After a few minutes, they heard the sound of bolts drawing back and a man peered through a chink in the door.

'What do you want, waking honest folks up at this time of night?'

Thomas produced a gold coin from his pocket and rubbed it between his finger and thumb. 'Our carriage shed a wheel on the road and my grooms were four hours mending it,' he said loftily. We require a room for the night.'

The man's expression brightened and he opened the door wider.

'Come in then.'

He goggled when he saw Eliza step from the carriage. Thomas led her inside and took her over to the fireplace where dying embers glowed in the ash-strewn grate. She spread out her hands to the faint warmth whilst he went back to the landlord. She couldn't help noticing the sly grin the man directed at her. A flush rose to her cheeks as she saw him laugh, then a sharp word from Thomas silenced him.

Thomas came back to where she sat. 'I'm sorry, Eliza, the ruffian says there's only one room left. We shall have to make do. There is, apparently, a large chair. I can sleep in that.'

'Won't you be very uncomfortable?'

He smiled gallantly. 'I've slept in far worst places on campaign.'

They drank some wine whilst they waited for the room to be made ready then followed the landlord up the stairs. The sickly light of his oil lamp illuminated a narrow passage with dingy walls, but when they reached the room, they found it clean and dry with a large, mullioned window overlooking the street.

The landlord put the lamp down on the table by the window. 'I hope this is to your liking?'

'It will do,' Thomas answered curtly.

When he had left them, Eliza stood uncertainly by the bed. Thomas came over to her and put a reassuring hand on her arm. 'Shall I turn my back whilst you get ready?'

She nodded.

He went to the window and stared out at the deserted street. Eliza took off her shoes and began to remove her dress. She was not used to managing without the help of a maid and her fingers fumbled with the ribbons and buttons. At last, she stood in nothing but her shift, the rough floorboards cold beneath her bare feet.

Climbing into bed, she pulled the much-mended, red eiderdown up to her chin.

'I am done now,' she whispered.

Thomas went to the oil lamp and blew it out. She heard a series of creaks as he crossed the floor, then a soft whoosh of air as he settled himself in the chair. She lay staring at the darkness and thought how silent it was. If there were other people staying at the inn, they slept very noiselessly.

After a few minutes, she heard Thomas shift in the chair.

'Are you all right?' she whispered.

'Damn thing has broken springs,' he muttered. 'It's like sleeping on a bed of nails.' He gave an awkward laugh. 'Might there be a bit of room for me in that big bed?'

She did not answer but a moment later she heard the straw in the mattress rustle and felt it sag.

'Thomas?'

'Eliza?'

His voice was much nearer than she had expected.

'I'll just lie here at the edge of the bed,' he whispered.

They lapsed into silence again but his breathing seemed very loud in her ears. She felt the heat of his skin. When his hand touched her thigh, she jumped.

'Don't be afraid,' she heard him murmur. 'I just want to hold you; it's cold in here, we could keep each other warm. You'd like that wouldn't you?'

His arm snaked around her waist and he pulled her to him. She felt the rough linen of his shirt but his legs were bare. His moustache scraped her skin as he nuzzled the soft place at the base of her throat then his lips travelled down to her breasts. Her voice was unsteady. 'Please don't do that, Thomas.'

'Just a bit of a kiss and a cuddle, my dear; what's the harm?'

'No, I don't want to.'

'Don't want to?' He laughed huskily. 'I know what you want better than you do, my pet. You pretty little things giggle and talk at school together, don't you? Wondering what a man has between his legs and what he'll do to you with it when he gets the chance?'

'Let me go.'

His lips closed over her nipple. As he sucked, the soft flesh hardened and she felt as if a string that connected it to the place between her legs had suddenly been pulled taut.

'No,' she gasped.

'Oh but yes: I think you are ready to find out, my darling,' he chuckled. 'Like a little flower, all ready for the bee.'

With a swift movement, he pulled her nightgown up to her waist and slid a finger inside her. She shuddered.

'That's it,' he crooned, as if he was gentling a horse. 'Good girl. Here we go: in with the old soldier.'

Eliza felt him withdraw his finger then press something thick and hard into her. The stab of pain made her scream. Thomas clamped his hand over her lips and began to move with an insistent rhythm, faster and faster, gasps and grunts drowning his endearments until at last he let out a long, visceral howl and slumped on her breast.

Terrified, Eliza looked down at him with a sensation even more alarming than the ache she felt inside her. What if he had died? When he looked up, there was a moment of relief before her tears came, trickling into the damp locks that stuck to her cheeks.

'Don't cry, my darling,' Thomas mumbled. 'My wonderful girl. It wasn't too bad was it? You'll see, you girls all love it in the end.'

He took her hand and pulled it between his thighs. 'There, the old soldier promises to be gentler next time. He didn't want to hurt you; it was just he'd waited for so long.'

Eliza gulped down a sob. 'You said you would be a father to me.'

He let her hand go with an awkward laugh. 'You weren't such a fool as to believe that were you?'

She shivered. Perhaps in her heart she had suspected but chosen to delude herself. Everything seemed so confused now; it was too difficult to remember.

'What will we do?' she asked in a small voice.

He got up and went to the window then pulled the curtain back a little. Moonlight crept into the room. When he came back and sat on the bed beside her, he had a rueful grin on his face.

'Do? I suppose we shall have to marry; that's if you'll have me. Not that I've left you much choice. No other man will take you after this.'

She drooped. He did not mention love.

'What's the matter?'

'Do you love me, Thomas?'

He leaned forward and kissed her lips.

'Of course I do. We can be happy together, trust me.'

Cautiously, she let him draw her into his arms. Her head rested on his shoulder and she closed her eyes. If he loved her, then this must be right.

'Tomorrow we'll take the road west and find a boat for Ireland,' he soothed her. 'We'll go to my family's house. We can be married from there.'

Chapter 6

Ireland.

Eliza sat on the window seat in the gloomy, over-furnished drawing room of the James family's ancestral home. She preferred to be as far apart as possible from the rest of the company.

Since they had argued at breakfast, Thomas had been gone all day. Irritably, she stared out at the gardens and the parkland beyond and wondered if it would ever stop raining. The steady downpour leached every colour but grey from the view, leaving dull smudges where trees and shrubs should have been. Beyond the parkland, sodden hedges divided the fields into a drab patchwork that eventually gave way to the dark slopes of Mount Leinster.

It seemed as if years rather than months had passed since they had left Bath. In those months, she had grown up a great deal and not everything that she had learnt was pleasant.

Unconsciously, her fingers went to the bruised place on her arm and she winced. Thomas as a husband had proved very different from Thomas as an admirer. With what I know now, she thought grimly, my advice to all young girls who contemplated a runaway marriage would be that they would do better to hang or drown themselves just one hour before they start. An admirer devotes himself to flattering and amusing you. Your smiles are payment enough. A husband thinks he owns you and never lets you forget it.

Her mother had refused to meet them and it had fallen to Thomas's family to arrange a hasty wedding. Eliza sighed as she remembered what a disappointing affair it had been. She had hoped to marry in one of the fashionable Dublin churches: the plain chapel at Rathbeggan had been a poor substitute. Thomas's brother, who held the living there, had conducted the service with a face as long as a dull sermon. The only other people present had been his wife and nephew who had acted as witnesses.

She drummed her fingers on the windowsill. It was no wonder that she and Thomas argued so. The lack of entertainment in this cold, rambling house oppressed her spirits and brought out the brute in him. She could not understand why anyone would want to spend their time here with no society but tenant farmers, and most of those too poor to be anything but an object of charity.

'More tea, Eliza?'

The voice of her sister-in-law, Sarah Watson broke in on her thoughts. She pretended that she had not heard the question. These endless cups of tea, drunk with methodical conscientiousness in the same quantity, in the same rooms and with such unshakeable solemnity drove her to distraction.

Before Sarah could ask again, the door opened. Thomas strode in and flung himself down in a chair.

Sarah looked at him sympathetically. 'Poor Thomas, what a shame there has been no hunting today.'

He grunted.

'Will you take some tea?'

'Can't abide the stuff.'

At least we have something in common, Eliza thought wryly.

He stood up and walked over to the window seat. His face was pale. 'I'm sorry if I hurt you this morning,' he muttered. 'Don't turn away from me, dammit.'

Neither of them spoke for a few moments. Deep lines furrowed his brow then he tried again and she heard the strain in his voice.

'Forgive me. I wronged you.'

Her heart softened. She knew it must be hard for him to ask forgiveness. She would not let him off too easily but perhaps she might unbend a little.

Turning back to the room, she raised her voice so that the others could hear. 'As there is no hunting and you do not want to drink tea, perhaps we should go to the library and read together?'

He brightened and offered her his arm. 'That seems an excellent idea. I hope you will excuse us, ladies?'

The library was a small, dusty room whose shelves contained little but tales of hunting exploits and musty tomes of Irish history. Early in her visit, Eliza had exhausted such pleasures as it afforded.

Closing the door behind them, he put his arm around her waist.

'There, that's better,' he grinned.

'Stop that, Thomas.' She pushed him away and took a book down from one of the shelves. 'Shall we read this?'

He swore under his breath. 'I don't want to read some damned book. I love you, Eliza; I want to make love to you.'

'If you love me, why don't you want me to be happy?'

He took a step towards her but she raised the book as if she would strike him with it. He groaned. 'All right, all right, if you hate this place so much, I'll do my best to get us back to Dublin. It may take some time though. The old man can be damned tight with money and I fear my army pay won't stretch far there.'

She turned on her heel and walked to the window.

'Eliza, look at me,' he begged. He ran a hand through his hair. 'I just need time. I'll find a way, I promise. I can't stand much more of this. Why must we always quarrel?'

'Because I detest this place and you are cruel to keep me here.'

'I've told you, we'll leave, but you must be patient.'

'You promise?'

'Yes.'

She stroked his cheek and he seized her hands and covered them with kisses.

At least there is one thing that we like doing together,' he muttered thickly.

She looked down at his bent head and felt a tremor go through her. Yes, she did like it and it was pleasing too that he was always in a much more pliant mood afterwards.

'Lock the door,' she whispered.

Letting her go, he hurried across the room. As she arranged herself on the roomy, button-backed sofa next to the fireplace, she heard the key turn.

Afterwards, as he dozed, flushed and sated, she felt the wave of sadness that often came over her. Edging quietly off the couch, she straightened her clothes and went over to the window. Through the leaded lights, she saw that the rain still fell. With a sigh, she twitched the curtains across to shut out the sight.

75

That day in Bath when she had thrown in her lot with Thomas seemed so long ago now. How she wished that she had not been forced to choose him as a means of escape; she did not love him; she never would. With a grimace, she thought of her mother. Did she ever feel any remorse for her part in the affair?

On the sofa, Thomas stirred.

'Eliza? Where are you?'

'Here, Thomas.' She went back and snuggled up beside him.

'Where shall we live in Dublin?' she asked.

In the house that he had rented for them in the city, she dressed for dinner.

She felt happy. After the dreary months in the country, she loved playing mistress of her own establishment. True, the house's parlour was smaller than she would have liked and furnished with cheap pieces. The hall and stairs were cramped and the dining room looked out onto a weedy alleyway frequented by stray cats. But what did that matter? With her wit and style, it was not hard to distract visitors from the place's shortcomings.

Her fingers brushed the pearls at her throat. Of indifferent quality, they still set off the luminescence of her complexion and the sultry intensity of her deep-blue eyes. She smiled. Her parties had become quite the rage in Dublin.

Tonight, one of her dinner guests was Thomas's brother, the vicar of Rathbeggan. How amusing that he now sought her invitations; in fact he even tried, rather comically, to play the gallant.

She picked up her fan. Some of Thomas's brother officers and their wives would make up the numbers.

'But I,' she told her reflection, 'shall out-dazzle them all.'

Through the half-open door of the bedroom, she heard the first ring of the doorbell and elderly Bridie, the parlour maid bustling to answer it. She had better have remembered to put on a clean apron, as I told her, Eliza thought. And if Cook burns the dinner again, I'll throw all of her saucepans at her.

Downstairs, the rooms blazed with candles and a bowl of yellow, hothouse roses, her favourites, stood on the console table in the hall, filling the air with spicy perfume. Thomas would carp about the expense later but she did not care. It would not be hard to mollify him. Indeed, Dublin seemed to have worked magic between them. Probably, she reflected dryly, because between the theatre and the opera, the parties and the calls, we are hardly ever alone in each other's company. And if that is what is needed for us to be civil to each other, long may it remain so.

Dishes of tough capons – at least Cook had not incinerated them entirely, Eliza thought - followed a tolerable soup and the party was merry with talk and wine when Thomas stood up and tapped the side of his glass with his fork.

Eliza put down her wine. Something about Thomas's expression raised her suspicions. He cleared his throat.

'Dear friends,' he began, 'a tremendous pleasure indeed it is, to see you all gathered here together.'

A murmur of agreement went around the table but Eliza's sense of foreboding increased. Thomas was not usually given to speeches.

'Sadly,' he went on, 'this may be one of the last times that it will be possible.'

Eliza stared at the claret in her glass. She felt a knot tighten in her stomach.

India; the Honourable Company; absent too long already; do not wish to harm my prospects. Thomas droned on with thanks and protestations of friendship but she had heard all she needed. She had always known the time would come, but every day she had prayed it would not come too soon. She remembered the journey to England all those years ago. Then she had been a child, indulged by the crew and petted by Mrs Innes. Four months at sea with Thomas presented a very different prospect.

As summer advanced, Thomas gave notice on the house and let Cook and the maids go. On arriving back in England, he and Eliza travelled north from Liverpool to Scotland to visit the Craigies and Aunt Catherine. The roads were rough and Eliza was soon weary and out-of-sorts. By the time the post coach lumbered over the final miles to Montrose, her patience was near its end.

The house had not changed since she had left it as a child almost eight years ago. The same olive-green wallpaper and prim chairs in the parlour. But I have altered, she thought, I am a grown woman now. And since I am, why is it that Aunt Catherine's sharp eyes can make me feel so uncomfortable? Perhaps it was because, remembering her kindness, of all the women she knew, it was Aunt Catherine whose approval she valued. She hugged her when the time came to say goodbye.

'Promise you won't forget me?' she whispered, tears brimming in her eyes. She saw Catherine swallow hard before she spoke.

'Dear Eliza, you must follow your husband now; I shall pray every day that you will do so with a willing heart.'

.

Chapter 7

Midnight approached as, below decks on the boat taking them from Calcutta to the garrison at Karnal, Eliza lay awake in the small cabin that she and Thomas shared. The swollen timbers wept resinous tears that filled the heavy air with their pungency, competing with the lingering smell of the curried mutton and rice that the native cooks had served for that evening's dinner. Beside her, Thomas snorted and twitched in his sleep. She rolled away trying to find a cooler part of the bed. If only they had been able to afford a cabin on the upper deck.

She sighed. If she never saw a ship again, it would be too soon. The journey out from England had been a daily penance. *The sea,* she confided to her diary, *makes women sick and men extraordinarily unpleasant. In the marital cabin, you are constantly bumping into one another. You cannot turn around without finding yourself in an unwilling embrace.*

To be fair, the shipboard routine had not been as exasperating as life in Ireland. She had found other passengers to talk to in the day and at night a small orchestra had played for dances. Thomas, however, had soon reverted to his boorish, insufferable manners. His breath stank from the endless glasses of porter he consumed, after which he grunted and snored all night.

In the moonlight that shone through the small cabin's porthole, she could just make out a flat shape on the bedside ledge beyond Thomas's sleeping form. It was the diary that he had kept since they left Ireland, but all that was written in it was a list of his complaints about her. What kind of husband kept a record of those? If she kept a list of his shortcomings, she would need far more than one book. With a grimace, she rolled on her side, closed her eyes and tried to sleep. She might go mad before the journey ended.

At Patna, she saw the same crowds of worshippers and monks that she dimly remembered from her childhood visit. A vivid memory of her father flashed into her mind. She could almost feel his strong arms around her and hear his voice, but the romance that his enthusiasm had given to the scene had been snuffed out like a candle flame. Now she noticed the dust devils that coated everything with red grit; the piles of fly-blown dung cakes stinking in the sun. The wails and shrieks of the mourners as they committed the ashes of their loved ones to the holy river chilled her blood.

When the boat stopped to deliver mail at Dinapore, she went on shore and walked to the dusty little graveyard where her father was buried. Close to the empty walls of a new, but half-built church, she found the stone tablet that marked his grave. A pair of ravens perched on a headstone nearby watched her with bright, cruel eyes. She picked up a clod of earth and hurled it them. Croaking, they wheeled into the air and flapped away.

She knelt down and traced the inscription with the tips of her fingers, murmuring the words under her breath.

Sacred
To the memory of
Ensign Edward Gilbert HM 44th Regiment
Who departed this life
The 22nd day of September 1823
Aged 26 Years

Bitter tears rolled down her cheeks. 'Oh Papa,' she whispered. 'If you were alive now, everything would have been different.'

By the time they reached Benares, the river was too dangerous to navigate. They travelled the rest of the way on palanquins carried by Indian bearers. Swaying over the bumpy roads, Eliza peeked out through the gap between the red silk curtains and felt the heat of the sun on her face. It was a wonder to her that the men could stay so cheerful. They sang all the time as they jogged along. She was glad that the palanquins were too small to take more than one person. It gave her a welcome respite from Thomas's company.

In Karnal, spring arrived, but to Eliza, apart from the distant view of the Himalayan foothills, it looked a dull, barren place. The garrison was small and the posting not much sought after.

'But at least we can afford plenty of servants,' Thomas remarked. He raised an eyebrow. 'I hope you won't become too idle, Eliza.'

'If I do, I'm sure you will make a note of it in your diary.'

Time dragged. Parties and entertainments were few in Karnal. It irked Eliza too that etiquette dictated that she could only attend them when Thomas was with her. At the end of a tedious week when he had been absent on recruiting duties, she lay on her bed in their bungalow. Apart from the chatter of a pair of monkeys in the baobab tree outside her window, the house was silent. She did not know where any of the houseboys or her maid had gone. When Thomas was away, she could not be bothered to direct their work.

Rubbing a hand across her eyes, she yawned. Her head had ached all day. No wonder, when she had to spend her time alone in this dreary place. It surprised her how much she looked forward to Thomas's return. At least then she would not have to miss her morning rides and evening outings.

A shiver went through her. Strange, she had been too hot a little while ago, now her hands were like blocks of ice and her toes felt numb. She tried to wriggle them but it made a pain shoot up her left leg. With difficulty, she hauled herself onto one elbow and reached for the bell pull. She was hot again now and the brass ring felt slippery in her clammy hand.

The effort of ringing exhausted her and she fell back onto the pillows. Her head swam as she waited for the sound of footsteps, but none came. Why didn't her maid answer?

Water, I need water, she thought, a rising panic turning the ache in her head into a noise like the pounding of a blacksmith's hammer. She made a fresh effort to reach the bell pull but it was impossible. Her stomach convulsed; bile rushed into her mouth and a stream of vomit splattered the dusty floor beside the bed.

By the time Thomas returned, there was no question of morning rides or evening outings. Shivering and sweating, Eliza was in the grip of a fever. The garrison's medical officer diagnosed malaria and prescribed large doses of quinine.

'Too bitter' she gasped as Thomas held the glass for her and she took a tiny sip. Her throat burned.

'But you must take it. It is the only remedy we have.'

She grimaced. 'Very well but I will hold it myself. She fumbled for the glass and drank.

'There, it's done.'

He stroked her forehead. 'We must get you better as soon as we can, my dear girl. Where would I be without you?'

She looked at his worried face. Poor Thomas. He meant to be kind.

'No more diary?' she asked with a weak laugh.

He smiled. 'No more diary.'

Sometimes, in the weeks that followed, she could not distinguish night from day, but she was dimly aware of Thomas by her side. In her lucid hours, he read to her as he had done in Bath. His concern touched her heart and as she recovered, she regretted the times when harsh words had passed between them. Perhaps they could be happy after all.

He came to her one afternoon with an envelope addressed in a strong, upright hand.

'It is for you. Shall I open it?'

She nodded.

He slit the envelope and pulled out the sheet of paper. After a moment, he whistled. 'It's from your stepfather.'

Eliza's eyebrows shot up. 'What does he say?'

'He and your mother are on their way to Simla. He suggests that we go up and meet them. See for yourself.'

She shook her head. 'My eyes are too sore to read. So do they forgive us?'

Thomas's brow wrinkled. Although Patrick Craigie claimed that Eliza's mother was anxious to see them too, she had not added any words of her own.

'It seems so,' he said cautiously, and then in a bluffer voice, 'we should accept and go as soon as you are well enough to travel. The climate up there will be excellent for your health.'

Eliza hesitated. 'I should like to see Simla, and I suppose that if my mother wants it, it is time that we made up our quarrel.'

His fingers brushed her cheek. 'Yes, it is.'

Privately too, he reflected that Craigie was comfortably off. A little help in lieu of a dowry would not come amiss: something to help pay for Eliza's expensive tastes.

Chapter 8

Simla

Pine and sandalwood perfumed the air as the little party arrived at the fair in the Annandale Valley. A month had passed since Eliza and Thomas had joined her mother and stepfather at Simla.

Elizabeth Craigie stepped from the carriage and squealed with delighted horror as a villainously-bearded young man in patched, ragged clothes and a scarlet bandana around his head strode up to them and bowed.

'Captain Crichton, is that you?'

He laughed. 'Indeed it is, ma'am. I am a gypsy for the day.' He pointed to a spot nearby where three other men crouched around a fire, one of them stirring a steaming cauldron. Beside them grazed a tethered donkey, decked with bright ribbons.

'The donkey is for the children to ride and we plan to tell fortunes.' He grinned at Eliza. 'What a pleasure to see you, Mrs James. I hope you will let me tell yours?'

Eliza laughed. 'Only if you promise to make it a happy one.'

'How could one so lovely expect anything else?'

Thomas looked on indulgently. He rather liked the admiration that Eliza excited. It flattered his choice of wife and he did not think of himself as a particularly jealous man. As long as no one turns her young head, he thought, there is no harm in it. He nodded to Crichton and offered Elizabeth Gilbert his arm.

'With your husband's permission, may I escort you around the fair, ma'am?'

She smiled coolly. 'How kind. Patrick, will you and Eliza follow us?'

They moved away to wander among the stalls, greeting friends and acquaintances as they went.

'I hear there will be races later on,' Thomas remarked. He turned to Patrick Craigie. 'I rode in Ireland a great deal but today I think I shall leave it to the younger men.'

Craigie nodded. 'Very wise: Annandale is the one place at Simla flat enough for a tolerable course, but it is still rough going.'

Eliza took a breath of limpid air and looked around her. Beyond the lush, tree-fringed valley, the sunshine bathed the snowy peaks of the Himalayas in rose and gold. 'How beautiful it is here,' she said. 'I am so glad you asked us to come.'

'There is nowhere in India as delightful as Simla,' Elizabeth remarked.

Eliza felt a stab of irritation. Perhaps she deserved no better, but she wished that her mother would not brush away every overture of friendship as if they were no more than acquaintances. Was it so hard to say that she too was glad? She was beginning to suspect that if it had not been for her stepfather, the invitation would never have been issued.

'And we are delighted that you could join us, aren't we, Elizabeth?' Patrick said quickly.

Elizabeth smiled but her eyes lacked warmth.

With an effort, Eliza quelled her anger and began a new topic.

In spite of her mother's coolness though, she found that the day passed very pleasantly. As usual, she collected a crowd of admirers. It seemed that every man there wanted to compliment her dress or give her tips on which horses she should back.

'Well done, Captain Crichton,' she smiled as the captain, smart once again in his regimentals, came over to her after he had won the final race. His steaming horse tossed its head and its foam-smeared bit jangled.

'Thank you.'

'And the beard has gone.'

He grinned. 'It was made of goat hair and boot black. I apologise for the stench. It must have been awful.'

'It was rather strong.'

He lowered his voice. 'I hope you know that I wanted to win for your sake alone, Mrs James.'

She reached up to stroke his horse's muzzle. 'You are teasing me.'

'No, I mean every word. But sadly, your husband has all the luck.' He straightened up and frowned. 'And here he comes now with your mother and stepfather.'

'Captain Crichton! Congratulations on your win. I am afraid that I must take my wife away from you. The Governor's sister has expressed a wish to meet her.'

Eliza rose from a low curtsey to find herself looking into a pair of shrewd, humorous, grey eyes. Their owner indicated the straight-backed chair set beside her under the canvas awning. Eliza smoothed out the skirt of her blue muslin dress and sat down whilst Thomas and the Craigies hovered at a respectful distance. Lady Emily nodded regally in their direction, then turned back to study Eliza through her lorgnette.

'Well, my dear, how do you like Simla?'

'I think it is the most beautiful place I have ever seen, Your Ladyship.'

'You like mountains?'

'Oh yes, I would climb them all if I could.'

Lady Emily chuckled. 'That might be rather unseemly, but at your age, I would have felt the same. Do you play the pianoforte?'

'Yes I do, Your Ladyship.'

'Excellent. And who is your favourite composer?'

'Chopin, Your Ladyship.'

'Mine too. You must visit us at the Residence. We have an excellent instrument that no one plays.'

'Thank you. I should like that very much.'

Eliza could not resist casting a triumphant glance in her mother's direction. She was gratified to see the strain in her polite smile.

By the end of the afternoon, Eliza went home with a promise from Lady Emily that she would send a carriage for her the next day. She became a frequent guest at the Residence and with the parties and picnics, the compliments lavished on her and the attentions of a stream of admirers, the five months in Simla flew by.

As they drew to a close, Eliza could count on the fingers of one hand the evenings that she and Thomas had been obliged to spend alone in each other's company. Whenever she thought about it, she frowned. November would soon come and with it, the end of their stay in the hills.

They were to return to Karnal for a short time then travel to a new post at the recruiting depot at Bareilly. From what she could gather, it was an even smaller place than Karnal and there would be very little in the way of parties and entertainments.

A grand ball marked the end of the hill season. Eliza wore a dress of pink satin that Lady Emily had given her. Fine Brussels lace embellished the low neckline and the cuffs of the full sleeves. She wore her pearl necklace and fastened a nosegay of shell-pink rosebuds to the waistband to emphasise her slim figure. When she stood back to study the finished effect in her dressing mirror, she smiled. The dress was very elegant and probably far more expensive than anything her mother could afford.

Her face clouded. This might be the last chance she would have to wear it for a very long time.

Walking up the Residence's sweeping staircase on Thomas's arm, her first glimpse of the ballroom, glowing in the light of hundreds of candles, dispelled such gloomy thoughts. A small orchestra played and in the long dining room, tables covered with fine linen clothes groaned with bowls of mangoes, papayas and melons and silver dishes of sweetmeats.

After supper, when the dancing began, Thomas watched as she swooped around the floor in the arms of captains and colonels. As time had gone by, he had tired of being just the husband of the popular Mrs James. It did not seem to have done his preferment much good. He would be glad now when they returned to duty and he had her to himself. Perhaps there would be a child. It often surprised him that she had not conceived yet. Goodness knew, the old soldier had been on campaign enough times for that. Some people said that too much junketing and dancing could stop a woman breeding. Well, if that was true, Bareilly would solve it.

On the other side of the room, the Craigies' attention was also on Eliza.

'I believe that her dance card has been fuller than any woman's in the room,' Patrick remarked, but no sooner were the words out of his mouth than he realised that the remark was unfortunate. He could not pretend that the experiment, in which he had placed such hope, had gone well.

'It is a wonder to me that Thomas puts up with her ways,' his wife replied acerbically, 'but then she was always headstrong. I could have told him that long ago.' She scowled. 'A thousand pounds on her education,' she muttered. 'A thousand pounds.'

Craigie stroked his moustache and frowned. He wished she would not harp on about the cost of Eliza's education.

He looked up to see Thomas bearing down on them.

'Hush, my dear,' he whispered.

'Evening Thomas, splendid occasion, eh?'

'Indeed it is, sir.' Thomas bowed to Elizabeth. 'If your husband permits, may I have the honour of a dance?'

'By all means,' Craigie smiled. 'You must enjoy yourself, my dear. As you know, I'm not much of a dancer.'

Elizabeth's smile did not quite reach her eyes but Thomas did not notice. Taking her hand, he led her onto the floor as the orchestra struck up a quickstep.

Craigie watched the couples dip and turn: a rainbow of silks and taffetas interlaced with scarlet regimentals and magpie evening dress. Across the room, he noticed Captain Crichton leaning against a pillar, watching Eliza with a dejected air. A very able chap Crichton, with a bright future ahead of him. Patrick was certain that nothing improper had occurred between them. In the goldfish bowl of Simla, nothing ever did without gossip spreading like a monsoon flood. But a fellow like Crichton would have been far more suitable for Eliza.

Not for the first time, Patrick felt a stab of guilt. He wished that he had not given in to Elizabeth over old Abraham Lumley. Still, there was nothing to be done now. In a few weeks, they would be back in the plains and Eliza would be on her way to Bareilly. He would be sorry to see her go. Even the candles seem to burn brighter when she was in a room. He only hoped that she could adapt to the quiet married life that awaited her.

Driving home in the carriage, Eliza looked up at the stars, sparkling like polished diamonds in the inky sky. She drew in a deep breath of crisp, pine-scented air and savoured it. She would miss Simla so much. She looked across at Thomas, dozing with his head bumping against the side of the seat. How would she manage when there was no society to fill her days? When she must make do with no company but his?

His growing paunch strained against the gleaming buttons of his scarlet coat. She could not help thinking of Captain Crichton's tall, slim figure; his mischievous sense of humour and the endearing way his chestnut locks seemed to resist his attempts to tame them. Life was not fair. She turned back to the window to watch the stars.

Two days later, the whole British community assembled with its baggage teams. Donkeys, elephants and camels groaned under the weight of the trunks, furniture and household equipment that had to be lugged back to the plains. Eliza stood with Lady Emily whilst she supervised the stowing of the grand piano. The next day, the slow procession down from the hills began.

Chapter 9

Winter in Bareilly dragged; Eliza and Thomas often
quarrelled.

As spring approached, the invitation to Simla was
not renewed. Bored and lonely, she faced the prospect
of a long summer of relentless heat.

On one of many sultry evenings, Thomas's heavy
boots clumped up the stairs of the verandah. As he
passed Eliza's scarlet macaw, it let out a raucous
whistle and rocked on its perch. Her pet monkey
scuttled off into the bushes, chattering angrily.

Lying down in their bedroom, Eliza heard him
shout for whisky. She winced. Why must he always be
so grouchy? He was not the only one who had to suffer
this dreadful place. She turned over and buried her head
in the pillow to shut out the noise he made. The blinds
in the room had been closed since morning to keep out
the sun and the air was stale and heavy.

She felt the bed sag and looked up with distaste.
Thomas sat mopping his sunburnt forehead.

'Go away and wash, Thomas,' she scowled. 'You
stink of sweat.'

'I'm sorry if I offend your delicate sensibilities. I'm
afraid that earning our bread is not always a refined

occupation. I hope the servants have prepared an edible dinner, I'm famished.'

'I don't know and I couldn't care less. I have no appetite in this wretched heat.'

'But I do. It's been a long day: I've ridden forty miles since this morning and inspected any number of these damned native troops. I want a decent meal. It would be nice if you had at least taken the trouble to arrange it.'

She did not reply.

He seized her shoulder roughly and twisted her round to face him. She tried to jerk away as his fingers dug into her.

'If you hit me, I'll scratch your eyes out,' she spat. 'If I had known what you are really like, I would never have married you.'

He raised his fist but then his shoulders slumped. 'I don't want to hurt you, Eliza.'

'Then let me go.'

He groaned. 'We have had this conversation a hundred times. You are my wife. Where would you go? What would you do?'

'I could go back to Calcutta.'

'To your mother and stepfather?'

She nodded.

'I doubt they would accept you. No, Eliza, we are married. It is your duty to be a good wife. Nothing can change that.' He stood up. 'I'll leave you now but I expect to see you dressed in half and hour and joining me at dinner.'

When the door closed behind him, Eliza turned her face back to the wall. 'You are wrong,' she whispered fiercely. 'This is no life. Things can change and I shall not give up until they do.'

Six weeks later, in Calcutta, Mrs Craigie paced her drawing room, her skirts swishing over the polished floor.

'Read me the letter again,' she snapped to her husband. 'No, don't. I feel as if every word is branded on my heart.' She clapped her hand to her forehead. 'I can't believe that this is happening. I don't want her here. First she shames me by eloping with him, now she wants to leave him. How much more must I endure? The scandal will kill me.'

'He is bringing her to Calcutta himself. Perhaps if I talk to them, there may still be a chance of reconciliation.'

She gave a bitter laugh. 'Not Eliza, she is stubborn as a mule. Anyway, why should he have her back when she has made it so clear that she no longer cares for him?' She barked her shin on a footstool and cried out with pain and vexation.

'Sit down,' Craigie said, his irritation rising. 'If there is nothing else for it, we must decide what to do with her. Thomas says he will provide her with what money he can, but it won't be much.'

Mrs Craigie pursed her lips. 'So we shall have to give her money as well?'

'I think so.'

Her eyes narrowed. 'You are too generous, Patrick. It is far more than she deserves.'

He frowned. 'She could go back to my family. I know that Catherine became fond of Eliza when she was a child.'

'Then write to her. Anything, as long as Eliza does not stay here to shame me.'

'Very well.'

Patrick Craigie stared into the depths of his malt whisky. Seated opposite him in a quiet corner of the smoking room at the officers' club in Calcutta, Thomas waited, rubbing a finger along the brass studs on the arm of the leather chair in which he sat. They felt hard and cold to his touch. On the wall above Craigie, a tiger's head, mounted on a gleaming mahogany plaque, snarled down in the rictus of death.

It was a mercy that the separation was not yet a matter of public knowledge, Craigie thought. He and Thomas might just be two comrades-in-arms chewing the fat over a pleasant drink. He cleared his throat. 'I have booked Eliza's passage on T*he Larkins*. It sails for Portsmouth in a few weeks. I have paid for the fare already. My sister Catherine Rae will meet her at the docks and arrange for her to go to my family in Montrose. Everyone is to be told that she has not fully recovered from a fall out riding, and has come home to convalesce.'

Thomas leaned forward. 'Thank you. I'm very grateful for all your help.'

'You will instruct your bank to pay the allowance we discussed?'

Thomas nodded. Craigie saw a muscle twitch in his cheek.

'I have an appointment in the morning to see the manager.' He looked away. 'I am sorry that it is not more.'

Craigie thought that he saw the Irishman's eyes mist but there was no point in holding out any hope of mending the relationship now. He and Elizabeth had marshalled all the arguments they could think of and Eliza still refused to budge. Probably best to bring an end to the interview now.

'Well,' he said briskly, 'you've behaved as honourably as any man might be expected to under the circumstance.' He stood up and held out his hand. 'Good luck.'

Thomas got clumsily to his feet and took the proffered hand. 'Thank you.'

Craigie stood and watched him as he walked to the door. He pitied him, whatever his faults, with nothing to look forward to but a lonely return to his duties in Bareilly. He pitied Eliza too. Perhaps they might be reconciled one day but it seemed very unlikely and if not, she faced a bleak prospect as a separated wife. He hoped that she understood the full implications of what she had done.

Chapter 10

Ten days out of Calcutta, *The Larkins* docked at Madras. The first part of the journey had been dull, and Eliza had suffered more than a twinge of guilt and anxiety over her decision, but now the sight of the teeming, colourful activity on the quayside cheered her. Beside her, Mrs Sturgis, an acquaintance of the Craigies who had agreed to be her chaperone, fanned herself.

'New passengers, I suppose,' she complained. 'How tiresome that we have to come in for them; it was far cooler out at sea.'

Eliza frowned. Few things could be more tiresome than the company of Mrs Sturgis, who lost no opportunity to remind her of her shame.

She leaned over the rail to watch the hordes of porters dragging trunks and bales of goods up the gangplanks and into the holds. They reminded her of a colony of ants.

'Really Eliza, that is most unladylike. Stand up at once.'

Eliza shrugged. 'There is no one who matters to see me.'

'That is not the point.'

Eliza was about to retort when she noticed a young man stroll up the gangplank. Tall, with golden hair, he sported the sabre and spurred boots of a cavalry officer. He paused and looked up at Eliza. Catching her eye, he doffed his solar topee and grinned.

Mrs Sturgis frowned. 'Eliza, I forbid you to smile back,' she hissed. But it was already too late.

After Cape Cormorin, the ground swell off the Malabar Coast set the ship bucking and rolling in choppy waters. Mrs Sturgis complained of sea sickness and stayed in her cabin. Glad to be free of her company for a while Eliza went up on deck alone.

'Is your companion indisposed this morning?' a voice behind her asked.

She turned to see the golden-haired cavalry officer smiling at her.

'She has been vomiting since breakfast.'

He suppressed a snort of laughter. 'I am sorry to hear it. We should be in calmer waters soon.'

Eliza raised an eyebrow. 'Not too soon I hope.'

The skin around his grey eyes crinkled. 'Permit me to introduce myself: Lieutenant George Lennox at your service.'

Eliza held out her hand. He took it and bent to kiss her fingertips. She felt a thrill run through her.

'Mrs Eliza James.'

'Is your husband already in England, Mrs James?' he asked after they had exchanged pleasantries about the journey and the weather.

'No, I left him in India.'

'I hope that he will be able to join you soon?'

'I am supposed to tell people that I am returning home to convalesce after a riding accident, but I never fell off a horse in my life. The truth is, I have left my husband and I hope never to see him again.'

Lennox's eyes widened. She was far more outspoken than any of the young women he had come across before. It intrigued him. She was also a great deal more attractive.

A wave buffeted the side of the ship sending spray over the rail. He noticed how the droplets of water glistened in her dark hair.

'Perhaps we should find a more sheltered spot,' he suggested, offering her his arm.

'Yes, perhaps we should.'

They spent the rest of that day and all the next enjoying each other's company, but on the third morning, Eliza could no longer ignore the notes with which Mrs Sturgis bombarded her. When she went down to the older woman's cabin that afternoon, Mrs Sturgis wasted no time in pleasantries.

'I have heard that you have been seen talking alone with Captain Lennox, Eliza.'

Eliza drew a deep breath. She wondered who she had to thank for this piece of spying.

'We have done nothing wrong, it was just conversation.'

Mrs Sturgis bridled. 'Conversation? Are you as foolish as to believe that you, a married woman, and one in a most invidious position at that, can afford to be seen alone with a single man? It is unseemly. It is scandalous. Your mother and stepfather entrusted me with your welfare. I cannot allow you to expose yourself to gossip.'

Eliza shrugged. 'Then I shall tell him I cannot speak to him alone.'

Mrs Sturgis was surprised. She had not expected Eliza to be so pliant. Should she believe her? She searched Eliza's face but her expression was inscrutable. Mrs Sturgis opened her mouth to make another protest, then could think of nothing to say and closed it again.

Eliza suppressed a smile. She looks like a cod on a fishmonger's slab, she thought. Aloud she said, 'Was that all you wanted to say to me? May I go now?'

Flushing, Mrs Sturgis nodded. 'If you wish, but I hope you will heed my advice.'

'But you are alone with me now,' Lennox laughed, as he and Eliza walked together the following day.

'Oh but we are not really alone. She gestured to the waves. 'We have the sea, the whales, the albatrosses to chaperone us.'

His face took on a serious expression. 'I doubt Mrs Sturgis would think that was enough. I do not want to get you into trouble, Eliza. Perhaps we should be more discreet.'

She went to the rail and leaned over, looking down at the waves beneath. ''I don't care what Mrs Sturgis thinks. She can't tell me what to do. I shall behave as I like.'

He squeezed her arm. 'You know Eliza, you're wonderful. I don't think I've ever met anyone like you.'

When Mrs Sturgis recovered, she seemed to have lost the will to oppose Eliza. It would have made no difference if she had, for Eliza was too happy to care. She gloried in Lennox's company: a companion of her own age with a spirit as gay as her own. Every day, she fell in love with him a little more.

At meals, with every sip of drink or forkful of food she took, she tried to imagine how his kisses would taste. Once, when she glanced across to where he sat, she saw him holding his glass of claret to his lips as if he wanted to savour it forever. He looked across the rim and caught her eye. Was he thinking the same?

At night, she lay awake in the darkness of her cabin and wondered what it would be like to lie with him. Compared with Thomas, he was an Adonis. There were six more weeks of the voyage left. If she dared to find out, by the time they reached Portsmouth she would know the answer.

It was a Sunday morning and as usual, Captain Ingram was preparing to go on deck to conduct the morning service. Struggling to fasten his white cravat, he swore as he stabbed himself with his gold pin.

'Let me do it,' Mrs Ingram said irritably. 'Hold still: there, that's better.'

'Did you speak with Mrs Sturgis?'

'Yes, the poor woman is at her wits' end. She says that Mrs James will not listen to reason. She has washed her hands of her. The whole ship sees how she and Lennox flirt but they seem to have no shame.'

'I'll speak with Lennox, although I doubt he will take any notice of me. He's affable on the surface but he's well aware that being a relation of the Duke of Richmond allows him to do very much as he likes.'

His wife frowned. To her mind, a connection with the aristocracy was not sufficient excuse for immorality. 'They've been seen sitting alone in his cabin again,' she retorted. 'Mrs James just laughed when I took her to task and said that it was only because his is cool and has a window, whilst hers does not. She can't seem to understand how serious her behaviour is. She has already abandoned her husband; is she determined to ruin herself?'

Her husband shrugged. 'That is her choice.'

'True, but what about your reputation? What will people say if you allow immoral conduct on your ship?'

The captain chewed his lip for a moment before he spoke.

'Yes, there is that to consider. You are right of course. I shall have to think very carefully about Mrs James.'

Lennox stood at the door to his cabin and glanced up and down the passage. 'I think we are safe,' he whispered to Eliza. 'In you come. I saw the captain go up on deck a few minutes ago.' He laughed. 'He will be leading the first hymn by now, out of tune as usual.'

Eliza giggled and slipped past him. Closing the door, he put his arms around her. 'I hope he gives a long sermon,' he murmured into her neck. I've been longing to have you to myself since dawn.'

He pulled her down on the bunk and she pressed her lips hard against his. He broke away and laughed.

'I see you've been impatient too.'

'George, I am so hot and my corset is suffocating me. I should like to take it off.'

His cheeks flushed. 'Do you want me to help you?'

She stood up and turned her back to him. 'Unfasten my dress.'

His fingers trembled as he fumbled with the buttons. 'Damn women's clothes,' he muttered. She laughed as she slipped the dress to the floor and stood in her corset and petticoats. 'There, now unlace me.'

'Eliza, do you really want me to?'

She turned and took his face in her hands, the soft curve of her breasts swelled at the lace edge of her whalebone stays. She saw beads of sweat on his forehead.

Yes,' she whispered. 'I do.'

'Your husband…'

'I hate him. He was cruel and never loved me.'

Lennox put his finger to her lips. 'He must be a madman. How could any man not adore you?'

'Do you adore me, George?'

'I haven't the words for it.'

She laughed softly. 'Then show me.'

'You must act,' Mrs Ingram snapped to her husband a few days later. 'The passengers are in an uproar. People are saying that you cannot command your own ship. A married woman flaunting her adultery for all to see. It is a disgrace.'

Her husband frowned. 'But can we be sure?'

'Of course we can. I told you, one of the maids saw them together in broad daylight. His cabin door came open when we went through those rough seas on Wednesday. They were both half-dressed, and he was on his knees helping her to put on her stockings.' She shuddered. 'What more evidence do you need?'

'So what do you want me to do?'

Mrs Ingram sniffed. 'I will not speak with her, or eat my meals with her anywhere near me, and I shall not ask anyone else to do so.'

'Very well, I shall inform her that she is not welcome to dine with us and the rest of the passengers. In future all her meals will be served to her in her cabin.'

'Dammit,' Lennox scowled when Eliza showed him the note. 'I thought there might be trouble when that door popped open. I shut it as soon as I could,' - he smoothed her hair - 'although we were rather busy at the time, weren't we, my sweet?'

He kissed her forehead. 'I'm sorry, my love, but the damage is done. We shall just have to brazen it out. At least when we get to England, we can go our own way. I must admit, I would rather not go to dine without you; the conversation at table was never very entertaining at the best of times, and now I shall be bored to death, but if the captain expects my presence, it would be rude to decline. You do understand that don't you?'

She bit her lip. It seemed very unjust that all the blame was to be laid on her, but his expression seemed so genuinely disappointed that she did not want to complain.

He put his hand under her chin and tilted her face to his. 'Poor Eliza, I promise to make it all up to you in London. One day, we shall laugh about this.'

He traced a line of kisses up her neck and let his tongue play in the soft hollow beneath her ear. In the distance, a bell sounded for dinner. His lips moved to hers and she shuddered. The bell sounded again. Lennox gave her waist a last squeeze then let her go.

'I'd better be off. Wait up for me. I'll be back when the ship's asleep.'

Left alone in her windowless cabin, she sat down on the bed, undid her stockings and rolled them off one by one. They felt stiff with sweat and dust. It was so hot. She wished she could wear fresh clothes each day but the rationing of water made washing a luxury.

Some time passed before she heard footsteps in the corridor and a knock at the door. A maid came in with a tray of food. She stared at Eliza's bare legs with a pert smile.

Eliza glowered at her. 'Put the tray on the table and get back to your work.'

Flushing, the maid banged down the tray and left. Eliza lifted the tin cover and her nose wrinkled at the smell of the pickled beef and watery, grey potatoes on the plate underneath. A pool of congealed gravy surrounded them. With a sigh, she put the cover on the floor and began to pick at the meat. The ship was not due to dock in Portsmouth for two more weeks. Every day would seem like a lifetime.

Chapter 11

It was a grey, February day when, at long last, they docked at Portsmouth. Evading Mrs Sturgis, Eliza strolled down the gangplank on Lennox's arm, ignoring the stares of the other passengers. Her stepfather had made arrangements for her to go to Montrose, but she and Lennox were gone before Catherine could find them in the disembarking crowd. They spent the night at an inn then travelled on to London the next day and rented rooms at the Imperial Hotel in Covent Garden.

'I must take the coach to Chichester today,' he announced the following morning. 'It won't be long before my parents hear that our ship is in, and I shall have a hard time explaining myself if I don't go to see them straight away. I'll be back as soon as I can.'

Whilst he was gone, Eliza found lodgings for them in Great Ryder Street. She unpacked her luggage and draped some of the Indian shawls she had brought with her over the chairs in the small drawing room, and over the bed that she and Lennox would share.

'There, that's better,' she murmured, standing back to survey the effect. The rich colours glowed like stained glass, banishing the drabness of the landlord's furnishings.

That evening, she paid for extra logs and candles. Sitting by the fire in their buttery light, she thought of Lennox and wondered what his family would be saying to his news. Surely they would want to meet her very soon? She pictured a fine old house built of mellow stone, with beautiful gardens and a long drive lined with daffodils in spring. She imagined the carriage bringing the two of them up to the grand entrance, where an elderly, distinguished-looking couple waited with smiles of welcome.

She hugged herself, thinking of the day when she and Lennox would marry. In some vague way, she was sure that Thomas could be persuaded to set her free. A match to a man with aristocratic connections would show her mother how wrong she was to despise her.

Lennox returned within the week. 'I decided not to tell my family about us just yet,' he said when she asked. He lifted her chin and smiled into her eyes. 'Don't look at me like that, Eliza. I will tell them soon, I promise. You must understand that they are old and need time to get used to things. Let them get over having me home for a little while before we visit them together.'

He pulled her into his arms and kissed her. 'You look very pretty,' he said, 'even when you are cross with me.' He smiled. 'I saw a magnificent ring in one of the jewellers' windows in Bond Street the other day. It is set with a circle of diamond chips around a fine sapphire as blue as your eyes. Shall I buy it for you?'

Eliza's pursed her lips. He stroked her cheek. 'Darling Eliza, don't be angry. You know how much I love you.'

He felt her body soften against his. 'There, that's better,' he whispered. 'I've missed you so much; it was all I could do to stay away for as long as I did.' His arms tightened around her. 'Come to bed, my love. Everything will be all right, I promise.'

The weeks passed pleasantly. They attended the theatres and drove in Hyde Park in Lennox's smart, canary-yellow brougham. At the opera one evening, Eliza noticed a dark, statuesque woman whose ivory satin dress was so tailored to her magnificent figure that she looked as if she had been sewn into it. Every inch of the fabric was embroidered with delicate seed pearls, and diamonds blazed at her wrists and neck.

'Who is she?' she whispered to Lennox, but he was too much occupied scanning the audience with his opera glasses to hear her.

His friend, Arthur, who often joined them on their outings now, leaned towards her, so close that his chestnut whiskers almost brushed her cheek.

'La Pavia,' he whispered. She's one of what the Parisians call *les grandes horizontales.* People say her mother was a Jewish merchant's daughter ruined by a cousin of the czar of Russia. In revenge, the child eats men for breakfast.'

He grinned. 'Not a sweet little piece like you, my dear.' He ran a finger down her cheek. 'Y'know I'm very fond of you, don't you Eliza? When you and old George are tired of each other, promise you won't forget that?'

Eliza coloured. 'That will never happen.'

Arthur grinned. 'What an innocent you are, my dear.'

In April, Lennox went to visit his family again.

Left alone, Eliza came back from a drive one morning to find a visitor waiting for her. With a jolt, she recognised her sister-in-law, Sarah Watson.

Sarah stood up from her chair, clasping and unclasping her gloved hands.

'Eliza, thank the Lord I have found you, we have all been so worried. There is no point in your trying to hide the truth. After Catherine could not find you at Portsmouth, she spoke to Mrs Sturgis who told her everything. My dear, you will ruin yourself if you go on like this. Come home with me.'

Eliza shook her head. 'I shall stay exactly where I am. George Lennox and I are in love. One day we hope to marry.'

Sarah frowned. 'But Eliza, you are married to Thomas.'

'Then I shall get a divorce.'

'It is not as simple as that. My poor girl, do you think that this man loves you enough to endure the shame that such a state of affairs would bring?'

Eliza flushed. 'I do.' She held out her left hand so that the diamond and sapphire ring caught the light. 'He bought me this. It is to show that we are bound to each other for the rest of our lives.'

Sarah looked at the jewel, her eyes full of concern.

'Eliza, this can only bring misery. I understand his family are wealthy and influential. They are bound to resist such a marriage. They might even cut him off. And then there is his career: the army does not countenance scandal, especially when a man has taken up with the wife of a brother officer. Faced with all that, do you really believe he will be loyal to you?'

Eliza tossed her head. 'I told you. We are in love.'

Sarah shook her head. 'They say love flies out of the window when adversity comes in at the door, Eliza.

Please, I beg you to reconsider. It is not too late. If you go to Scotland, we may be able to keep what has happened from becoming too widely known.'

Eliza turned away and did not speak.

'I'll leave you for tonight,' Sarah said sadly. 'May I come again tomorrow? Your Aunt Catherine would like to see you too.'

Eliza raised an eyebrow. 'So that she can scold me as well?'

'Oh my dear, I do not want to scold you and neither does she. We only want what is best for you. If you are not happy to go to Scotland, you would be very welcome to live with me in Ireland.'

Eliza gave her a watery smile. 'You are very kind Sarah, and I should be glad to see Aunt Catherine but I promise you both, I shall not change my mind. If you could only meet George, you would understand why. We are so happy and I belong here in London with him. I don't want to be anywhere else.'

As summer followed spring, Eliza and Lennox left Great Ryder Street and moved to more fashionable lodgings in Mayfair.

'What are you thinking about?' she asked one morning as they lay late in bed. The sun shone through the sash windows making oblique patterns on the blue and gold bedspread.

He stroked her cheek. 'Nothing much.'

She propped herself up on her elbow. 'Georgie, when will you tell your family about us?'

He looked down and picked at the hem of the sheet. 'Last time I went, you know Father had an attack of gout. It would not have been a good moment to talk about serious things.'

She grimaced. 'And the time before his favourite hunter was lame. Why do you always make some excuse?'

He frowned. 'Don't nag me Eliza. You don't understand how careful I have to be. The old man can be dashed difficult. I must find the right time or I shall ruin everything. As it is, he had a few things to say about this month's bills. We'll have to draw in our horns a bit.'

She pouted. 'I am beginning to wonder if you will ever talk to him.' She lowered her eyes. 'And if you really want us to be married at all.'

Lennox flushed. He got out of bed, pulled on a pair of breeches and went over to the window. Picking up a small, wooden elephant with ruby chips for eyes that stood on the sill, he weighed it in his hand. He remembered seeing many like it in India. How he wished that his life was as simple now as it had been then.

'Of course I do, but there's a lot more to it than that: your divorce for a start. That might take years and your husband hasn't even agreed to it yet.'

Tears sprang to her eyes.

He swallowed. 'I'm sorry, please don't cry. I'll go back soon and try again.'

Summer drew to a close. Within a few weeks, the leaves on the trees in the parks fell in great drifts of red and gold. When Lennox returned from his latest visit to his family, Eliza was determined that she would wait no longer.

'More lies,' she said scornfully when he trotted out his string of excuses.

Her tone cut him. 'Don't call me a liar,' he snapped.

'What should I call you then? I can hardly call you a man who honours his word.'

He took her by the shoulders. 'You don't understand how the world works, Eliza.'

She tore herself away. 'I understand very well,' she blazed. Raising her hand, she slapped his cheek before he could duck away. Wincing, he rubbed the place as a red patch flared up.

'It is lucky for you that I am a gentleman, or I would strike you back for that.'

'You are no gentleman. Hit me if you dare. I think you will find that I am a match for you.'

His eyes widened as she came towards him, her hands reaching for his throat. He grabbed her wrists and shoved her away. With a scream, she fell, but straight away scrambled to her feet to lunge again. White with rage, Lennox backed towards the door. His voice was harsh with the effort of controlling his temper. 'I am going to my club, Eliza. I hope that you will have come to your senses by the time I return.'

She flashed him a glance of pure loathing. 'Go then,' she spat. 'And don't come back.'

But a moment after the door slammed behind him, her face crumpled and a storm of tears overwhelmed her.

'Lovers' tiff, eh?' his friend Arthur grinned, finding Lennox slumped in one of the club's high-backed, leather chairs, staring gloomily into his brandy.

'Sometimes I think I should never have started this.'

Arthur settled himself in the chair opposite and took a sip of his brandy. Ironic, he thought, that his chance seemed to have come at last when he had just taken up with a very spicy little dancer from Covent Garden. Such was life.

'It's always difficult finishing these things,' he said when Lennox had unburdened himself.

'You think I should? Finish with her, I mean.'

'Why of course. Even if the husband lets her go, Mrs James ain't the kind a man marries. You know your family would never accept it. I'm surprised you've managed to keep it from them for so long. They're sure to find out some day and then where will you be? Your commission will be at risk too if the regiment finds out you've taken up with a runaway like her, especially when her husband is a brother officer.'

He looked at Lennox's glum face. 'Do it, my friend or you'll have as much chance of getting on as a cock in a convent. Plenty more fish in the sea.'

'But what can I tell her?'

'Oh, you'll think of something. You could go back to India. You'd be at a safe distance then. Find yourself an heiress instead. Your family would approve of that, I'll be bound.'

'Thank you for the advice.'

'My pleasure.'

Lennox groaned and banged a fist down on the arm of his chair. 'Damn! You're right, I know. I just have to find the courage to tell her.'

'Yes, you do.'

On the way back to their lodgings, Lennox bought tickets for a play that he knew Eliza wanted to see, as well as a bunch of chrysanthemums from a stall at the corner of Grosvenor Square. Heart thumping, he mounted the short flight of stone steps to his front door and let himself in.

Night had fallen outside, but no candles were lit and in the drawing room, the fire was almost out. Eliza crouched by the cooling remains of the logs in the grate. He saw that she had been crying. Putting down the flowers, he went to her. She jumped up and ran into his arms.

'I'm sorry,' she gulped.

He kissed her hair. 'It's I who should be sorry. I've behaved badly. I know it.'

She raised her head with a tremulous smile. 'Then I forgive you. Let's pretend it never happened and be happy again.' She looked at him anxiously. 'We are happy aren't we, Georgie?'

His mouth was dry. 'Of course we are, my love. Of course we are.'

The play that night drew uproarious applause from the audience, but Lennox did not join in the laughter. His silence distracted Eliza. She wished they had not come and was glad when the curtain went down for the last time.

Back at home, Lennox threw down his top hat and cane and went straight to the sideboard. She heard the brandy decanter clink against a glass as he poured a full measure. He took a swig, then another one.

'I'm afraid the play bored you,' she observed.

'Not at all, I was simply tired.'

She put her arms around his neck and reached up to kiss him. 'Shall we go to bed then?'

He ducked away. 'Mind my brandy,'

She frowned. 'What's the matter? Don't you want to?' She noticed that the brandy shivered in his glass. There were beads of perspiration on his brow.

'I'm sorry,' he faltered. 'I have a lot on my mind just now.'

'Can't I help?'

He drew a deep breath. 'Eliza, I have to go back to India.'

'India? Why, we can go together.'

He hesitated.

'Don't you want me to come?'

'Of course I do, but it is not for me to decide.'

She heard the catch in his voice and saw him moisten his lips with his tongue.

'It's no use. I can't lie to you. I haven't been ordered back to the regiment yet. I don't know when I shall be, but we have to part. If we stay together it will be the ruin of us both.'

'But you said you loved me. I thought we would be married.'

Dismayed, she saw that he could not meet her eyes. 'It would never work,' he mumbled. 'We'd only end up hating each other.'

'No, that's impossible.'

He shook his head. 'It's better this way. Maybe your husband will have you back, or you could go to your stepfather's family. I'll give you all the money I can spare and the rent is paid here until the end of the month'

She got up and went across to the mantelpiece. Her knuckles were white against the dark surface of the wood.

'So you just want to be rid of me? How dare you. Do you think I am some little whore to be thrown aside when you're bored?'

'Eliza, don't be like this.'

Seizing a brass candlestick from the mantelpiece, she hurled it at him. It caught him on his right ear and he gave a howl of pain.

'Stop that!' He ducked as she grabbed a second one. It flew through the air, narrowly missing him, and smacked into a windowpane, shattering the glass. Lennox lunged at her and pinioned her arms. His strength was greater than hers and suddenly, she felt exhausted. She went limp in his grasp and tears pricked her eyes.

'You have deceived me,' she said miserably. 'How can you be so weak, so faithless?'

'Eliza, please…'

She shook her head 'I don't want to hear any more. Go. I don't want anything from you.'

Lennox rubbed his throbbing head. 'Very well,' he said in a tight voice. 'I'll send a man for my things.'

She heard him pick up his cane and hat and walk to the door. When it shut behind him, she sank to the floor and wept.

Chapter 12

As the weeks went by, Eliza often regretted that her pride had prevented her from accepting the help that Lennox had offered. She still received Thomas's allowance; obviously the news of her affair had not reached him; but she had never needed to manage her own finances before. Even though she moved to a cheaper part of town, the rate at which money slipped through her fingers alarmed her.

The freezing winter weather did not help. Logs for the fire, food and warm clothes seemed to cost a great deal. She hated her drab rooms. To escape them, she spent hours walking. And even in this weather, she thought wryly, it makes me much warmer than I would have been if I had stayed inside.

Sometimes she rode one of the horse-drawn trams to the West End and looked in the shop windows, but there was nothing in them that she could afford to buy. Sadly, she remembered her shopping trips with George and the stacks of prettily-wrapped parcels that had followed them home.

Coming back to her lodgings one icy afternoon, she met her landlady in the hall. A sour woman with a bulldog face, she had a bundle of Lola's underclothes in her arms.

'I suppose you want the maid to wash these,' she sniffed. 'Soap costs money you know. In future, I shall expect you to provide your own.' She stomped off through the door to the washroom leaving Lola scowling at her retreating back.

'Stupid woman,' Lola muttered. 'What if I was late with the rent last week? You should be grateful that anyone will take your poky rooms.'

Upstairs, she looked at the paltry fire that the maid had prepared whilst she was out. It wouldn't last more than an hour or two but she doubted the landlady would let her have extra logs on account. Not after the exchange they had just had. Perhaps it was time to leave London. But where should she go? Not to Ireland, that was for sure.

Later that night, she thought of Catherine Rae. She had always been so kind. Perhaps she would be prepared to help. In the morning, she wrote her aunt a long letter, then went out to spend some of her precious money on sending it to Edinburgh to where Catherine had moved some years ago.

Caherine replied with an invitation for Eliza to stay for as long as she liked. On the post coach north, she reflected that such generosity was very likely more than she deserved.

Her life in Edinburgh was quiet and unassuming, but at first, she was glad of it. She did not want to be noticed and she was content to spend her days helping Catherine or reading. She immersed herself in the novels of Sir Walter Scott, and when she had exhausted them, the poetry of Burns. How fortunate his lover was, she thought wryly. He promised to love her until all the seas ran dry. The merest puddle had barely had time to seep into the dry earth before George Lennox fell out of love.

One damp, gusty Monday, she and Catherine had spent the morning baking. The windows in the stone-flagged kitchen streamed and the smell of warm, fresh bread, nutmeg and cinnamon filled the steamy air.

Catherine wrapped a thick cloth around her hands and pulled a tray of scones out of the oven. 'I'll take some of these to Mrs Anderson. The poor soul has been in bed all week with a chill.'

Eliza looked out at the grey sky and scudding clouds. 'I think I'll stay here and read for a few hours.'

Catherine tipped the scones onto a rack to cool. 'I'll go and get ready then,' she said.

When she had gone, Eliza sat by the fire. Her attention soon wandered from the book in her lap. She had been in Edinburgh for five months now. She was fond of Catherine but she did not want to stay with her forever. With a sigh, she put down her book and stood up. Perhaps she should have gone to visit Mrs Anderson after all. Going out into the hall, she climbed the creaking stairs to her bedroom to find her sewing basket. A pile of stockings needed mending, a dull chore but at least it would pass the time.

As she came downstairs again, one of the maids was talking to a man at the front door. When he saw her standing at the bottom of the stairs, he pushed past the girl.

'Mrs James?'

Eliza frowned. 'Yes, but what business of yours is it who I am?'

He came closer. She caught the smell of mothballs on his rusty black suit.

'I have come to inform you that your husband, Thomas James, has petitioned for divorce on the grounds of your adultery with one George Lennox.' He held out a paper sealed with red wax.

Eliza took it and broke the seal. She felt numb as she scanned the words. Then anger welled up inside her.

'How dare he do this? He drove me away with his cruelty.'

'The rights and wrongs of the matter are not my concern, Mrs James. I am only the messenger. I wish you good day.'

When Catherine returned, she found Eliza sitting on the bottom stair.

'Whatever has happened?' she asked anxiously.

Eliza held out the paper. Catherine's frown deepened as she read.

'It has taken a long time for the news to reach Bareilly,' Eliza said bitterly, 'but Thomas has found me out at last. He wants his revenge. He intends to divorce me but it will not be the quiet affair I once hoped for: I shall be branded as an adulteress. The whole of society will shun me.'

Catherine's hand flew to her mouth. 'Oh Eliza! I had so hoped that one day you and Thomas might live together again as man and wife.'

Eliza felt Catherine's strong arms around her, rocking her to and fro. The older woman's sympathy overwhelmed the last vestiges of her self-control and she gave way to tears.

'There must be something we can do,' Catherine soothed her. 'I'll write to Sarah Watson straight away. Thomas is very fond of her. Perhaps she can persuade him to change his mind.'

Eliza gulped down her tears and shook her head. 'It will do no good. Why should he? I was not happy with Thomas, but I can't deny what I did.'

'You are a brave girl, Eliza,' Catherine said gently. 'Whatever happens, I promise that there will always be a home for you here with me.'

Slowly, winter lost its grip on the grey city. Icicles melted from railings and eaves and darkness no longer fell in the middle of the afternoon, but there was still no news of when the trial would begin. Eliza read in the newspaper reports that Thomas had not only named Lennox in the divorce proceedings in the ecclesiastical courts, but also lodged a claim against him in the civil courts for substantial damages on the ground of seduction. As far as she could ascertain, Lennox had bolted to France to avoid the hearing. She did not feel any sympathy for him.

In the days that followed, Catherine was tactful and never mentioned Eliza's predicament, but Eliza read the newspapers and knew that her disgrace was common knowledge. She feared that her kind friend's reputation would be tainted by her plight and she tried constantly to think of a way she could leave Catherine's house and support herself. Work as a governess or lady's companion – the least regarded person in any household – would have been respectable, if not at all congenial, but even that would be impossible now.

It was a while before the idea that she might make her way in a more glamorous sphere, perhaps as an actress, formed in her mind. The more she considered the prospect, the more attractive it seemed. 'I have always been complimented on my looks,' she mused. 'They should be an advantage.'

She remembered a celebrated, elderly actress she had met in London, who had planned to set up a school of acting after her retirement. It was a moment before the name came back to her – Mrs Fanny Kelly.

'I've made up my mind to go to London,' she announced to Catherine one day.

'To London! But why? How will you support yourself there?'

'I shall become an actress.'

Catherine's eyes widened. She opened her mouth to protest, but Eliza held up her hand.

'Dear Catherine, you have been so kind. I know there are probably a hundred reasons why I should not go, but I have to do something. I shall go mad if I don't.'

Catherine sighed. She knew how stubborn Eliza could be. If there was a rift between them now, it might never mend.

'If it is what you really want,' she said at last, 'I won't try to stop you. Will you at least promise to come back if you need help?'

Eliza hugged her. 'Thank you for understanding,' she whispered. 'Of course I shall.'

The journey south, on a succession of post coaches, was slow and tedious. The inns were noisy with other coaches coming and going half the night. Food was expensive and poor and the beds were lumpy and damp. By the time she reached London, Eliza had spent most of what she had left over from Thomas's allowance. She found cheap lodgings and went straight to see Fanny Kelly.

Fanny Kelly's life on the stage had inclined her to favour a bohemian mode of dress. She was tall with a narrow, olive-skinned, aristocratic face which she accentuated by concealing her greying hair with elaborate turbans fastened with jewelled brooches. She wore flowing, heavily-embroidered robes in the oriental style. The effect was imposing and, Eliza thought, a little intimidating. She was glad that Fanny did not ask too many questions and agreed to take her on as a pupil for a fee that she could just afford.

In the months that followed, some of the lessons went well but others were not a success.

'How many more times must I tell you to speak up?' Fanny snapped after a difficult morning. 'London theatres need big voices, or the audience will not hear a word.'

Eliza bit her lip. 'I'm doing my best.'

Fanny's tone softened. 'I know you are.'

Eliza sighed. Over time, she had developed an affectionate respect for Fanny and had come to confide in her and trust her opinions.

'I shall never be good enough,' she said sadly. 'What am I to do, Fanny?'

'Life is precarious for us women without the protection of marriage or family. Are you are still determined not to return to Thomas?'

'Determined.'

'It is always possible to find other men to pay the bills.'

Eliza gave her a wry smile. 'You know that I already do, but…'

'You do not love any of them,' Fanny finished for her. 'And I think that you have too much heart and spirit to go on that way for ever. So you must support yourself. But not in the way you have chosen.'

She touched Eliza's cheek. 'You are a beauty and you fill a dress splendidly, but you will not make an actress. Don't look so downcast; all is not lost. If you are determined to go on stage, there is another way.'

She stood back and surveyed Eliza. 'You move gracefully. It's true you are too old to train as a ballerina but other styles are less demanding. Spanish dancing, for example, is very popular at the moment and you have the looks. I could send you to someone who could teach you all you need to know.'

'Do you think it would work?'

'I believe it would.'

Eliza thought for a moment. Perhaps she should try a different approach. Her mother had been born in Ireland, but had often claimed to have Spanish blood. The famous Fanny Essler had danced a bolero at the opera house a few evenings previously. It had looked far less difficult than the classical dances she usually performed.

Fanny smiled. 'Shall I send a note to my friend?'

'May I think about it?'

'Of course; you must take your time.'

Eliza went to the door and collected her bonnet and cloak. In the hall, her escort for the evening waited. Stepping out into the dusk, she felt the nightly fog that descended on London sting the back of her throat. She was glad that she could look forward to an evening at the theatre and a late supper, with a warm carriage to drive her home afterwards. Lightly, she put her hand on her companion's arm and gave her full attention to what he was saying. This latest one was younger than many of the men who squired her about town, and rather handsome. She would be glad of that when the time came to reward his generosity.

Two days later, she returned to Fanny Kelly and accepted her offer. On her first lesson with her new teacher, she knew that she had found her niche. The dancing master, Don Diego Montez de Leon, an impoverished aristocrat exiled from Spain during the Carlist civil war, applauded as she completed the simple steps he had shown her.

'Marvellous! I must admit I was not sure when Mrs Kelly sent you to me, but you have fire and passion: my job is already half done.'

The lessons continued to go well and Eliza grew fond of the elderly, dapper man who was, in spite of his large paunch, still very nimble on his feet. It was too soon to seek any engagements, he told her, but she was confident that would change.

A month went by and then another. As the year drew to a close, the newspapers trumpeted the imminent hearing of the case against Lennox, which would be followed by the case of *James v. James* in the Court of Arches. Eliza began to fear that her carefree days were doomed.

'What will become of me?' she asked Don Diego. 'Half London will turn out to watch the trial. I shall have to endure endless pointing and whispering and at the end of it all, no theatre will employ me.'

'People forget,' he shrugged.

'But not soon enough.'

'You do not have to stay in London.'

'What do you mean?'

'Spain is pleasant at this time of year. My family there would help you and you could perfect your dancing.'

'It is an interesting suggestion.'

'You might even consider a more radical course.'

'Yes?'

'Your dancing has improved a great deal, but if you returned as a true Spaniard, how much more romantic and fascinating your audiences would find you.'

'Change my name?'

'Why not? At a stroke, Mrs James would disappear.' He flourished the cane he used to beat time. 'Pouf, she is gone.'

Eliza thought for a moment. It was a bold plan, but it tempted her. The alternatives were not appealing: at best public ridicule, at worst hostility. A life dependent on the whim of any man whose fancy she caught and loneliness and fear when her looks faded as one day they must. Don Diego's suggestion offered the possibility of a different course, perhaps one that would allow her to control her fate.

She raised her head. 'I'll do it,' she said.

Chapter 13

To raise the fare, she sold the jewels she had been given by her more generous admirers and, with Don Diego's letter in her trunk, set sail from Southampton a few weeks later, bound for Cadiz. Winter seas made the crossing a rough one, but she had always been a good sailor. As the ship neared port, the days grew warmer and she felt full of hope. In the harbour at Cadiz, bright flags fluttered at the mastheads of a huge assortment of steamboats and sailing ships. She noticed that many of the fishing smacks had eyes painted on their bows. She remembered her ayah's tales from long ago of the magic eye that warded off bad luck. She would be glad of such a talisman now.

Disembarking, she joined the crowds on the quayside. Don Diego's family lived in Seville and she knew that the steamer did not leave for two days. As she stood wondering which way she should go, a swarthy man with sharp, black eyes smiled at her.

'Can I help you, senorita? You need somewhere to stay?'

'Do you know of a cheap place?'

'Si, si, I will take you.'

He grabbed her valise and hurried off at such a speed that she had difficulty keeping up with him. He led her through a maze of narrow streets – she feared that she would never be able to retrace her steps – until he stopped at a battered wooden door through which she saw a small courtyard surrounded on three sides by shabby houses. Her heart thumped. She was alone in a strange city. Perhaps she should not have followed the man but it was already too late. He had disappeared through the door of one of the houses.

Inside, she found a cool, dark hallway. At the far end of it was a narrow flight of stairs. She was just in time to see the man shoulder her valise and bound up them.

When she reached the top, she saw an open door. She entered the room cautiously and, as she did so, heard a swift movement behind her. A sinewy arm encircled her neck. She smelled sweat and fear.

'You give me your money and I will not hurt you.'

Eliza fought for breath. The blood roared in her ears and her eyes clouded as panic mounted.

'I have no money,' she gasped.

Summoning all her strength, she kicked at him and caught him on the shin. He howled with pain and, for a vital instant, his grip slackened.

She wrenched away and swung round to rake her nails down his face, then, before he could recover, she flew down the stairs and out into the courtyard. She did not stop running until she had exhausted her last ounce of strength.

Panting, she sank down on a bench beside a fountain and splashed her face with the cool water. Her hand went to the bodice of her dress where she had sewn a small packet before she left England. She closed her eyes and gave thanks. The wretch had her valise but she still had her money. And she had learnt a valuable lesson. She would need something more than courage if she was to protect herself.

For several hours, she tramped the streets until she found a cheap lodging house. The owner eyed her lack of possessions suspiciously, but thawed when she paid for two nights in advance. The following morning, she asked for directions to the nearest market and brought some clothes. She also sought out a stall that sold knives and chose a small dagger with a carved bone handle and a short, keen blade. As she tucked it in her belt, the old man who kept the stall nodded. 'You are alone, senorita?'

'For now, yes.'

'Then you are wise to take that. The city can be a dangerous place.'

Two days passed before she was able to embark on the paddle steamer that would take her up the Quadalquivir to Seville. The countryside they sailed past reminded her of India: brown and dusty with few creatures apart from herons and storks fishing in the shallows, and even fewer people. At last, rounding a bend in the river, Seville came into view. It was evening and the setting sun gilded the venerable city walls and turned the rosy brick of the imposing Giralda tower to violet.

She went first to the house of Don Diego's relations. It was even more humble than she had expected.

'I fear that the war has left us in greatly reduced circumstances,' his sister, Carmela Montez said sadly on the first evening, 'but you are very welcome to stay for as long as you like.' Later, Eliza discovered that her generous hospitality was typical of Sevillians.

In contrast to Cadiz, where the steep terraces of tall, white houses seemed to peer over their neighbours' shoulders for a view of the sea, Seville was a city of low buildings on a broad plain, huddled round the gigantic silhouette of its great cathedral. Many people whitewashed their houses three or even four times a year and the predominant colours of the city were pristine white and the hot blue of the Andalusian sky.

Finding work was hard. The manager of the Teatro Real was courteous but Eliza left his office with nothing. Summoning all her resolve, she set off to find some of the famous theatre's humbler cousins.

Day succeeded day as she trailed around the city's different quarters, until one afternoon, she stopped in a bar in a shabby part of town to buy a glass of wine to revive her spirits. Practising her Spanish on the bartender, she learnt that a nearby theatre often needed chorus girls. She found the place in a small square where a central fountain splashed into a stone bowl. A peasant stood by it watering his donkey. In answer to her question, he pointed to a house that was half-hidden by a jacaranda tree.

As was the practice in Seville, from the street the theatre was indistinguishable from the private houses that flanked it. The only sign that it was a place of entertainment was the trio of lamps that hung above the entrance door. Inside, the floor was of plain earth and the air reeked of tobacco – she soon discovered that Spanish audiences smoked incessantly.

After a brief talk with the manager, she obtained a place in the chorus, dancing six nights a week. As she left with the small advance on her wages that she had succeeded in winning from him, she noticed a man putting up gaudy posters beside the ticket booth. She gave a wry smile. Her theatrical debut was to be in the

131

company of a troupe of gypsy acrobats and a strong man who went by the name of Hércule.

Her first week at the theatre was a moderate success. She found that she could keep up quite easily with the steps that she needed to perform. Hércule turned out to be a charming native of Granada who taught her to smoke in the Spanish fashion – inhaling the smoke deep into her lungs. At first, she felt dizzy and he laughed at her, but she soon became accustomed to the habit.

As she grew more familiar with Seville, it surprised her to find that unlike in England, here it was acceptable for unmarried women to meet and talk with their suitors without being overheard by a chaperone. It seemed a sensible arrangement. At least the parties to a marriage would have a good chance of understanding each other before they agreed to marry. She might never have made her own mistake if she had known Thomas better, before it was too late.

One evening, strolling along La Cristina, the fashionable promenade by the Quadalquivir, she stopped to light her cigarillo at one of the posts wrapped around with burning, sulphur-coated rope that the Sevillian authorities provided for the purpose, when she heard a voice call her name. Turning, she saw Bibiana, one of her fellow chorus girls walking on the arm of her young man.

'Eliza, come and meet Felipe, *mi novio.* We are going to eat ices at our favourite café. Will you join us?'

Seated in the café, they chatted in a mixture of Spanish and English – both Bibiana and Felipe spoke a little of the latter - and watched the crowds passing by. A young man dressed in blue velvet breeches with silver filigree buttons and carrying a long, white stick attracted Eliza's gaze. He wore an egg-yolk yellow sash around his waist and his black jacket was cut short to the waist and lavishly decorated with arabesques of scarlet leather and silver thread. His three-cornered hat was high-crowned and glossy-black.

'A *majo*,' Bibiana remarked. 'They like to show off the traditional costume.'

'It's splendid; I'm surprised more people don't wear it.'

Felipe frowned. 'We are a modern people now, not just picturesque curiosities for foreign artists to paint.'

Bibiana shot him a reproving look.

'Forgive me, I did not mean to be rude, but it is important to say it.'

Eliza smiled. 'I'm sorry too. I did not mean to give offence.'

'If Eliza does want to see some of the old ways,' Bibiana observed, 'we should take her to visit the gypsies up in the caves.'

Felipe raised an eyebrow. 'It is a long way and often dangerous.'

'Eliza is brave,' Bibiana laughed. She had heard the story of the robber and seen the dagger.

'Well, if she would like to come, we shall take her.'

A few nights later, mounted on donkeys, they trotted out of the city and up into the wild countryside beyond. Eliza had not ridden since the days in India with Thomas, and the donkey could not match her old mare's smooth gait, but she felt exhilarated by the cool crisp air and the stark beauty of the landscape. She breathed in the scent of wild fennel and thyme.

The moonlight had turned the stony path to a ribbon of mother of pearl and cast fantastical shadows on the rocks through which it wound. Her donkey picked out the way gingerly and she leaned to pat his neck, feeling the rough tufts of gaily- coloured wool that decorated his harness.

'Well done, little fellow,' she murmured.

'Nearly there,' Felipe said, drawing up in front of her. At that moment, there was a sharp command and a shadowy figure stepped out from behind a rock. He wore faded brown breeches and a ragged jacket. A wolf-skin cap was pulled low over his eyes.

'It's all right,' Felipe whispered. 'He's one of the gypsies. He won't hurt us but we have to lead the donkeys from here; the path gets much rougher.'

He dismounted and went up to the gypsy. Eliza heard a few words pass between them, then the chink of coins. A few minutes further on, the gypsy motioned them to tie their donkeys to a nearby tree. He went to a place where a large piece of coarse tapestry hung against the rocks and pushed it aside. Inside the cave, the gypsy families sat around a central fire. One old man stood up and spoke in rapid, guttural Spanish that Eliza could not follow.

'He's saying we are welcome,' Bibiana whispered. 'They are asking us if we will eat with them.'

A huge pot hung on a tripod over the fire and in a while, a raddled old woman dressed in a faded green dress ladled food into wooden bowls. Eliza took hers and smiled her thanks. She watched everyone dive into the food with their hands and followed suit.

The meal was simple but tasty: rice with a few pieces of coarse, garlicky chorizo and scraps of strongly-flavoured meat.

'Goat,' Bibiana whispered. 'It's good, yes?'

Flagons with long spouts were passed round. The wine was strong and almost black. Eliza felt her head swim.

'There will be dancing now,' Bibiana said as the meal ended.

The dying fire was shovelled away from the middle of the cave and the light now came from the oil lamps smoking on the walls. A striking young woman stood up and came forward. Her black hair hung to her waist and she wore a flounced, blue dress powdered with stars. Her bare calves were tattooed with henna lilies and birds and her feet were shoeless. Skeins of amber beads swathed her neck and wrists. She had a long, sallow face with an aquiline nose. Eliza suspected that as she aged, she would become as gnarled as the older women in the cave but for now, she was beautiful with a presence so commanding that Eliza could not take her eyes off her.

The girl raised her arms above her head and a pair of black castanets snapped between her slim fingers. A guitar struck up and she began to dance, languorously at first then with mounting intensity. Sweat beaded her forehead. Her undulating limbs seemed to write poetry on the air. As she strutted and stamped, it seemed to Eliza that it was the poetry of avenging contempt.

'*El Olano,*' Bibiana whispered. 'A poisonous spider has walked up her skirt. You will see: she will find it and crush it to death.' She smiled. 'It shows how she would do the same to a lover if he betrayed her.'

When the last chords died away, the girl stood completely still then shouts of 'Brava! Brava, Lola!' set the echoes flying around the glistening walls of the cave.

A man walked into the circle.

'Brava, Lola,' Eliza heard him say more softly. He put his arms around the girl and they kissed as if there was no one else in the world.

Eliza felt a pang of envy twist her heart. How she wanted to be like the girl. No, that was not quite the truth. She wanted to be her: to have the power to bewitch her onlookers with her dance and then be held in arms of the man she loved, savouring his kisses and hearing him speak her name like a caress.

Part 2

1843 - 1846

Lola

Chapter 14

Few English newspapers reached Seville, and those that did were weeks old, but in a while, Eliza managed to ascertain that the court cases Thomas had brought against her and Lennox were both over. Lennox had paid a hundred pounds in compensation.

She grimaced. 'So that is my price,' she muttered. 'But at least I am free of Thomas at last.'

There was no need to stay out of England now, she reasoned. She doubted that her career was likely to progress any further in Spain. In London, however, if she presented herself as a real Spanish dancer, she would be more of a rarity and perhaps any deficiencies in her dancing might not be so obvious.

The more she thought about it, the more convinced she became that it was time to go back and try her luck. As her new name, she chose Lola for the gypsy dancer and Montez for the family who had welcomed her so warmly.

At Southampton, she waited whilst the Spanish consul scanned her papers. She felt a qualm when she saw him frown.

'It is not clear to me where you come from in Spain, Dona Montez,' he said. 'Forgive me for saying so, but your accent is unusual.'

'I have lived in many places; no doubt that it why.'

'There are some irregularities here,' he said after a few more moments, 'and certain documents that I would expect to see are missing.'

Silently, Lola cursed the back-street trader who had prepared the papers and promised her that they would pass the keenest scrutiny.

'So much was lost when my husband died,' she sighed. She dabbed her eyes with a small lace handkerchief and gave the consul a wan smile. 'It is very painful for me to remember those terrible times. All I want now is to go to my friends in London.' A lie, but she had already decided that it would be best not to appear friendless.

The consul rolled up the papers and re-tied them with their red ribbon. 'Then I shall not distress you any longer. I wish you luck, Dona Montez, and a safe journey.'

At the station, locomotives screeched and steamed, filling the glass and iron canopy over the platforms with sooty vapour. Luggage carts trundled by and she picked out one piled high with brass-bound, leather trunks, emblazoned with gilded coronets. She observed with interest the distinguished-looking gentleman giving instructions to the sweating porter. When he stopped at a first-class carriage and went up the steep steps, she halted abruptly.

'I shall get in here,' she told her own porter. 'Take my bags down to the luggage car.'

She slipped a few coins into his hand. As she disappeared into the train, he looked at them with disappointment. The amount was considerably less than he had expected from a woman who bore herself like a lady of quality, but come to think of it, her black cloak and dress had been a bit rusty. He shrugged and pushed the trolley onwards. You got all sorts on Southampton station.

As the train steamed through the fields of Hampshire, Lola sat back in the plush velvet seat opposite the Earl of Malmesbury. She congratulated herself on her choice. He seemed very ready to be affable.

'Tell me more, Dona Montez,' he said, stretching out his long legs.

She gave him her most soulful look and continued the story that she had rehearsed so many times on the voyage home.

'My late husband, Don Diego Montez, was executed for his support of the liberal cause in the civil war. I had no other family and I could not bear to stay in Spain alone. It was dangerous too, so I came to England. Don Diego left me a little property in London. I hope to sell it.'

'And you have no one to turn to? No friends?'

She shook her head. 'No, but as a young girl, I trained as a dancer. Before I married, I was a principal at the Teatro Real in Seville. I shall try to make my living from that.'

'Your courage is admirable, Dona Montez. If I can be of any assistance, I hope that you will not hesitate to ask me.'

'You are so kind. I was not sure what I would find in England. I had been told that the English people are very cold.'

'Slanderous!' he laughed. 'I shall do my utmost to prove that that is a base lie.'

She lowered her eyelashes. 'I am so glad to hear you say this,' she said softly. 'Especially as I think no one will deny that we Spanish are a very passionate race.'

141

A week later, as the first act of *The Barber of Seville* romped to its end at Her Majesty's Theatre, Benjamin Lumley, the theatre's manager, felt a twinge of apprehension go through him. He had taken a risk employing this unknown woman to perform the interval dances, but the Earl of Malmesbury had been most pressing and he was a very important patron of the theatre. Of course, Spanish dancers were becoming all the rage now; that should give a good chance of success. He just hoped that this Dona Montez knew how to dance as well as she knew how to charm.

Through the peep hole at the back of the stage, Lola surveyed the audience. In the lighted auditorium, she saw row upon row of men in evening dress, their black and white alleviated here and there by bright spots of women's dresses.

She placed her hands on her hips and smiled. In a tight, black velvet bodice that segued into a yellow-and-black-striped, Andalusian skirt, she knew that she looked her best. A mantilla of delicate black lace, fastened at each temple by a crimson camellia, covered her hair.

After the singers had taken their bows, the curtain was lowered for a few moments to allow the stage hands to change to the backdrop for her performance. As they rolled it down, she heard the crackle of stiff, heavy paper. She closed her eyes and pictured the painted vista of the Alhambra with its marble domes, silvery fountains and emerald and blue peacocks. Tonight she would be in Spain and the audience with her.

'Places!' a voice shouted. The corps de ballet's satin slippers pattered over the bare boards as they

142

hurried to their positions to await her entrance. She looped the strings of her castanets around her wrists and stepped onto to the stage. An expectant hush fell.

She strutted through a *bolero* and finished to a smattering of applause, but it was far less warm than she had hoped for. The corps de ballet joined her in the next dance. This time, to her relief, the response was more encouraging. When the music ended, she came to the footlights. Her heart fluttered as a sea of faces looked up at her. Were they smiling? She hoped so. *Brava, brava, Lola*, she repeated under her breath.

'Ladies and Gentlemen! Thank you for your kindness. When I came to London, a refugee from my homeland, I did not dare to hope that your country would welcome me as generously as it has done. I should like to show my gratitude by performing a dance that is very close to my heart. I learnt it when I was a child from the gypsies who live high in the hills and caves of Andalusia. It is the story of a young girl who is attacked by a dangerous spider, and must defend herself.' She waved an imperious hand to the conductor.

'Play for me: *El Olano.*'

At first, as she mimed the search for the spider, the audience watched in silence, then some of them started to clap and cheer her on. The mood was infectious. When she had thoroughly crushed her imaginary insect, displaying as much as she dared of her shapely ankles and calves, the theatre erupted in applause.

After she had given an encore and left the stage for the last time, a throng of admirers jostled to get into her dressing room. Laughing and joking, she accepted their compliments. But amid all the excitement, she did not notice Lumley's absence. He was talking with a small group of men who had stopped him by the stage door.

All of them were well-known in society and connoisseurs of the arts.

'What the devil's going on, Lumley,' one of them growled. 'That looked like little Eliza James on stage. Surely you remember her? She went about with a young fellow called Lennox a year or two ago when she already had a husband in India. When he found out, he divorced her for adultery. She's no more Spanish than my dog.'

Lumley felt a flush creep up his neck. If the damned woman has lied to me, he thought, I have a disaster on my hands. It was not worth risking his reputation for a quick profit. Lax morals were not uncommon amongst dancers but an adulterous wife was a different matter, and the disaster would be compounded if she wasn't Spanish at all. He had made a great point of her authenticity, and the public did not relish being tricked out of the price of their ticket.

'I engaged her in good faith, gentlemen' he spluttered. 'But I assure you, if what you say is true, tonight will be the last time she appears on my stage.'

'Glad to hear it,' one of the other men cut in. 'Her Majesty's has always had an excellent reputation. I am sure you would not want anything to change that.'

Lumley's hands were clammy with sweat. 'You have my word as a gentleman. If she has lied to me, I shall dismiss her at once.'

Lola rose late the next morning and read her reviews. She was gratified to see that they were flattering. Lumley had sent a note requesting her visit him but she did not bother to go until early evening. When she arrived, his gloomy face surprised her.

'What is the matter?' she asked. 'Surely I was a great success?'

'There is more to it than that,' he muttered.

As he levelled the accusations against her, Lola's face darkened.

'I have been insulted,' she spat. 'I insist that I be given the chance to face my accusers personally.'

'So none of this is true?

'Not a word. I have a right to defend myself and I shall.'

'But these are men from eminent families.'

Lola drew herself up to her full height. 'And I am a Montez!'

She saw how he frowned and chewed his thumbnail.

'Will you take their word or mine?' she snapped.

Lumley leaned across the desk towards her. 'Forgive me, Dona Montez, my theatre's reputation is at stake. No doubt there has been some misunderstanding, but I think it would be better if your engagement came to an end.'

She drew herself up. 'I thought that in England I would be free from persecution, but I see that I was wrong.'

'I'm sorry: there is nothing I can do.'

'You will regret this. I have many friends in the aristocracy.'

Lumley leaned back in his chair. He was starting to feel angry. 'Then I suggest that you look to them for help. Good afternoon, Dona Montez.'

The newspapers were soon at war over her identity. She had a choice: to flee or to fight. She chose the latter. *Sir,* she wrote to the editor of *The Age*

*Since I have had the honour of dancing at Her
Majesty's Theatre, when I was received by the English
public in so kind and flattering a manner, I have been
cruelly annoyed by reports that I am not the person I
claim to be, and that I have long been known in London
as a disreputable character. I entreat you sir, to allow
me, through the medium of your respected journal, to
assure you and the public in the most positive and
unqualified manner, that there is not one word of truth
in such a statement.*

*I am a native of Seville and in the year 1833, when I
was ten years old, was sent to a catholic lady in Bath,
where I remained seven months and was then taken
back to my parents in Spain. From that period until
April last when I landed in England, I never set foot in
this country and I never saw London before in my life.
The imperfect English I speak I learned in Bath, and
from an Irish nurse, who has been many years in my
family.*

She put down the pen and flexed her fingers,
cramped by the ferocity of her grasp. Perhaps she had
deviated a little from the truth but it was permissible.
She felt confident and powerful, ready to make her own
future. And if she could do that, she could also remake
her past.

London society buzzed with speculation. Lola had her
supporters amongst the press, but her most vociferous
detractor, the editor of *The Age* was determined to
discredit her.

Reading his latest piece, Lola stubbed out on the
page the cigarillo that she was smoking and narrowed
her eyes. 'It is time that we met,' she muttered and as

she stood up, her fingers brushed the Spanish dagger that she still carried at her belt.

When she swept unannounced into his office, the editor recognised her straight away. He sprang to his feet. 'This is most unorthodox,' he spluttered.

'And your conduct has been most shameful.'

'Be careful, madam. If you were a man, I would challenge you for that.'

She gave a cool smile. 'As I am a woman, I am happy to accept.'

He snorted. 'You are wasting my time. Please leave.'

'No I will not: there are a great many things I wish to tell you.'

He gritted his teeth. 'Very well, I will spare you five minutes but not one second more.'

He looked at the curious faces of his staff peering through the door. 'Get back to work,' he shouted.

Lola perched on the side of his desk. She picked up the tinderbox that lay there, lit her cigarillo, then exhaled a curl of blue smoke.

'I can recommend these,' she remarked. 'I have them sent to me from Seville. May I offer you one?'

The editor scowled. 'Thank you, no. And do not forget, I said five minutes, madam.'

She laughed. 'We Spaniards do not like to be hurried. Now tell me, sir, are you acquainted with my country?'

'As it happens, madam, I am not, but I do not see what that has to do with the veracity of your position.'

'Ah, but there you are wrong. You cannot judge me if you are not familiar with it. If you were, you would know that Seville is full of people, people of importance, who would vouch for me if they were here.'

'I have only your word for that.'

She tossed her head. 'If you wish, I can obtain letters.'

She would write them herself if she had to. She saw the look of uncertainty on the editor's face and felt her confidence rise. This man would not find it as easy as he might have thought to beat her. She still had plenty of arguments up her sleeve.

When the clock struck three an hour later, she was still there, and when the hands passed four and five. Eventually, six o'clock approached and she stood up. The editor was slumped in his chair. He had said very little for the last hour.

She gave him her most charming smile.

'Thank you for your hospitality, sir. I must leave you now and dress for the evening. I hope that I may assume that you will print a full apology in your newspaper?'

He grunted. 'Your capacity for argument outstrips even my own, madam. I shall think about it.'

She nodded. 'Good. But please do not think for too long.'

Her belief that she had triumphed over the editor of *The Age* buoyed Lola up for a while. But as days passed and she scanned the paper in vain for an apology, her exasperation grew. She marched to his office once more, but this time, he was ready and the door was shut in her face.

She lobbied Benjamin Lumley with no more success. Her frustration increased as people started to cut her. Even though there were still men willing to foot her bills, their numbers dwindled rapidly.

When gossip spreads, she thought glumly, doors close. She reviewed her prospects with a grimace. She could take a lover, but the life of a kept woman was not always all it was reputed to be. Visited once a week perhaps, when her protector could sneak away from his wife, then for the rest of the time, left to languish in some little love nest, bored out of her wits. Even life with Thomas might have been less dreary than that.

Then one evening at a party - one that she might formerly have declined in favour of something grander - she was touring the room on the arm of her host, a banker with European connections, when there was a stir by the entrance doors. A portly, middle-aged man, resplendent in a white dress uniform loaded with gold braid and ostentatious decorations had just arrived. A small entourage surrounded him.

The host put his monocle to his eye. 'Ah, here is Prince Heinrich.'

'A prince?' Lola's ears pricked up.

'Indeed, Prince Heinrich the Seventy-Second of Reuss-Lobenstein-Ebersdorff.'

Lola laughed. 'What an absurd name.'

'You must not let him hear you say that. He may have more syllables to his name than lands, but he is a god in his own country and he has a powerful sense of his own dignity, even if he is rather out of his depth in the big, bad world.'

'You mean he is pompous?'

Her host chuckled. 'A good man for all that. Let us go and greet him. By the way, he speaks very little English, so unless you have a good command of German, I suggest you talk to him in French.'

'I have heard much of your dancing,' the prince said in his ponderous French after they had been introduced. 'I look forward to seeing it for myself before I leave London.'

'I fear that my engagements here are at an end, Your Majesty.'

'A great pity.'

She thought quickly. 'But I have many invitations to perform my work in Europe. I plan to leave for Germany soon.'

'Then you must favour me with a visit at Schloss Ebersdorf.'

Lola looked at him over her fan. 'What a delightful idea.'

By the time the carriages arrived to take the guests home, the prince was captivated. He even found himself offering to settle some of Lola's more pressing debts, and they parted with mutual promises to renew their acquaintance in Reuss-Lobenstein-Ebersdorff.

Chapter 15

Lola sailed from Blackwall to Hamburg not long afterwards.

Before she left England, she had not realised how much the weight of malicious gossip and newspaper attacks had oppressed her. Standing on deck as the ship crossed the North Sea, she gazed at the rolling waves and felt the wind in her hair. Reuss-Lobenstein-Ebersdorff. It sounded like a setting for a comic opera. It might be just what she needed. She was glad she had decided to go.

In Hamburg, she wrote to her new friend Prince Heinrich telling him that she would arrive shortly, and would travel as far as Leipzig by train. The court was thrown into a whirlwind of preparations for her arrival. The servants grumbled as they cleaned corners of the palace that had been home to spiders for decades and polished mountains of silver and crystal glass. Gardeners worked from dawn until dusk weeding and pruning borders to display the prince's precious plants to their best advantage, and the courtiers dusted off their gala uniforms.

Six of the prince's finest horses were harnessed to the great state coach and dispatched to meet Lola at Leipzig. She clapped her hands when she saw the equipage and pointed to the trunks that the station porters were dragging out to the courtyard.

'Strap those to the roof of the coach,' she ordered in French.

Heinrich's men looked at her blankly. She was about to tell them off when she realised that they probably did not speak French. Having a natural ear for languages, in the last few weeks, she had already picked up some German, so she tried again with that. This time they understood her but their expressions were still perturbed.

'We have brought a separate wagon for the luggage, my lady,' one of the men said. He indicated a covered cart drawn by two mules.

'No, I want it on the roof,' she said, giving him a sharp tap on the arm with her fan.

He shuffled his feet. It had taken hours of hard work to bring the state coach to its spotless condition, the trunks might scratch the gleaming paintwork, but on the other hand, the Serenissimus had given orders that his guest was to be treated with great deference. Reluctantly, he motioned to the footmen to do as she said.

'Everyone who is not needed to drive the coach must ride inside with me,' Lola went on. 'I cannot bear to have no one to talk with. Come along,' she laughed. 'I am a guest of your prince and must have my way.'

As the coach swayed along the dusty roads, Lola rolled cigarettes and, between puffs, practised her newly-acquired German on Heinrich's servants. They hardly spoke at all. 'Have we much further to go?' she asked after several hours of this one-sided conversation.

'We have just crossed the border,' the eldest man said.

Lola pulled down the window and peered out at the dusty road. All she saw was dense woodland, broken up by a few fields and small farms. 'What does the prince do here all day?' she asked.

'The Serenissimus hunts and visits his villages and farms.'

'Is that all?'

'Yes, my lady.'

'How dull,' she yawned.

The man's jaw dropped.

She leaned her arm out of the open window and banged on the crested door. 'Stop,' she shouted over the rattling of the wheels. The coachman hauled on the reins and the coach juddered to a halt. Lola jumped out and began to climb up onto the box. He watched her open-mouthed.

'I am bored,' she declared. 'Give me those.' She pointed to the reins.

The horses snorted and pawed the ground. An expression of horror came over the man's face. 'It is too dangerous,' he said.

Lola glowered, then, as suddenly as it had come, her irritable mood faded. She gave a brilliant smile. 'Oh, if you insist, I suppose I can go the rest of the way inside.'

A few hours later, the coach rumbled into the cobbled main square at Ebersdorf. A drum roll rang out and the guard of honour which had waited to greet Lola since early morning snapped to attention. She climbed down from the coach and marched along the line of blue and white uniforms, studying each man as if she was a general inspecting his troops. An aide hurried to fetch the prince and, in a few moments, with a broad smile on his florid face, Heinrich arrived to welcome her.

Ebersdorf was a modest town where, in the course of five centuries, the half-timbered houses had settled into a cock-eyed geometry of crooked gables and tipsy roofs. Heinrich's palace had, however, replaced the medieval castle and it was in the classical style.

That evening, the cream of Reussian society gathered there to meet Lola. In the gilded state apartments, huge vases of musk roses and lilies stood on every surface; champagne flowed and the dining tables groaned with game from the forests, and peaches, melons, figs and pomegranates from the hothouses.

After dinner, the court orchestra played waltzes and polkas so that the guests might dance. The music would not have passed muster at Her Majesty's Theatre, but Lola was having far too much fun to notice. Chatting in the mixture of German and French at which she was becoming very adept, she impressed everyone with her candid charm and good manners.

After a few days, however, life at the small court began to pale. The gala welcome over, the prince returned to his usual occupations of hunting and inspecting his villages and farms. Lola loved to ride, but she disliked hunting and the allure of inspecting the tiny villages and farms, picturesque as they were, soon faded. It also irked her that the whole country seems to treat the prince as if he was a god.

'The dynasty of Reuss-Lobenstein-Ebersdorff must be a very ancient one,' she observed as she rode with him early one morning. 'Seventy-one Heinrichs alone before you.'

'All my predecessors have been called Heinrich; indeed every male member of my family has the same name. My father was Heinrich the Fifty-First but twenty-one male children were born between us.'

Lola laughed. 'Did no one have the wit to choose any other names? A few Wilhelms, Franzs or Josephs would have made a pleasant change.'

The prince coloured. 'It has always been arranged this way.'

Lola shrugged. 'I meant no offence.'

She struck her horse's flank with her riding crop. 'Come on, I'll race you back,' she called over her shoulder as the animal broke into a gallop. The prince spurred his stallion to follow her, but to add to his indignation, she reached the stables first.

Lola had developed a fondness for the prince's St Bernard, Turk, which the big, shaggy dog returned whole-heartedly. That afternoon, he followed her into the palace gardens to walk in the sunshine.

'Your master is a pompous old fool, Turk,' she muttered scratching him behind the ears. His eyelids drooped with ecstasy and his pink tongue lolled from his jowls. 'I have never known a man spend so much time on primping and preening as he does,' she went on. 'As for the way he likes to run his court, I cannot understand how everyone endures so much tedious ceremony and solemn conversation.'

They passed a bed of pinks and she flicked at them with the switch she carried, decapitating a few. 'I know,' she chuckled. 'I'll make Heinrich a gift.' Soon, she had picked every flower and, sitting on the sun-warmed grass with Turk at her side, she wove them into a garland. When she reached the royal stables, she found the prince's stallion in his stall drowsing in the afternoon heat. He lifted his head as she approached and whinnied.

'Good fellow,' she murmured. She reached up on tiptoe and dropped the garland over his head, then stood

155

back and surveyed the effect. 'There, you look splendid.'

A groom came round the corner of the stable and stopped short at the sight. His hand flew to his mouth, but Lola wagged her finger at him. 'It is a surprise for the prince. If you take it off before he sees it, I shall be very angry.'

The stallion still wore the wilting garland when Heinrich came early the next morning. He fumed as he rode out to the hunt. If he had known what a trial this woman would be he would never have invited her.

The hunt bagged a fine stag that morning and when Heinrich returned, he was in a happier frame of mind. Noticing the dead flowers scattered on the muck heap where one of the grooms had tossed them, he remembered Lola. Perhaps he should do more to amuse her. He beckoned to his master of ceremonies.

'You wish for something, Your Majesty?' he asked, riding up on his bay gelding.

'I have been thinking. We should organise an entertainment for our lovely visitor. What do you suggest?'

The man thought for a moment. 'An outing to your hunting lodge might amuse her. It is very beautiful there at this time of year and she has not seen it yet.'

Heinrich smiled. The hunting lodge was one of his favourite spots. 'Excellent idea,' he beamed. 'Make the arrangements at once.'

Dew still silvered the grass as the royal party rode out to the hunting lodge the following morning. Lola feared that she might have gone too far with her joke the previous day and she tried to please Heinrich by showing great interest when he insisted on taking her round every nook and cranny of his beloved building, stopping at each stag or boar's head on the walls to tell the story of the animal's final hours.

When he had finished, the party moved to a pretty glade nearby where they sat down at long tables covered with crisp, white cloths and tucked into a hearty meal of bread, honey, sausage, fresh eggs and ham, washed down with tankards of foaming wheat beer. As they ate, music drifted through the oaks and lindens surrounding them.

'What is that?' Lola asked.

'I have asked the band of the local foresters and miners to entertain us,' Heinrich replied and, still playing, the band came into the clearing, the sunlight gleaming on their instruments.

Lola smiled. 'How charming they look.'

The tune came to an end and Heinrich turned to his master of ceremonies. 'Tell them to keep playing. They must wait for their beer and sausage.'

After a hurried conference, the band struck up a new tune. This time, however, they did not know their parts so well and at each discord, Lola winced.

The prince scowled. 'The music does not please you?'

Lola rolled her eyes as one of the trumpets wobbled and died away with a squeak. The prince's ears reddened.

Just then, a small procession of children, the boys in short leather trousers and white shirts with brightly embroidered braces, and the girls in colourful dresses and kerchiefs, marched into the glade and began to climb up into the trees.

'What are they doing?' she asked.

'They are going to sing.'

Lola sat with her fork halfway to her mouth and listened to the high-pitched voices labouring through a Reussian folksong. Suddenly she dropped the fork with a clatter and sprang up, clamping her hands over her ears.

'I beg you, make them stop,' she cried. 'It is too horrible.'

The prince jumped to his feet as well. 'Stop the music,' he roared. He seized Lola by the wrist. 'Sit down, Madam, you forget your manners.'

Her eyes blazed and her hand went to the dagger that she still carried in her belt. A gasp of horror rose from the rest of the party and for a moment everyone held their breath.

She blinked and let her hand drop. 'Forgive me. I was alarmed.'

The prince's mouth was dry and his hand shook.

'The concert is at an end,' he barked.

The band slunk away to find their beer and sausage and the chorus of children scrambled down from the trees. As he passed the royal party, one of the boys stared at Lola and pulled a face. In a flash, she leaned over to Turk who was sleeping at her feet and tweaked the scruff of his neck.

'Get him!' she commanded, pointing at the boy.

As Turk lumbered to his feet, the boy broke into a run, but he had not gone ten yards before the dog caught him and sank his teeth into his leg. Heinrich was beside them in a moment. He grabbed Turk by the collar and hauled him off the shrieking boy who limped sobbing into the trees.

The prince rounded on Lola. 'This must not happen again! I am the master here.'

'And I am the mistress.'

The courtiers froze, their eyes exchanging anxious glances. His face purple, Heinrich stomped off in the direction of the stables. At the edge of the glade, he swung round.

'You, come with me,' he growled, pointing to his most trusted aide. 'The rest may stay here and continue with the entertainment. I do not wish to see anyone back at the palace before evening.'

For a few moments after he had left, no one spoke. Then Lola stood up. 'I fear that the prince did not find my little joke amusing.'

Her smile encompassed the whole party and it was irresistible. Soon everyone was laughing at her witty apologies. 'And so,' she ended, 'I hope we can still enjoy the day. Who will come with me to explore the woods?'

At the top of a low hill, they stopped to admire the sea of trees below. Lola turned to a good-looking young man with soft, fair hair and a sparse beard.

'Will you dance with me?'

He blushed to the roots of his hair at her attention. 'I am not much of a dancer,' he said.

She swayed from side to side humming a tune then reached for his hands. 'But I am a very good teacher.'

Soon the whole party joined in, enjoying themselves enormously as they tried out the steps that she showed them.

The air was cooling by the time the party returned to the hunting lodge and the grand banquet that awaited them. Everyone was mellow with good food and wine when the prince's aide entered the dining room. Lola looked up in surprise as he touched her shoulder.

'I should like a word in private.'

She nodded and followed him into a small ante-chamber where he handed her two envelopes.

'What are these?'

'I suggest you read them for yourself.'

Lola tore them open in turn. The first letter was from the prince and the second a letter of introduction to the Kapellmeister at the Court Theatre of Dresden.

She looked up. 'So your master wishes to be rid of me?'

'The prince has enjoyed your visit, Dona Montez, but he regrets that affairs of state oblige him to ask you to cut it short.'

'When would he like me to leave the country?'

'He suggests tonight.'

Lola laughed. 'At least it is not a long journey.'

The aide bowed stiffly. 'I have a carriage waiting outside. If you will permit me, I shall escort you back to the palace.'

'Oh very well, but you must wait whilst I make my adieux.'

An hour later, she came out to the courtyard. Doing his best to conceal his irritation, the aide handed her into the carriage. All the way back to the palace, she talked gaily in spite of his monosyllabic replies.

'You must accompany me to my apartments,' she said as the carriage clattered into the courtyard.

'I do not think that would be appropriate.'

'What nonsense, I merely want to give you something.'

He followed her up the grand staircase, preferring not to risk a scene that was likely to increase the prince's outrage. In her room, she rummaged in one of her trunks and pulled out a pair of castanets. 'There,' she tossed them to the surprised man, 'wish your master goodbye from me and tell him they are a gift to remind him of my visit.'

Chapter 16

Dresden

Lola sat in the drawing room of her suite with the morning's newspapers strewn around her. Picking one up, she thumbed her way through the theatre pages, looking for her reviews.

At the moment we are seeing a curious and lovely vision on our stage, one began. That was good; she read on. *In London she had the greatest success and was received with distinction by Queen Victoria herself; indeed she was allowed to demonstrate before that august personage her second and not inferior talent, the playing of native Spanish songs on the guitar, something she does not perform in public.'*

She put the paper down. She had given that last version of her career in London to the correspondent of the *Deutsche Allgemeine Zeitung* two nights ago. She was glad that he had not, as she had feared, been too drunk to remember it.

She turned to another report and frowned. This critic was less kind. *'We found in Dona Montez little grace in her poses or movements...* She tossed the paper away. Why should she care for a fool's opinions?

Her performance the previous evening had been the last of the three guest appearances the Kappelmeister had booked. She had few regrets that she would now be leaving for Berlin, the capital of the kingdom of Prussia. She had exhausted her repertoire, and the audiences' reactions had been very mixed. The citizens of Dresden were clearly fonder of opera than ballet. Everyone raved about a young composer, Richard Wagner, whose opera, *The Flying Dutchman*, had been premiered that winter, to great acclaim. From what she had heard, it sounded a very gloomy piece, but if that was what these Dresdeners wanted, they were welcome to it.

She breakfasted on rolls and coffee whilst her maid finished packing the trunks. The journey to Berlin would take several days. Once there, she planned to take the letters of recommendation she had managed to obtain in Dresden to the Kappelmeister of the Royal Opera House.

When she arrived in Berlin, however, she found that it had suffered a disaster that thwarted her plans. A few days beforehand, a fire had broken out at the Royal Opera House. The building, one of the city's jewels which had stood on Unter den Linden since the days of Frederick the Great, was a ruin.

When the post coach that she travelled in stopped for its passengers to view the damage, Lola looked with dismay at the heaps of blackened masonry and twisted iron. In many places, acrid smoke still rose into the air. Workmen stood about, unsure of what to do.

'Ground's so hot, you'd scald the soles of your feet if you were fool enough to walk on it,' one of them remarked, shaking his head. 'Don't you come too close, lady.'

'Were many people hurt?' she asked.

'God be thanked, no. The fire started after the place had closed for the night.'

'So where are they all now?'

'The company? At the Schauspielhaus. The Kappelmeister hopes to set up there for a while.'

She thanked him and as the coach trundled on, decided what she must do. It would not be a good time to approach the Kappelmeister, but she needed money. She must try.

'He is too busy to see anyone,' his assistant said when she presented her compliments. 'We have no costumes, no props and all the scenery is burnt or ruined by the firemen's hoses. Everything has to be made again or borrowed.'

'I'm sure he will see me.' She sat down on a chair and lit up one of her cigarillos. 'I am happy to wait.'

The man shrugged. 'If you wish, but it might take all day.'

Hours passed before the Kappelmeister, harassed and puffy-eyed from lack of sleep, appeared. He scanned her letters briefly. He had heard that she had not found favour in Dresden but it did not surprise him. Opera was all they cared about there. He studied her for a moment or two: a face that was vivacious and arresting rather than classically beautiful and a magnificent figure. Yes, she could be the novelty he needed to fill the theatre at such a difficult time.

'Spanish dances, you say?'

'I am a Spaniard, sir. They are in my blood.'

He pursed his lips. 'Very well: three dances in the interval. We will agree the fee when I have seen them.'

He was gone before she could argue.

Back in the street, she walked briskly home to her hotel. At least she had an engagement. Now she needed to make some friends: as wealthy and influential as possible.

It did not take her long to collect admirers and as soon as she could, she moved to a better hotel. There, she entertained them in her suite and champagne flowed until the early hours of the morning. The men who vied for her favours paid the bills but she was careful not to prefer any of them above the others. They were more generous if one kept them guessing and in any case, she had had enough of love with George Lennox.

The reception given to her dancing, was, however, a disappointment. Her coterie of admirers could be relied upon to attend her performances and applaud vigorously, but their cheers and the flowers they tossed onto the stage could not hide the fact that a large part of the audience was not impressed.

Then one morning, she received a letter embossed with the royal crest. She knew that the king had come to her performance at the City Theatre in Potsdam and declared himself an admirer. Perhaps he wanted to see her dance again.

Eagerly, she slit the envelope and pulled out the card inside. Embossed in red and gold, it was a command to dance at a performance to honour the state visit of the Czar of Russia. She hugged the card to her: so much for the Berlin audiences and their pernickety complaints.

The sun had almost set when the carriage sent to fetch her turned into the Grand Drive that led to the Neues Palais. Ahead, rosy evening light suffused the palace's long, brick façade and stone columns. Closer to, she saw that gilded eagles topped the domes and the rooflines bristled with statues.

One wing of the palace contained an exquisite, rococo theatre. The royal chamberlain had informed her that, after the king and his guests had dined, there was to be a performance of Donizetti's opera *The Daughter of the Regiment*. She would dance *Los Boleros de Cadix* during the interval.

Backstage, once her maid had helped her on with the black dress embroidered with gold thread that she had chosen to wear, she sat quietly in front of the mirror for her hair to be arranged, thinking about the dance she would perform.

The door to the dressing room was half-open and she heard the first act of the opera come to an end, followed by applause from the royal party. Leaning forward, she tested the ribbons that fastened her shoes to make sure that they were secure then she stood up. Her heart pounded, but a surge of pride went through her too. In a few moments, she would be dancing for two of the greatest men in Europe. As she walked to the wings, she repeated the magic words: *brava Lola, brava.* Then she stepped into the light.

The following day, she woke late, glowing with pleasure as all splendour of the evening came back to her. The czar had looked magnificent in full dress uniform and the theatre and its audience had glittered. At the reception afterwards, both the czar and the king had congratulated her.

Throwing off the bedclothes, she jumped up and pirouetted around the room humming snatches of her music. She had just one more performance booked at the Schauspielhaus. Surely after last night, the manager would beg her to stay, and let her name any fee she liked?

She dressed that evening with a light heart, but from the moment she stepped on stage, she knew that something was wrong. The murmur from the audience was hostile, not approving. The atmosphere distracted her and she stumbled in the faster passages of her dance. It was a relief to leave the stage but she was also angry. What did these people want? Had she not received their king's seal of approval?

In her dressing room, she scrubbed her face with a cloth smeared with cold cream. No one came near her while her maid helped her to change out of her costume. She felt her anger mount. When she was done, she stormed to the manager's office.

He looked up and coloured when he saw her.

'Dona Montez. How can I help you?'

'What is the matter with these Berliners?' she stormed. 'Don't they know that I danced for His Majesty and the czar?'

'I fear that does not always assure the approval of His Majesty's citizens.'

She frowned. 'So they insult his opinion? I am sure he would not be pleased to hear that.'

He sighed. 'I hope he will not, but I also hope that you will understand that I cannot renew your contract.'

Her anger flared. 'But I gave a command performance. I was honoured by the king.'

'As I said, Dona Montez, the king is not the only arbiter of taste in Berlin.'

'I challenge you to say that to his face.'

His lip curled. 'My decision stands.'

Lola scowled. 'Then you are a fool. There are other cities and other theatres where people appreciate artistry. The czar himself told me that I would be welcomed in Russia. I shall be delighted to be finished with Berlin. My talent is wasted here.'

He bowed stiffly. 'I doubt we shall meet again, I wish you good luck and goodbye.'

In the early hours of the morning, Lola sat alone in her hotel room. The ashtray beside her held a pile of stubs. She jabbed another half-smoked cigarillo into them. Her mouth felt dry and stale. How she wished she had someone to talk to. In the heat of the moment, it had been easy to stand up to the manager, but the bravado she had shown a few hours ago was hard to sustain now that she was alone. Had she been right to abandon Eliza James? Lola was just a fiction: perhaps not a very good one at that. It might not be too late to go back.

She rubbed her hands over her face, massaging the tense muscles that made her head throb. If she did go back, who would be Eliza's friends? Certainly not Thomas. She had heard too that when the news of the court case reached India, her mother had put on black and announced that her daughter was dead. Her stepfather was too loyal a man not to support his wife.

Her mind went back to Bath and dear Fanny. They had exchanged letters for a while, but Fanny was married with children of her own now. No place in her household for a woman of ill-repute. That left Catherine Rae and she had already done enough.

She got up and stretched. She felt so weary and cold. What was the point in thinking about all this tonight? It was better to go to bed.

It was almost mid-day when she woke. She got up and threw the windows open wide to find that the day sparkled with sunshine. As she took a deep breath of warm air, the problems of the night before seemed surmountable. It had been weariness speaking. Of course Lola had a future. She would be mad to go back when Eliza had nothing but a past.

She remembered the czar's smiles and his flattering words. That was it: she would go to Russia, but first, she would attend the final grand parade in his honour. He might even notice her again. That would show Berlin what it had lost.

Thirty thousand Prussian troops had assembled for the parade, every one of them resplendent in the smart, dark-blue uniforms that the king had commissioned for the occasion. By five o'clock in the morning, crowds of people were gathered at the Friedrichfelde to the east of Berlin to watch the preparations. For weeks, rain had been scarce and when the sun rose, dispelling the early morning mist, the pounding feet of the troops and horses stirred up clouds of gritty dust from the parched ground. The discomfort did not, however, spoil the good-humoured atmosphere.

Lola came out alone from the city. She had hired an expensive and spirited grey mare for the occasion and she knew that she looked splendid, riding side-saddle in her full, black skirt and tight-fitting jacket, a glossy, high-crowned hat swathed with a black veil on her head. Lengthening her reins, she let the mare amble around the edge of the crowds for a while, looking for her opportunity to go into the royal enclosure. She saw that the police were turning away anyone who could not show a pass, but she was sure that she could find a way of evading them.

From her vantage point, she watched the advance guard of the cavalry riding down the parade ground, their gilded helmets glinting in the sun. Somewhere, a canon boomed. With a snort of alarm, the mare reared and skittered sideways tossing her head. Lola brought her under control, and by then, an idea had flashed through her mind. When the next salvo rang out, she was ready. Wheeling the mare around, she dug her spurs into the animal's flanks. The mare bucked, sending the people nearby scurrying to avoid her flying hooves. Crouched low on her neck, Lola set her at the entrance to the royal enclosure. Astonished onlookers jumped aside as they charged through the open gate. Inside, Lola made great play of pulling up the mare as a policeman hurried over to them.

'Your pass, lady?'

She ignored him.

'Your pass?' he repeated.

'Do you know who I am?'

He gave her a stony look. He had been a king's officer for twenty years; he had always done his duty with pride. He was not going to be outfaced by a mere woman.

'If you cannot show a pass, you have no business here, whoever you are.'

'My horse bolted. What would you have me do?'

He took hold of the mare's bridle. 'You must leave at once.'

Lola raised her whip.

'Let go of my horse or you will regret it. The king will tell you I am welcome here.'

The policeman shrugged. 'I do not think so. If you were, you would have a pass to enter.'

The whip hissed through the air and struck him hard across the mouth. With a yell, he let the horse go. Blood oozed from the cut on his lip.

Lola glared at him as a gasp went up from the people watching the scene. He wiped the blood from his mouth with the back of his hand.

'You'll pay dearly for that,' he growled.

Her heart thudded, but she would not let him think he could alarm her. She raised an eyebrow.

'On the contrary, you should be grateful for the lesson in how to treat a lady. Be thankful that I do not intend to report you,' she snapped, and before he could reply, she had wheeled the mare around and cantered away.

Chapter 17

Prince Ivan Fedorovitch Paskievitch, viceroy to Czar Nicholas of Russia, governor of occupied Poland and censor of public entertainments, studied the report on his desk and frowned. He looked up at his chief of police, Colonel Abramowicz.

'So she assaulted a Prussian police officer and was allowed to go free?'

'It seems so. I presume that the man preferred to forget the incident, rather than suffer ridicule at a trial.' Abramowicz's lips twitched. 'He was a well-set up, muscular fellow, I understand. Dona Montez is small and slight.'

Paskievitch's frown deepened. 'She will not find us so accommodating in Poland. What do we know about her intentions?'

'She plans to stay for a while then go on to Russia. She claims that the czar himself has invited her to perform in St Petersburg.'

Paskievitch raised an eyebrow. 'And yet she mixes with people like that banker, Steinkeller and the publisher, Lesnowski, dangerous intellectuals who criticise Russian policy. Either she is a fool or she is arrogant enough to think that her behaviour will be overlooked for the sake of her charms.' He scrawled a

171

few notes on the dossier and handed it back to Abramowicz. 'Continue to watch her and report to me again in two weeks.'

'The Grand Theatre's manager has asked whether he may engage her for a few performances. What shall I tell him?'

'I see no harm in it for the moment. Tell him he has my permission.'

On the journey from Berlin, Lola had decided to stake the funds she had left on securing an entry into wealthy society. Accordingly, she set herself up in a grand suite at the finest hotel in the city. It was in the luxuriously furnished drawing room that she entertained her new Polish friends that evening. She had ordered up the best champagne and the party was going well.

'You are a born revolutionary, Lola,' Piotr Steinkeller smiled when she had finished regaling the company with her opinions on the Russian authorities. 'I have seldom heard such an impassioned speech against oppression and foreign rule.'

Lola looked round the group. 'Is not any person of spirit a revolutionary? How can anyone not want to be free?'

Antoni Lesnowski frowned. 'Of course Poland longs for freedom but it is not so easy. Russia's power is far greater than ours. Her army would crush us like flies.'

She sighed. 'I suppose you are right.'

'Sadly, he is,' Steinkeller shrugged. 'We have to bide our time; meanwhile, we try to persuade the authorities to agree to some changes that will make our lives easier.' He grinned. 'And when the opportunity presents itself, we make theirs harder.'

Lola extended her hand to him. 'I must not neglect my other guests. Will you take a turn with me, Piotr?'

'With pleasure.'

He bowed to the others and led her away. 'Be careful, Lola,' he murmured as he did so. 'Warsaw is full of spies. You seem to be among friends here, but one can never be sure. I would advise you not to speak so freely again.'

Her eyes danced. 'I am not afraid.'

'But you should be.'

She squeezed his arm. 'You are a dear friend, Piotr. If they dare touch me, I shall feel safe if I have you on my side.'

Abramowicz returned to Paskievitch with his report as he had been instructed. The viceroy read it, nodding as he went.

'I see Steinkeller is a frequent visitor,' he remarked.

Abramowicz cleared his throat. 'The man is no friend to Russia and he is just one of many. I think that it may have been unwise to let Dona Montez stay, Your Highness. She seems determined to stir up trouble. Strange when she hopes to perform for the czar, but she does not seem to connect the two. Apart from anything else, she is everywhere; watching her takes up too many of our resources.'

Paskievitch stroked his beard. Abramowicz fell silent. It was a gesture that told him not to interrupt his superior's train of thought. After a few minutes, the prince leaned back in his chair and closed the dossier. 'I would prefer to avoid a fuss. Let our fair guest finish her contract, then we shall find a way of persuading her to leave quietly.'

'How can you endure being spied on all the time?' Lola asked Steinkeller as they took a morning walk around the city together. She shuddered. 'I hate spies and I feel their presence everywhere. The maids take far too long arranging my flowers and tidying my rooms; I have begun to recognise the men standing in the shadows when I come and go from the hotel.'

'I'm afraid they are a fact of life that we Poles have learnt to live with.'

'If it was up to me, I would poison all the Russians and take my country back for those who have the right to it.'

A mischievous smile came over her face. It would be amusing to start a little rumour and see where it led. 'As for that toad, Abramowicz, not long ago, he begged to accompany me in my carriage to the theatre then had the gall to make advances. I threw him out in the rain, I can tell you.'

Steinkeller let out a bark of laughter, but soon, his native caution returned. He lowered his voice. 'Lola, you know I hate the Russians, most of us do, but I urge you: take care.' He glanced at a group of men nearby. 'Never speak too freely in public. Men have been imprisoned and tortured for our cause.'

She touched his arm. 'I'm sorry. You and your wife have been so kind to me, I must not jeopardise your safety. Let us change the subject. Will you come and see me at the theatre next week? I am performing a new dance called La Saragossa.'

'I should be delighted, and I'll bring the usual supporters, shall I?'

Watching Lola's performance, Abramowicz gritted his teeth as she received enthusiastic applause for the new dance. He had heard rumours that Piotr Steinkeller regularly sent some of his workers to ensure that her performances received a good reception.

He moistened his lips with his tongue. Perhaps it was time to arrange a trick of his own, especially as she seemed to have been spreading scurrilous rumours about him. He had denied them of course, but plenty of people were prepared to believe that there was no smoke without fire.

The following evening, he ordered some of his officers to dress in plain clothes and mingle with the audience. Lola was only halfway through her dance when hisses and whistles rose up from the auditorium. Her supporters countered with cheers and applause but the noise grew so loud that she could barely hear the orchestra. With difficulty, she finished her dance then stood waiting for the hubbub to subside. She saw Abramowicz in one of the boxes. It was not hard to guess who was behind the outrage. He would see that she was not afraid to match him at any game.

She raised her hand and a hush fell. 'First, I wish to thank those who have been so gracious in their applause and made me so welcome in their charming city, but look up, ladies and gentlemen,' she pointed to the box where Abramowicz sat, 'see the coward who insults me; who has persuaded his supporters to disrupt your enjoyment simply because I would not submit to his infamous proposals!'

The theatre erupted. With Lola's outstretched hand pointing at him like an avenging angel's, Abramowicz seethed. She had turned the tables and made him look a fool. He would not rest until he got her out of Warsaw. Paskievitch had already gone to his country estate for the autumn hunt. It would be unwise to expel Lola without discussing it with him first. But there was something he could do.

Early the following morning, he called in two of his officers.

'You are to go to Madame Montez's hotel and place her under arrest,' he said. 'Tell her she is not permitted to leave the hotel until further notice.'

'But what reason shall we give?' the elder of the officers asked.

'Tell her she is accused of seditious talk against the Government.'

The men hesitated, exchanging glances.

'What are you waiting for?' Abramowicz snapped.

'The lady has a fiery reputation, sir,' the man said.

'Are you afraid of a woman?'

The man hung his head. 'No, sir.'

'Then go and do your duty.'

After they had made their reluctant exit, he sat back, rubbing his hands together. That would teach the Spanish woman not to tangle with him.

Locked in her suite, Lola paced the rooms like a lioness in a cage. Several days had passed and none of her friends were permitted to visit her. She saw only the hotel staff when they brought her meals.

When Paskievitch returned, Abramowicz went straight to see him.

The viceroy frowned.

'The circumstances are not what I should have wished, but we cannot turn back now. Escort her to the Prussian border.'

He looked at Abramowicz's triumphant face and gave a wry smile. 'I suggest you leave the job to others. It would not add greatly to your dignity if she resists.

Send some of your best men and warn them to take care. We do not want an embarrassing scene. I hear that the lady wears a dagger in her belt.'

Lola was at breakfast when she received the officers detailed to escort her. She gave them a charming smile. 'Please thank Colonel Abramowicz, but tell him I am very content here and the weather grows too cold for travelling. I have decided to stay.'

Outmanoeuvred, the men returned to the colonel and made their report.

Abramowicz banged his fist on his desk, scattering a pile of papers and making the inkwell jump.

'And you let her get away with it?'

'W did not know what to do, colonel,' one of them said.

'Idiots! Get out of my sight.'

Alone, he tried to compose a note to Paskievitch asking for his advice, but everything he wrote made him sound whining and incompetent. He threw the drafts away and thought for a long time. Perhaps he would not involve his superior yet. There might be a way he could defeat Lola on his own. If he ordered his men to drag her from her hotel and throw her into a carriage, it would be bound to cause an uproar. But taking advantage of her loyalty to her friends might be effective. He took up his pen once more and wrote a note to Piotr Steinkeller, summoning him to a meeting.

Steinkeller's face was impassive as he sat in Abramowicz's office. Wariness was a habit he had learnt well. Abramowicz's remarks seemed innocuous enough, but there might be danger behind the affable smile.

'I believe that you and Madame Steinkeller see a good deal of Dona Montez?' Abramowicz asked.

'She visits us from time to time.'

'Prince Paskievitch was very displeased by the disturbance at the Grand Theatre after her last performance.'

'I am sorry to hear it, but why are you telling me?'

Abramowicz's lip curled. 'Do you really need to ask?' He pulled a dossier out of the top drawer of his desk and pushed it towards Steinkeller. 'Her activities make interesting reading – as do yours.'

Steinkeller felt a chill creep up his spine and paw at his neck.

'You look pale, meinherr. I hope you are not in ill-health? You must take more care.'

Steinkeller glanced through the first few pages of the dossier.

'I imagine that there is something I can do to persuade you not to use this?'

'It is such a pleasure to deal with a man of your intelligence. Dona Montez seems unwilling to leave Warsaw. All I ask is that you persuade her to change her mind. A quiet departure would be best for everyone.'

Steinkeller swallowed. 'I will see what I can do.'

'You have twenty-four hours.'

On his return home, his wife rushed into his arms. 'What did he want? I've been so worried.'

He kissed her cheek. 'He wants me to persuade Lola to leave Warsaw.'

'What did you say?'

'I agreed to try. She may be angry, but I have to think of all our safety. I hope she will understand that. Now all we need to do is think of a way.'

Later that afternoon, Madame Steinkeller arrived at Lola's hotel and was admitted to her suite. The two women hugged each other.

'I am so happy to see you,' Lola beamed. 'I have been very lonely here.'

'I have come to ask you to join us on a visit to our estate in the country.'

'But what about Abramowicz? I do not want to put you in danger.'

'Piotr has already spoken with him'

Lola looked at her suspiciously. 'And he agrees?'

'Yes.'

Lola turned away and walked to the window. Glancing out into the street, she saw one of the usual watchers loitering on the other side of the road. She turned back. 'Will it harm you if I decline the invitation?'

'I fear that it will.'

'I suppose it is a very short way from your estate to the border?'

Her friend nodded. 'Forgive me. Lola.'

Lola stepped forward and took her hands. 'There is nothing to forgive. Of course I shall come.' She smiled. 'But I won't go return Prussia. I always intended to go on to St Petersburg. I should delay my journey no longer if I am to reach there before the snows come.'

Chapter 18

The fastest route lay along the coast of the Baltic Sea. Day after day, the post coaches in which Lola travelled struggled through sleet and snow over roads rutted with frozen mud. She had very little money left, but she kept her spirits up imagining the triumph she would enjoy when the czar heard that she was in the city: a command performance at the very least.

They arrived late at night. It was freezing and needles of rain stung Lola's face as the coach rumbled away over the cobbles, leaving her and her maid outside the small hotel that the driver had recommended.

'My cousin, Mrs Vitebsky owns it,' he had said. 'Very clean and comfortable. She'll see you right.'

Lola's maid looked around apprehensively at the deserted street. 'It seems very quiet everywhere, madam.'

Lola strode up to the door. 'We'd better get in before we both die of cold. Hurry up with my bags,' she called over her shoulder.

She rang the bell several times before a sleepy woman with a lined, weathered face opened up. She wore a rusty black dress and a thick grey shawl pulled tight around her stout frame. When she saw her visitors, she barked something in Russian that neither Lola nor her maid could understand.

'Do you speak French?' Lola asked.

The woman nodded. 'A little.'

'So my cousin sent you, eh?' she grumbled when Lola had explained. 'He should know better than to be sending people to me at this time of night. Still, now you're here, you can come in. Lucky I've got a room free.'

She jerked her thumb in the maid's direction. 'She can sleep in the kitchen if she wants. It's warm by the range and there's a straw pallet she can use.'

'We've not eaten all day. Give her something in the kitchen and send supper up to my room.'

The woman's eyebrows shot up. 'Do you think this is the czar's palace? It's late missy and as soon as I've shown you where you'll sleep and locked up again, I'm off to bed myself.'

Lola bit her lip. She was very tired. For once, she did not have the strength to argue. In silence, she followed the woman upstairs. The room was plain, but the coach driver had been right: it was clean and the bed quite comfortable.

'How many nights do you want?'

Lola shrugged. 'I'm not sure; not many. I'm a friend of the czar and a celebrated dancer. Once he knows I am here and I have an engagement at the opera house, I shall need a much larger place where I can entertain.'

For the first time, the woman smiled, showing brown, stumpy teeth. 'Of course you will,' she chuckled. 'Well goodnight to you. You can breakfast in the kitchen in the morning if you want, and your maid can heat your washing water on the copper and bring it up.' As she went off down the stairs, Lola heard her cackling.

'Damn you, you old fool,' she muttered.

She stayed up half the night composing a letter to the czar. In the morning, she handed it to her maid.

'I need you to take this to the palace.'

The girl looked doubtful. 'I can't understand the barbarous language they speak here, madam. I shall get lost and never find my way back.'

Lola glared at her. 'Nonsense, if I can find my way about, so can you.' She looked at the girl's downcast face. 'Oh very well, I'll ask old Vitebsky to send a servant. You had better spend the morning darning my stockings and cleaning up my clothes. God knows they need it.'

Her visit to the opera house later that day was not a success.

'The manager is in the middle of rehearsal,' the doorman said firmly. 'It is impossible for anyone to see him without an appointment.'

She left a message and went back to the hotel. There she waited for the rest of the day, but no news came. At midnight she gave up hope and went to bed.

Fresh snow fell on each succeeding night. In the mornings, before the street sweepers had done their work, it lay so deep on the pavements that it was almost impossible to walk through it. Carriages struggled along the streets, stopping frequently for the coachmen to knock gluey lumps off the wheels.

Icicles a foot long hung from the eaves of the houses. Walking back from the opera house one dark afternoon, after yet another attempt to speak with the manager, Lola hands throbbed inside her thin gloves.

As she passed the gates of the royal palace, she slipped on a patch of ice.

Scowling, she stumbled up and brushed down her dress. It was already splashed with muddy slush, now her petticoats were soaked as well. She shivered and felt an ache in her side where she had landed on the frozen ground. Nearly two weeks had gone by and there was always some excuse from the theatre. She had delivered many notes to the palace too but no reply had come.

She grimaced. What a fool she was. She should have realised that this might happen after the way she had been treated in Poland. And, she reflected ruefully, I probably didn't help myself.

'Damn all Russians!' she burst out, stamping her foot. A passer bye huddled in a greatcoat and fur-flapped hat looked alarmed and hurried on. 'And damn Abramowicz in particular,' she muttered. He was the one who had had her blackballed, the spiteful, lecherous toad. As she ploughed on through the snow, she faced the fact that this time, he had won and perhaps it was time to accept defeat.

'We are leaving,' she announced to her maid the next day. The girl's face fell at the thought of losing her nightly place by the warm kitchen range.

'But won't it be dangerous to travel? Mrs Vitebsky was saying yesterday that we are coming to the worst time of the winter, when the wild animals are so hungry that they come into the city to look for food.'

'Nonsense you goose, Mrs Vitebsky is a silly old woman who enjoys frightening you. I won't spend the rest of the winter in this miserable place. We're going back to Berlin.'

It was hard to find anyone who would take them, but eventually Lola secured two places on a coach going south. They would have to change many times before they reached Berlin, but she was determined not to wait for spring.

Day after day, she stared out at the louring skies and the flat, featureless countryside. Her spirits were so low that all she wanted to do was sleep. If only the coach would not jolt so over the frozen roads, she might have been able to do so. She ignored her fellow passengers' attempts to engage her in conversation, and during the long, freezing waits as the coachmen dug through the frozen drifts that often blocked the roads, she brushed away offers to share flasks of brandy or travelling rugs.

Doubts clouded her mind and she found it hard to think. She had told her maid they were going to Berlin, but what was there for her? She had to face the fact that her previous visit had not been a great success. If she was honest with herself, the last few months had been more notable for set-backs than triumphs. Perhaps after all, it would not be so bad to be kept by some man and give up chasing the limelight.

At one of their stops at an inn to change horses, she picked her way over the slippery, cobbled yard and went to find a place to sit on her own inside. In the small, cosy parlour, a blazing fire roared on the hearth. The warmth sent the blood rushing to her cheeks.

Ordering a glass of wine, she picked up a newspaper that lay on a table nearby. She took it over to a chair and sat down to read. It was good to find out what was happening in the world. In Russia, she might as well have been on the moon.

On one of the inside pages, she saw a name that pricked her interest: Franz Liszt. The innkeeper's wife bustled over with the wine.

'Ah,' she smiled, 'I see you are reading about Maestro Liszt. He travelled this way just recently on one of his concert tours. He was gracious enough to stay a night at our humble inn. He praised the wine I served him too. I hope that you will approve of it.'

Lola smiled. 'I'm sure I shall.'

Another customer clicked his fingers for attention and the woman went away to serve them. Lola put down the paper and rested her chin on her hand. So Maestro Liszt: was close by. He was an artist and a man of passion, a kindred soul. Perhaps fate had meant her to leave Russia after all. If she could meet Liszt, it would make up for all her disappointments.

She scanned the list of dates and venues for the concerts he was about to give then folded the paper with a smile. She might just catch up with him before he left Prussia.

Chapter 19

The tables in the vast, crowded banqueting hall were laid with fine china and silverware that gleamed in the light of a thousand candles. A small army of servants darted about carrying steaming platters of schnitzel and creamed potato. The aroma of the food mingled with the scent from great vases of white lilies. At one end of the room, a small orchestra struggled to be heard over the buzz of conversation.

Lola looked around her. Here she was at last, at the dinner in his honour, just a short step from her goal. She must not fail now.

The attractive woman opposite her stroked the bracelet that she wore on her slim wrist. When she saw Lola watching her, she smiled.

'It is my most precious possession.' She curved her wrist to show off the narrow band of plaited wire. 'See, it is woven from the broken strings discarded from Maestro Liszt's piano.' She turned to glare at a voluptuous woman in crimson satin and a magnificent jet necklace seated half a dozen places away.

'I had a piece of the handkerchief that he dropped yesterday,' she said loudly, 'but that bitch grabbed it right out of my hand.' The other woman shot her a triumphant smirk.

'You all seem to admire him a great deal,' Lola laughed.

'Of course: he is a genius.'

A waiter arrived and began to serve them, but Lola waved him away and stood up.

Her neighbour looked surprised 'Are you leaving already? He might speak after the meal is finished, you know. Sometimes he even walks around the tables.' She lowered her voice. 'Once, I touched the hem of his coat.'

'Oh, that wouldn't be enough for me. I think I shall go and meet him properly.'

The woman gasped. 'You wouldn't dare! No one approaches the Maestro unless they are invited.'

'What nonsense. I grant you he is a brilliant musician, but he is a man like any other.'

The woman's hand flew to her mouth. She watched with envious horror as Lola threaded her way between the packed tables until she reached the platform where the high table stood. A waiter tried to bar her way, but she evaded him. Now only a few paces separated her from Liszt and the air around him seemed charged with life. His blue-black hair sprang in shining coils to touch his collar. His pale, Olympian profile thrilled her. He was deep in conversation with a distinguished-looking man whose chest dripped with medals, but as her perfume wafted towards him, he broke off and looked up. A lazy smile hovered on his lips.

'May I help you, madame?'

Lola bent down and whispered something in his ear. His smile turned to a roar of laughter then he stood up and kissed her hand. A buzz of curiosity swelled through the other tables.

'Bring a chair and another place for my guest,' he commanded, 'and be quick about it.'

Two waiters hurried to carry up a chair and Lola sat down. Liszt motioned to one of them to pour her wine then he raised his glass. She felt a wave of hatred reach her from every corner of the room as she chinked her glass with his.

'I am honoured, Maestro,' she smiled. 'I have waited for such a long time to meet you.'

She stirred from sleep a few weeks later to find the bed cold beside her. Her brow furrowed. In the beginning Liszt would have woken her to make love, but now, in the half-light coming through the drawn curtains, she saw that he was already dressed.

She sat up. 'It is so early. Come back to bed.'

He finished fastening his cuffs and flicked an invisible speck of dust from the quilted sleeve of his black velvet coat.

'I can't. I need to go down to the concert hall.' He flexed his long, narrow fingers. 'The cold has made these stiff. I must practise to loosen them up.'

'You said that we would spend the day together, just the two of us.'

'Perhaps tomorrow. No, it will have to be the next day. Tomorrow the mayor and the city fathers are holding a reception in my honour and I have promised to tour the city.'

She scowled. 'Why is there always something? We have visited three cities in as many weeks. You never have time for me.'

He drew a sharp breath. 'Not this again, Lola. You knew what it would be like with me. And I've told you over and over again that you are welcome to accompany me wherever I am invited.'

'And be ignored by everyone? No thank you.'

He grimaced. 'You are behaving like a spoilt child.'
'How dare you!'

A cut-glass decanter of brandy stood on a table near the bed. She leapt up and grabbed it by the neck, but he was already gone. As he walked down the corridor, he heard the crash of breaking glass.

'There has been an accident in my suite,' he remarked to the startled chambermaid that he passed. 'You had better go and help Dona Montez.'

In the bedroom, Lola watched the brandy trickle down the door and pool around the shards of glass on the floor. Her eyes misted and she clenched her fists. Picking up a jagged fragment, she pressed it to the pale skin on the underside of her wrist and winced as beads of blood appeared. She would cut herself and he would be to blame. She pressed harder and the beads of blood swelled.

'But he probably wouldn't care if I died,' she muttered and threw the glass away. She put her wrist to her lips. The blood tasted salty but the cut was not deep and the flow soon stopped. She slumped on the bed. He had the power to make her so angry. He was too vain to love anyone but himself. Why had she been such a fool as to fall in love with him?

There was a timid knock at the door and the chambermaid sidled in. Her eyes widened at the mess on the floor and Lola's furious stare. 'The Maestro sent me, Dona Montez.'

Lola rallied. 'Clear this up and call my maid to dress me. I am going out.'

The chambermaid got down on her knees and began to collect up the pieces of broken glass.

'Didn't you hear me, you stupid girl? Get my maid. I am in a hurry.'

The rich sound of a Hungarian rhapsody filled the concert hall. His head inclined a little to the right to catch every note and nuance, Liszt was deep in concentration when Lola stormed down the central aisle, the manager and two of his assistants running to catch up with her. Skirts flying, she rushed up the steps to the stage and slammed her fist down on the piano keys.

Liszt threw up his hands. 'I will not put up with this! I am not to be disturbed when I am playing.' He looked at the perspiring manager who had just reached the stage. 'Show the lady out, if you please.'

Lola stamped her foot. 'I suggest that none of these men touch me if they value their eyes.'

The manager and his assistants backed away.

Liszt jumped up from the piano stool. Darting at Lola, he grabbed her left arm and twisted it behind her back. 'Then you will go by yourself,' he hissed, 'unless you want me to break this.'

She gasped with pain, but anger outweighed it. 'I'm not afraid of you,' she spat.

'You should be. I warn you, I shall not tolerate your tantrums much longer. You will not embarrass me in public.'

'I shall do so if I choose,' she panted.

He lowered his voice and spoke through gritted teeth. 'Lola, I have never made it a secret that my music comes first with me. If you cannot accept that, there is no future for us.'

Suddenly the rage went out of her and she went limp. He shook her.

'What is it?' There was a note of guilt in his voice.

'You are not all to blame,' she sobbed. 'It is my fault too, but I cannot help it.'

He let her arm go and she clung to him. He felt her chest heave.

'My poor darling,' he murmured. 'I make life hard for you, don't I?'

She drew back and took the handkerchief he held out to her. She wiped her eyes and gave a shaky laugh. 'At least I do not have to fight for scraps of this with the other women.' She folded the square of fine, scented linen and handed it back to him. 'Forgive me. I love you too much.'

He bent down and kissed her cheek. 'Go back to the hotel. I shall follow you as soon as I can.'

She nodded and turned to go. He stood and watched her as she walked away past the bewildered manager and his assistants and disappeared into the shadows of the aisle then he sat down at the piano and started to play once more.

Lola's head throbbed as she walked back to the hotel. Waiting there for him – he did not return until early evening – she examined her heart.

She had told him that she loved him too much, but was it true? Was what she felt simply a passion nourished by his beauty and fame? Before she met him, she had said that she was tired of love. There was no denying that it would be wiser to forget him. A life with a man who eclipsed her in the eyes of the world as he did would never make her completely happy. But was some happiness better than none at all? She had no answer to that.

The waiter held a taper so that Lola could light her cigarillo then offered it to Liszt to kindle his cigar. Candlelight flickered over the cut-glass balloons of brandy that stood on the pristine white tablecloth.

'Will you be requiring anything else, Maestro?'

Liszt shook his head. 'You may leave us.'

The waiter closed the door softly behind him. There was no sound in the private room except the tick of the ormolu clock on the mantelshelf. Liszt sipped his brandy and watched Lola.

Two months had passed since she had invaded the concert hall. In those months, not a day had passed without an argument between them.

'Have you nothing to say?' she asked after a while.

He raised an eyebrow. 'There is more than enough, wouldn't you agree? But you must promise not to lose your temper for once.'

She frowned. 'I will try.'

'Not much of a promise,' he chuckled.

Her eyes flashed. 'As much as you deserve.'

He opened his mouth to retaliate then changed his mind. 'I don't want to quarrel any more, Lola. I know you think I let you down, but there is nothing I can do about it. In my fashion, I love you, but it is not enough, is it?'

He leaned forward and gripped the stems of the brandy balloons. 'It is better that we part but I hope we can part as friends.'

Lola looked down at his elegant hands, the knuckles white against the tawny glasses. To her surprise, she was glad he had been honest. She knew that he was right. The passion between them had faded a little more with every sharp or resentful word. Soon there would be nothing but bitterness. It was madness to cling on to an image of love that did not meet the reality. Gently, she prised his fingers from the glasses.

'You need not be afraid,' she smiled. 'The brandy is too good to waste.'

The look of relief that came over his face made her laugh.

'What fools we are,' she gasped when she had finished. 'You and I are far too much alike to be happy. I should have known it from the start.'

He did not answer and her expression grew sad.

'Will you be so glad to be rid of me?'

He clasped her hands. 'When I told you I wanted us to remain friends, I meant it.'

She nodded. 'I should like that too.'

He raised his glass. 'Then let us drink to friendship.'

Her glass clinked against his. She drank and felt the fiery liquid scald her throat before its warmth suffused her whole body, bringing comfort with it.

'Where will you go?' he asked.

'I'm not sure. Not to England, that at least is certain. I hate that damp, miserable country.' She traced a line on the tablecloth with the tip of her finger. Paris perhaps, I should like to dance at L'Opéra.'

He nodded, although privately, he wondered if she was aiming too high.

'Will you give me a letter of introduction?'

'With pleasure, although it may not do you much good.'

She gave him a mischievous smile. 'Surely you are too modest?'

He leaned back in his chair and laughed. 'I never thought that I would hear that from you.'

Chapter 20

Paris

Lola found her way to the stage door of the Opéra and handed Liszt's letter to the porter. 'Please tell Monsieur Pillet that I have come all the way from Prussia to see him and I bear greetings from his dear friend, Franz Liszt.'

The porter gave her an admiring look. He had seen a lot of would-be stars in his time, but very few had been as beautiful as this one. He grinned. 'For you I'll go straight away.' He gestured to the small room inside. 'Will you wait there?'

'Thank you.' She sat down and lit one of her cigarillos. The man hovered in the doorway and she smiled. 'Are you going then?'

He chuckled. 'Yes of course.'

An hour passed before she was called to Pillet's office. By then, she had regaled the porter with a dozen stories and taught him how to smoke in the Spanish way. He scratched his head as he watched her walk away down the corridor. He had never met anyone quite like her.

Pillet stood up from his desk and bowed.

'I am sorry that you were kept waiting, Dona Montez. I see from his letter that my friend Liszt commends your talent, but I hope you will not be offended if I say that I have a very difficult decision to make. My patrons expect the highest standards to be maintained at the Opéra. As far as I have heard, you have not been dancing for very long and the public's reaction to you has been mixed.'

She had anticipated some resistance and already thought of a scapegoat. A flash of anger crossed her face, 'It is true that I have not been well-received everywhere but that had nothing to do with my dancing.'

He raised an eyebrow. 'How is that so?'

'Ever since I was forced to flee from my homeland, I have been persecuted.'

'Persecuted?' he frowned.

'The Jesuits: they are my mortal enemies. In Spain, my husband opposed their evil ambitions. He died for his beliefs and they can no longer torment him, but in revenge, they have turned their spite on me.'

Pillet went to the window and looked out. She studied his back. Did he believe her? There was no truth in what she said, but the Jesuits were a good target. For many people, their very name aroused suspicions of sinister dealings.

'I was a principal dancer at the Teatro Real in Seville,' she added. 'Surely your patrons will be interested to see Spanish dances performed by a native of Spain?'

He turned around and she searched his face in vain for a sign of interest.

'I am afraid that I cannot help you.'

'Will you at least let me show you what I can do?'

Her smile was so charming that to his surprise, the hard-bitten director found himself shepherding her to the auditorium and summoning his rehearsal pianist to bring a sheaf of Spanish dance music.

As the pianist thumped out the opening bars of the *bolero*, she raised her arms above her head, knowing that the pose showed off her full breasts and slender waist to perfection; then languidly, she launched into the dance.

When she had finished, she felt a flutter of nerves as she waited for Pillet to speak. His severe expression betrayed nothing. She looked out into the auditorium behind him. There was no magic to help you in a theatre by day, she thought. No blazing chandeliers; no hum of anticipation. Somewhere up in the galleries, carpenters hammered and sawed. In the shadowy stalls behind Pillet, a cleaner clattered about with a bucket and mop.

Pillet cleared his throat. 'I am sorry, Dona Montez, but my answer has not changed.'

'Oh, but I have not finished.' She turned swiftly to the pianist. Play *El Olano.*'

The pianist hesitated until Pillet shrugged and nodded to him.

'Very well.'

Ignoring her surroundings, Lola cast her mind back to the Sevillian cave. Perhaps the gypsies would bring her luck. When she came to the part of the dance where she looked for the spider, she raised her skirts demurely at first, then glancing at Pillet, who seemed to be watching her with more interest, took the risk of going higher. As the last chord echoed through the auditorium, she saw a ghost of a smile on his lips.

'All right,' he said with a grudging nod. 'You will perform the *Olano* and a *bolero*: five francs.'

'Ten.'

The smile vanished and for a moment she feared that she had gone too far. Then he laughed.

'Seven.'

'Agreed.'

A few days later, posters went up announcing that she would dance in the interval of the following evening's performance of Die Freischutz. By late afternoon, thanks to the curiosity her name by now aroused, every seat in the theatre was sold.

Pillet watched from his box as he waited for her performance to begin. 'I have to admit,' he remarked to his wife, 'in all the years I've been in the business, I've rarely felt such a buzz.'

She surveyed the audience through her lorgnette. 'Everyone is here,' she remarked, 'from the Jockey Club to the hoi polloi; hoping for a breath of scandal, no doubt.'

The scarlet velvet curtains swept aside to reveal a backdrop of a whitewashed Spanish village with a Moorish castle on a distant hill. Lola stepped out onto the stage and bent down to unfasten a ribbon from one of her stockings before walking to the footlights. A seductive smile hovering on her lips, she let the ribbon dangle from her hand then threw it into the stalls. A ripple of surprise and amusement ran through the auditorium. The music of *El Olano* wound its way up from the orchestra pit. She began to dance.

At first, the audience observed her in silence, but slowly, they grew restless.

'What is she doing?' one man whispered to his mistress. 'I don't think she understands the rules of style. Look at her feet; a soldier on the march has more grace.'

The woman giggled. 'I can't imagine how she persuaded Pillet to engage her, or rather I can.'

A mere scatter of applause greeted the end of the dance. Lola curtsied but she felt shaken and confused. She hurried off-stage and two of the house's regular stars came on to perform their piece. Watching from the wings and hearing the cheers they received, a lump came into her throat. She closed her eyes and took a deep breath. She must stay calm, it was not over yet: one more dance to go. She would make them love her.

But as she stepped out onto the stage, her courage wavered and her eyes brimmed. As was customary, the auditorium remained lit, and the blaze of thousands of candles in the crystal chandeliers blinded her. She was not ready for her cue and she stumbled through her *Bolero de Cadix*.

Watching from his box, Pillet grimaced as the dance dragged to its conclusion. How could he have let his judgment be swayed? 'Tell the stage manager to call everyone back on stage as soon as the music stops,' he hissed to the runner waiting in the entrance to the box. 'Don't stand there with your mouth open. Get on with it.'

On stage, Lola felt hands snatch hers and sweep her forward. She found herself in a line with the rest of the cast. Forcing a smile, she sank into a curtsey. A bouquet of red roses was suddenly in her arms.

She returned to her dressing room in a daze. In front of the mirror, her shoulders sagged. Snatching up a piece of cloth, she began to wipe away her makeup, angry tears mixing with the powder and rouge. 'Pompous fools,' she hissed.

Her maid scuttled in and Lola swung round. 'Bolt the door before you help me change. I won't have anyone in here tonight.'

'But what if Monsieur Pillet asks for you?'

'Monsieur Pillet can go to the Devil.'

'Only you had anything kind to say about me,' she said sadly the following evening as she dined with her new friend Pier Angelo Fiorentino. He was one of several she had made since she arrived in Paris and like most of them, a journalist.

'Your dancing deserved praise.'

She shook her head with a rueful smile. 'It didn't and you know it. I realised when I saw the others perform that I could not compete with them.'

'You are too harsh on yourself.'

'I think not. It is as well to know one's own strengths and weaknesses. Last night, I certainly had a lesson in the latter.'

'So what will you do?'

'The Opéra is not the only stage in the world. I shall go elsewhere; but before I do, I intend to enjoy Paris.'

He grinned. 'I'm glad to see you so philosophical.'

She shrugged. 'What else can I be?'

He leaned forward and touched her hand. 'Then I shall be honoured if you will let me help you to enjoy my city.'

A few days later at Lepage's shooting gallery, he watched as she practised her aim with a pistol. How fragile she looked, yet there was a glimmer of steel in her eyes as she took aim. It made a piquant contrast.

The attendant took down the target and brought it over to where they stood. Fiorentino studied the neatly-perforated card and whistled. 'Every bullet found its mark. Congratulations, Lola.'

'You have a natural eye, madame,' the attendant said.

She smiled. 'Thank you.'

Fiorentino looked over at a tall, thin young man with prematurely-receding black hair who had just walked in. He stopped at the entrance to their booth and smiled. Fiorentino gave him a friendly nod.

'If you are waiting to take this place, you have a high standard to live up to.'

The young man's grey eyes crinkled at the corners. 'So I see. If the lady was to challenge me to a duel, I think that I would be very afraid indeed.'

He bowed. 'May I introduce myself, madame? Alexandre Dujarier, at your service.'

Lola held out her hand for him to kiss and felt a tremor as his lips brushed her skin. He straightened up smiling. 'Of course I already know who you are, madame, but nothing that I have heard has done justice to your beauty.'

Fiorentino looked from one to the other. I might as well not be here, he thought glumly.

Dujarier smiled. 'I am giving a dinner at L'Escargot tonight. Perhaps you would both care to join me?'

'We should be delighted, shouldn't we, Pier?'

Dujarier did not wait for his answer. He kissed Lola's hand once again. 'Until tonight then.'

'Tell me about him,' Lola whispered as she and Fiorentino walked away.

Fiorentino shrugged. 'Very clever: whatever he touches turns to gold. He made a fortune in banking by the time he was twenty-five then when he was bored with that, he bought a bankrupt newspaper. People thought he was mad but he turned it around in six months. Of course he hasn't time for much except work. Some people find him rather dull.'

Lola looked at him sideways and squeezed his arm. 'Please don't sulk, Pier. I want us to be friends.'

'And that is all?'

'I have never pretended to be in love with you,' she said gently. 'And I don't believe you are really in love with me.'

Fiorentino gave her a wry smile. 'I suppose you are right. But it was worth a try.'

There were many guests at the dinner at L'Escargot, and although Dujarier welcomed Lola and Fiorentino warmly, they hardly spoke for the rest of the evening.

At midnight, as Fiorentino's carriage rattled away from her lodgings and she was left alone, Lola could not ignore the bitter taste of disappointment in her mouth. It angered her. Had she not sworn such a short time ago that she had no need of a man? How weak her resolve was if she could change so quickly. Yet she could not expel Dujarier's image from her mind, vexing herself over whether she had read more into his gallantry than was really there. The question was like a stubborn knot that refused to unravel.

The next day, she had no heart for company. She rose late and took a fiacre to the Bois de Boulogne. As she walked, she tried to compose her emotions and thoughts.

The sky, blue as a duck's egg, was feathered with hazy clouds. On the lawns, children dressed in neat pinafores and panama hats played with hoops and balls, supervised by their starched nurses. Couples strolled arm in arm in the sunshine and carriages bowled past on the broad avenues. Paris was going about her business, it was an ordinary day. Why then did she feel so agitated? Dujarier was just a man. If she could not have him, there would be others.

But the wrench of pain that the thought caused her made her afraid. She would be a fool to admit love into her life again, she knew it. Love brought with it humiliation and despair. When she parted from Liszt, she had vowed to build strong walls around her heart. But was it already too late?

By the time she returned to her lodgings, she had still not found an answer. As she passed the landlady's door, the woman came bustling out.

'There is a gentleman waiting for you, madame,' she said. 'I told him that I did not know where you had gone or when you would be back, but he would not leave. He has been here for two hours already.'

Lola's heart leapt. It could not be Fiorentino, he had told her he was going out of Paris for a few days and in any case, he would never wait so long. She felt her hands shake as she thanked the woman. Her legs would hardly carry her up the last flight of stairs to her door. When she opened it, she saw a tall figure in black standing at the window. He swung round as she came in. The low sun beat through the windowpane, throwing his face into shadow. The breath seemed to have left her body and she could not speak. Then he took a step towards her, his hands outstretched, and she knew that there was no need for words.

Chapter 21

Lola touched the ring that Dujarier had given her that morning and felt a glow of happiness. Since the day that she had returned from the Bois to find him waiting, her life had changed utterly.

Her mind strayed from the conversation in the group around her as she watched him across the room, talking with his friend, the celebrated novelist, Dumas. She could not help smiling. Dujarier had a particular way of tilting his head to one side when he considered a point, but his serious expression became delightfully boyish when he laughed. After a few moments, she excused herself and went over to the two men.

'Good evening, Monsieur Dumas.'

Dumas kissed her hand. 'Lola! What a joy to see you. As usual, you do my old heart good.'

Dujarier tucked her arm into his. 'Lola is dancing at the theatre at Porte St Martin next week. I hope that you will come?'

'Of course: I'll make up a party and perhaps you would dine with us afterwards?'

Lola smiled. 'It is my turn to be honoured.'

They chatted for a while then Dumas moved away to talk to someone else.

'Thank you,' Lola whispered when they were alone.

'When everyone has gone, you may thank me properly.'

She raised an eyebrow. 'Of course I am quite capable of organising my own publicity.'

He chuckled. 'I know you are. But not, I hope, above accepting help from someone who adores you?'

'Flatterer.'

'No. I always tell the truth,' he grinned. 'I'll shout it out for the whole room to hear if you want.'

She brushed her hand across his cheek. He caught it and pressed it to his lips. Across the room, Dumas saw them. Dujarier is a lost man, he thought with amusement.

The Porte St Martin was a large theatre but not in the same class as the Opéra. Its seats were shabby and the walls needed a coat of paint. Nevertheless, it was a popular venue and Lola's notoriety and Dujarier's patronage had drawn an exceptional crowd in spite of the freezing night. In the queue for last minute tickets, people stamped their feet to keep warm and their breath rose in clouds of steam in the frosty air.

In the best box the place could offer, Dujarier leaned over the balcony to observe the audience. There were quite a few critics there, many of them men who professed to be his friends or owed him favours. If they did not measure Lola's dancing by the rigid standards of excellence the Opéra demanded, and gave her credit for the charm and character of her style, the reviews should be good.

It was of the greatest importance to him that they should be. He had never felt like this before. He knew that his happiness was inextricably linked to hers. As the curtain rose and the audience quietened, he closed his eyes for a moment and willed her to succeed.

The morning was almost over when he woke the following day. Beside him, the rumpled sheets were cold and he heard Lola moving about in the little bathroom next door. He called out to her and she flew through the door and pounced on him.

'Lazybones, I thought you would never wake up.'

He gasped as she tickled his ribs. 'Stop it.'

'Only when you tell me I am the best dancer in Paris.'

He grabbed her wrists. 'I'm not so sure about that.'

She pouted. 'You heard the applause and saw the flowers the audience threw. By the end, I could hardly find a place left to dance on the stage.'

'All right,' he laughed, 'it's true. All the others are mere glow worms to your blazing star. Now come here.'

She leant forward and nipped his neck with her small, white teeth. Alexandre shuddered and stroked her bare shoulder, his other hand sliding round her waist to pull her close. She felt his heartbeat and the rhythm of his breathing.

'We shall always be together, shan't we?' she murmured.

He kissed her lips. 'Until death. Now come back to bed.'

Hours later, they woke again. The winter afternoon had leached the colour from the sun and as it sank towards the horizon, it was almost indiscernible against the grey sky. Lola stretched. Rubbing the sleep from her eyes, she turned to look at him. How much she loved every inch of his pale, gangly body. She still found it hard to believe that she had found a man she could love so deeply who loved her in return. Her success at the Porte St Martin had been exciting. Once it would have meant everything, but now nothing was as important as being with him.

He sat up suddenly, swung his legs off the bed and stood up. 'I have to go out for a while. There is some business I need to see to,' he said.

'You will come back soon? I want to celebrate tonight.'

He frowned. 'I'm sorry my love. That will have to wait until tomorrow. I have accepted an invitation to dine at Les Trois Frères.'

'Take me with you.'

'Impossible,' he bent down and kissed her forehead. 'It's no place for a woman, my love. All the men go to gamble and the company can be rough.'

She felt a twinge of jealousy. 'Why do you want to go without me?'

He pressed her hand to his lips. 'I don't. I promise I won't accept any invitations after this one, but I've told some people I'll join them tonight. I can't go back on my word.'

'What people?'

'No one of importance: business associates.'

'You are sure there are no women?'

He laughed and kissed her cheek. 'If there were, I would insist you came too.' He took her face between his hands. 'I swear on my honour, Lola, you are the only woman I desire.'

She kissed him 'Then you may go.'

The dinner at Les Trois Frères was a rowdy affair. After the meal ended, everyone adjourned to the gaming room to play cards. Dujarier found himself sitting opposite a man whose company he always tried to avoid.

Jean-Baptiste Rosemond de Beaupin de Beauvallon was a tall, well-built man whose chestnut hair and whiskers framed a patrician face habitually set in a supercilious expression. He wrote theatre criticism for a rival paper and was the brother-in-law of its editor.

St Aignan, who had agreed to act as banker, dealt the cards. Dujarier's spirits rose when he saw his hand although he was careful to keep his expression neutral. He cast a covert glance at Beauvallon. He would enjoy taking the rat's money.

An hour later though, Dujarier was losing; reaching out for the brandy bottle, he poured himself another glass. His luck must turn soon. He knocked back the brandy in one gulp.

'Gentlemen,' he said loudly. 'I propose that we raise the stakes.'

St Aignan frowned. 'The bank will not stand it.'

Beauvallon exhaled a cloud of cigar smoke and curved his lips in a smile that did not reach his eyes.

'If the stakes are raised I'll take the bank. What do you say Dujarier? Shall we be partners?'

A low murmur went around the room; most of the gamblers knew of the animosity between the two men.

'It will be my pleasure,' Dujarier replied. 'St Aignan, do you wish to remain in?'

St Aignan nodded.

Beauvallon raised his glass. 'To our success.'

Just after three o'clock, the party began to break up. The private room reeked of cigars and alcohol. Dujarier's head throbbed. He rubbed his eyes and waited whilst St Aignan made the final computations. He felt too tired and irritable to be bothered to take part in the desultory conversation around him. The evening had been a bore. Even though he thought he had recovered his losses, he doubted that his winnings would amount to much. He would far rather have spent the evening with Lola. Perhaps she would be waiting for him when he returned.

St Aignan frowned and cleared his throat. 'I'm ashamed to say that I made a mistake earlier this evening; the bank's losses are heavier than I thought, but as the fault is mine, I will find the money.'

'We wouldn't hear of it, would we, Dujarier?' Beauvallon interjected.

If it had been anyone else, Dujarier would have agreed immediately but Beauvallon's assumption annoyed him. 'If St Aignan says the fault is his I can't see why he shouldn't pay,' he said shortly.

'Times must be hard at *La Presse*.'

The table rocked as Dujarier started from his seat, the blood rushing to his face. The men on either side of him tried to pull him down.

Beauvallon smirked. 'Whilst we are on the subject of debts, perhaps you would like to settle the trifling one that has been outstanding for six weeks? Eighty-four louis if I remember rightly.'

The rest of the table watched the exchange with apprehension. A man like Dujarier did not get to where he was in life without being stubborn and Beauvallon's ruthless, belligerent nature was well-known.

Dujarier's eyes narrowed as he reached into his breast pocket and pulled out a roll of notes. One by one he threw them across the table to Beauvallon. 'I hope that will satisfy you?' he spat.

'Thank you. Shall we shake hands on it?'

Glowering, Dujarier looked at Beauvallon's outstretched hand. There was a long pause then he shook his head. 'I think not.'

A gleam of triumph came into Beauvallon's eyes. Dujarier snorted then turned on his heel and walked to the door.

He slept badly that night and in the morning, he cursed himself as he went over the events of the previous evening. Beauvallon was not a man to forget an insult and they had been at loggerheads for so long that he would probably welcome the opportunity for a challenge.

Dujarier bowed his head and pressed his knuckles into his bloodshot eyes, the blackness fizzed with pinpricks of crimson light. He had never fought a duel before but he knew that if it wasn't with Beauvallon, one day there would be someone else. The world of Parisian newspapers was full of jealousies and feuds. Sooner or later, he would have to be bloodied. If Beauvallon chose to pursue the argument, it might as well be now.

The Comte de Flers and the Vicomte d'Ecquevillez, came to see him at *La Presse* early that afternoon.

'We are here on behalf of our friend, Beauvallon,' d'Ecquevillez said. 'I imagine you know why.'

Dujarier waited.

'He is prepared to overlook your insulting behaviour last night in exchange for an apology,' de Flers chimed in.

Dujarier leaned back in his chair and put his feet on the desk. His pride was at stake. 'You must tell Monsieur Beauvallon that the answer is no.'

Silence fell. 'Won't you reconsider?' de Flers asked after a moment.

Dujarier shook his head. 'Not for the world. I'll send my seconds to you as soon as possible. Good day, gentlemen.'

His friends Charles de Boigne and Arthur Bertrand exchanged worried glances when he asked them to act for him.

'Beauvallon is a formidable opponent,' de Boigne said. 'Why don't you let us deal with this? I'm sure we can come to some arrangement with his seconds.'

'Would you have me apologise after all? No, I won't humiliate myself.'

Bertrand pursed his lips and frowned. 'He has fought many duels; you none at all. You are mad to do this.'

Dujarier scowled. 'I won't back down.'

De Boigne sighed. 'At least as you have received the challenge, you can choose the weapons. Swords would be best. Beauvallon is a gentleman. When he sees that your skill is inferior to his, honour will compel him to do no more than inflict a minor wound and disarm you'

'I shall choose pistols.'

De Boigne looked aghast. 'What? Don't you know that Beauvallon is a crack shot?'

Dujarier raised an eyebrow. 'I have fired a pistol before, you know.'

'A few visits to Lepage's shooting gallery? That hardly qualifies you to take him on.'

'I won't give him the satisfaction of sparing my life. I mean this to be a serious encounter.'

De Boigne sucked air through his teeth. He had tried his best but he knew Dujarier's nature. When he had set his mind on a course, it was no use trying to persuade him to give it up.

'Very well, shall we ask them to agree a time in the afternoon? You know you are fit for nothing before midday.'

Dujarier shrugged. 'Let Beauvallon choose.'

Lola had returned to her own lodgings on the night of the dinner but she slept fitfully. When morning came, her head ached from lack of sleep and a feeling of unease assailed her. She rose and dressed, then after breakfast, set off for her morning rehearsal at the Porte St Martin. There, she could not help noticing that groups of people fell silent when she passed. The rehearsal proceeded as usual but the feeling of unease grew.

That evening, Dujarier called to take her to dinner as he had promised, but during the meal, he spoke very little and hardly seemed to notice what he ate. With alarm, Lola noticed that people were casting curious glances in their direction. It was unusual too that no one came to their table to pay their respects.

'I want to know what happened last night,' she said abruptly when she could endure it no longer.

He shrugged. 'Nothing of importance.'

'Then why are people looking at us as if we have the plague? They were talking about me at the theatre too, I'm sure of it.'

Dujarier stabbed his steak and blood oozed out. 'People talk too much. There was some foolish difficulty over the bank last night, but it was soon forgotten.'

'I don't believe you, Alexandre.'

She scrutinised his face. 'There is something more, I can tell, and anything that happens to you is important to me.'

He put down his knife and fork. Suddenly, his expression was so sad that she was really afraid.

'An argument over the cards? That's it, isn't it?'

He nodded.

She crossed herself. 'Oh God, say it isn't true.'

'I wish I could, but you have no need to worry.'

Her voice rose. 'No need?'

He tried to give her a confident smile. 'These things happen. It will be nothing, you will see, a mere formality.'

'A duel? That is what you mean, isn't it? A duel is not nothing. Your life is not nothing.'

He put his finger to his lips. 'Hush, do you want the whole room to hear?'

She looked around defiantly and several of the other diners lowered their eyes.

'It seems I am the last to know,' she said. Her voice was quiet now. 'Who has challenged you? What weapons? Has the time been set? You must tell me everything.'

'No, my love, I cannot.'

Tears sprang to her eyes.

'Trust me,' he said softly.

She bit her lip and nodded. In her heart she knew that she must not meddle in an affair of honour. If he withdrew from the challenge now, he would be branded a coward. He could never endure that.

'May I stay with you tonight?'

He shook his head. 'No, my love, I think that I must spend the night alone. We can be together again when it's over.'

Later he sat in his study, staring at the blank sheet of paper on the desk before him. He had sent the servants to bed hours before and the fire was almost out. Clumsy with cold, he got to his feet and went to pick up the poker. The embers stirred into life and then died again.

He huddled into the old cloak that he had thrown around his shoulders and returned to his desk. The blank sheet of paper stared up at him. He took a swig from the glass of brandy at his elbow and adjusted the wick of the oil lamp to cast a brighter glow. His inkwell was almost empty and a pile of letters addressed to his family and friends lay sealed and ready to send, but he had reached the hardest task he had to perform. He had to compose the words that would tell his Lola how much he loved her.

It snowed in the early hours of the morning and when, after too few hours sleep, he woke at dawn, a white shroud covered the deserted streets. His hands shook as he dressed: in black as the code duello required, putting his warmest flannel shirt under his coat. He did not want to be seen shivering in the cold. The bottle of brandy stood on the night table. He poured himself another glass and swallowed it in one gulp before stuffing the bottle into the pocket of his coat.

Downstairs, his coach waited and his principal second, de Boigne stood by the door. 'I'll ride with you,' he said gravely. 'Bertrand has gone to fetch a doctor. He will meet us at the Bois.' He pointed to the bottle sticking out of the top of his friend's pocket. 'Dutch courage, eh? No harm in it but I hope you've just had one.'

The carriage jolted through the quiet streets. It was too early for anyone but delivery drays and sweepers to be out.

'Do you want me to go over the arrangements with you now?' de Boigne asked.

Dujarier listened but he found it hard to take in his friend's careful explanation of how the duel was to be conducted.

There was no sign of the challenger, Beauvallon, or his seconds when they arrived at the clearing in the woods near the Madrid Restaurant, the traditional place for such meetings. As Dujarier got down from the carriage, a twig snapped under his foot. He flinched and de Boigne put a reassuring hand on his arm.

It was bitterly cold. Bertrand arrived with the doctor and they all paced up and down in the snow stamping their feet and blowing on their reddened hands to keep warm. De Boigne looked at his watch for the hundredth time. 'They're late.' There was a tinge of hope in his voice.

'I'll go and look around,' Bertrand said. 'There shouldn't have been any confusion about the site but I suppose we must make sure of that.' He turned to Dujarier. 'We needn't wait much longer before you can depart with your honour intact.'

When Bertrand returned with no news of Beauvallon and his friends, de Boigne's numb lips cracked in a wide grin. He clapped Dujarier on the back. 'A lucky escape, you can stand us all a good breakfast.'

'Not yet. We must wait a little longer.'

Bertrand exploded. 'Do you want to be killed? The appointed time has passed. There's no shame in leaving.'

'If I leave now, I shall only have to face him another day. Better to get it over with.'

De Boigne opened his mouth to speak but he was cut short by the sound of hooves on the frost-hardened ground. The drumming grew louder and a carriage bowled into view and slowed at the junction of paths. Blood roared in Dujarier's ears and his vision clouded. He forced himself not to move as, slowly, the coachman negotiated the corner and drove towards them. A moment later, he saw Beauvallon step from the carriage.

'A thousand apologies gentlemen,' he smiled.

His nerves taut, Dujarier hardly heard the excuses. He felt the pressure of de Boigne's hand on his arm. 'Remember, you stand thirty paces apart,' his friend muttered. 'When I clap three times, you advance no more than five paces and fire. If he shoots first, you must stand still and return fire immediately.'

The pistol felt like a shard of ice when de Boigne put it in his hand. He gripped it and heard the click of the trigger. De Boigne leapt backwards.

'For God's sake man, if the powder had ignited, you would have killed me.' Ashen-faced, he snatched back the pistol and cocked it once more. 'Take it: I'm going to step away now. Fire as soon as you hear my signal. That way he won't have the advantage of narrowing the gap.'

Only the creak of snow under their boots disturbed the silence as the two men paced out the distance and turned to face each other. When the signal came and Dujarier fired, the explosion almost deafened him. He could not control the pistol and it jerked up and sideways. With a high-pitched whine, the bullet passed to the right of Beauvallon, a few feet above his head. Beauvallon levelled his own weapon and took aim.

With surreal clarity, Dujarier saw the black circle of the muzzle against the snow: a well of darkness ready to suck him in.

'For God's sake,' de Boigne hissed. 'Stand sideways! Shield your head with your pistol!'

Dujarier did not seem to hear him. De Boigne felt a pulse hammer in his ears. He glared at Beauvallon across the bleak clearing.

'Get it over with, damn you,' he shouted. 'Fire!'

Snatching up a cloak, Lola flung it around her then raced to Dujarier's house. She could not bear to wait any longer.

''Where is your master?' she shouted at the servant who answered her frantic knocking. He looked at her in astonishment; her hair straggled from its pins and she was panting.

'I don't know, madame. He left very early and didn't say when he would be back. Will you wait or shall I give him a message?' His voice tailed away for she was already running down the street.

In the Chaussée d'Antin, she pounded on Dumas' door.

'Monsieur is breakfasting,' the servant who opened it said. 'If you would like to wait, I shall announce you.' He recoiled as she barged past him.

'Where is he?' she cried, bursting in on Dumas. He put down his coffee cup and stood up, his expression full of apprehension.

'The Bois, but I'm sure there is no cause for alarm. He will probably return with a flesh wound at worst. A few days should suffice to mend that.'

Lola's eyes glinted. 'Who is he fighting? Tell me.'

Dumas shifted his weight from one foot to the other. 'I'm not sure I…'

'I will find out soon enough. Tell me now.'

'Jean-Baptiste Beauvallon,' Dumas said quietly.

'The weapon?'

'Pistols.'

She gasped. 'Then he is a dead man. You must help me find him. If I have to, I shall take his place.'

'Don't be absurd, Beauvallon would never fight a woman.'

'I can shoot as well as any man.'

'And shame Alexandre?' He took her hands. 'This is his quarrel.'

Tears welled up in her eyes. She broke away and hammered her fists against his chest. 'No, no, no: I shall never bear it if he dies.'

Dumas grabbed her hands again and held her away from him. He felt her body shake.

'Alexandre won't die,' he said gently. 'All Beauvallon wants is a little of his blood, then honour will be satisfied. You can nurse him to your heart's content when he comes back. I know it is hard, but you must go home and wait. Do you want me to come with you?'

Lola shook her head. 'Thank you, but I shall go alone.'

At Dujarier's house, she sat in the drawing room watching the hands of the brass clock on the mantelpiece creep forward. Every carriage that rattled by, every shout in the street sent her racing to the window. At last, a fiacre stopped in front of the house. She saw Bertrand climb out followed by de Boigne. Unsmiling, they glanced up at the window where she stood. Her heart jolted.

On the stairs, hampered by her full skirts, she almost fell but she kicked her legs free and rushed on. At the bottom, she stopped short as the door opened. De Boigne stood there with his hand raised in warning. He recoiled at the wildness of her expression. 'Don't, Lola; don't come out,' he faltered trying to take her arm.

She shook him off. He had not expected her to be so strong.

'Get out of my way,' she screamed.

He let her go and turned to the wall, his head in his hands. Then he heard a long, long cry that he would never forget and knew that she had found Dujarier's body.

For days she would not leave her bed, not touching the food her maid brought her and refusing to see any of the friends who called. On the day of his funeral however, she rose at dawn. Going to the mirror, she stared at her puffy, red-rimmed eyes and dull, tangled hair then she rang for her maid. I must look my best today, she thought. He would have wanted it.

In spite of the steaming water with which the maid filled her bath, she shivered. Afterwards, she sat in silence as her hair was brushed. When it had been twisted into a knot at the base of her neck and her swollen eyes were soothed with rosewater, she stood up. Her maid laced up her corset, helped her into a black dress and carefully placed a veil of black lace over her head.

On her way out of the room, she noticed a pair of leather gloves on a table. They were his. He must have left them there. She picked them up and held them to her cheek. The clean, masculine smell of the leather, mixed with the aroma of his favourite cigars brought tears to her eyes once more, but she choked them back. Today, she must not cry.

Dumas had sent a carriage to take her to Notre Dame de la Lorette. When she entered, she saw that the church was almost full. Unacknowledged by the ushers, she slipped into a seat at the back of the church.

Dujarier's family filed in silently and walked to the seats at the front of the church. The essence of respectable grief in their mourning weeds, they seemed to belong in another world.

Lola knelt to pray, but when a sound like a sigh spread through the church, she raised her head to see that the rest of the congregation were on their feet. Shaking, she stood too and a moment later, the coffin came into view. The bearers, Dumas among them, bore it at shoulder height to the altar, then lowered it onto a platform covered it crimson velvet.

She closed her eyes. The sweet sickliness of incense and lilies nauseated her and her head swam as the priest intoned the supplications for the dead. All she could think of was Dujarier as he had been in life, impatient of formality, serious when seriousness was called for, but swift with a witty remark when it was not. Her mouth quivered in the ghost of a smile. He would probably have made a joke about all this fuss. Then she remembered that she would never hear his laugh again and the grief flooded back. Guilt too pierced her heart. She had heard the whispers as she entered the church: her love was a curse.

In the weeks that followed, the world seemed to have blurred into a morass of grey. Her friends tried to rouse her but she wanted to be alone. Day after day, she remained in her lodgings. Sometimes she read the books that Dumas brought her and it was to a sonnet of Shakespeare's that she returned over and over again.

Let me not to the marriage of true minds admit impediment, it began. Yes, she thought, what we had was a marriage of true minds, but how can I deny the fact of death? No words can cheat death, however beautiful they may be.

'Do you need money?' Dumas asked when he visited her one day.

She shook her head mutely.

'You cannot live on air, Lola. Have you any expectations from Alexandre's estate?'

'He left me his shares in the Palais Royal Theatre, but his family have made it very clear that they will oppose the bequest.' She tossed her head. 'I shall not demean myself by fighting them.'

'I understand, but then you must let me help you. Have you decided what you will do?'

She sighed. 'I have tried to, believe me, but my head aches all the time. I cannot concentrate on anything.'

He put his large, swarthy hand over her pale one. 'It is almost August; Paris will be empty. You need life and activity, Lola, if you are to recover your spirits. Why not go to the spa at Baden Baden or to the coast where there will be plenty of diversions?'

She smiled sadly. 'Perhaps you are right.' But she knew that it would be a long time before the pain of losing Dujarier went away.

Chapter 22

Palais de Justice, Rouen

Under the gilded ceiling of the medieval hall, the public
galleries bulged with onlookers, packed so tightly that
when the procession of judges entered, majestic in their
red robes, the crowd struggled to stand. Heat squatted
on the courtroom like a toad. Even when the president
departed from convention and permitted the windows to
be opened, hardly a breath of air stirred.

On the witness benches, Lola sat and waited for
Beauvallon's trial to commence. Across the courtroom,
she saw him, stocky and bewiskered, talking with his
counsel Pierre Antoine Berryer.

She had heard of Berryer, who had not? He had the
reputation of being a veritable bulldog. She prayed his
feared tenacity would do Beauvallon no good. Opposite
her, Dujarier's family sat in silence. Their counsel
Duval, on whom the burden of prosecution as well as
the family's claim for damages lay, was deep in
conversation with the advocate-general.

Lola took her eyes off the two groups and bowed
her head. The ferocity of the attention directed at her
from the public galleries was almost tangible, but she
was determined not look round. She did not want to see
the scribblers from the Paris press or the curious public.
After she had left Paris, she had tried to drown her grief

in an endless round of parties. She knew that every indiscretion had been gleefully seized on.

She scowled. What did people want of her? If she had entered a convent, it would have denied them all the fun of damning her. She doubted they would have liked that.

The court stilled as the act of accusation was read out and the opening statements commenced. Then it was Beauvallon's turn. She watched him closely as he answered Duval's questions. He was fluent and assured. Not a twitch of a muscle or a faltering word betrayed any doubt of his innocence. Her knuckles whitened at the rising murmurs of approval from the onlookers as he reached the end of his testimony.

'Order!' the president's voice rang out. 'The defendant may stand down.'

The doctor who had performed the autopsy on Dujarier's body took the stand. Lola was unprepared for the evidence he brought with him. When he produced a bulky parcel and opened it, all the horror flooded back and her head reeled.

A bundle of blood-stained clothes tumbled out. An usher took them to the bench and the president stroked his beard as he inspected the garments.

'Have you anything else to show us, doctor?' he asked when he had finished.

The doctor held up a small, flattened piece of metal. Fresh murmurs rose from the crowd. *The bullet: the bullet that killed him.*

The president's gavel struck the bench, making Lola jump. The doctor continued.

'Observe how the shape has been distorted due to passing through the deceased's face and brain, then smashing into the back of the skull.'

Lola gasped. The mess of blood and bone that had once been the face she loved so much rose before her. The room went dark and she swayed.

Duval approached the bench and murmured something to the president. The old man nodded.

'Dona Montez, I realise that these details may be distressing for you. Do you wish to leave the court?'

With an effort, she recovered her composure and shook her head.

'Do you have any more questions, Monsieur Berryer?'

'Thank you, my lord, I do not.'

Monsieur Duval?'

'No, my lord.'

'Then we shall hear the next witness.'

The court rose at six. By then Lola was exhausted. What a charade, she thought miserably. The truth was plain.

The following morning at ten, the session resumed and Dumas was called. Lola smiled for the first time. How magnificently he swept through this gaggle of parasites and fools. He would turn the jury against Beauvallon.

But Berryer was too skilled to allow Dumas to dominate him. When he stepped down and Lola heard her name called, she still sensed that Beauvallon's advocate had the courtroom in his hand.

Taking Dumas' place, Lola raised her black veil and removed the glove from her right hand. She rested it lightly on the leather-bound bible placed before her and swore to tell the truth.

Every question that Berryer asked stirred painful memories of her life with Dujarier and their last evening together. He seemed to ask the same thing in many different ways. She knew what he was doing.

Under a veneer of politeness, he wanted to discredit her and show that anything she said was worthless. Normally, she would have fought back, but today, all spirit had deserted her.

At last, she could endure no more.

'Always the same questions,' she said brokenly. 'No more I beg you. I will always repeat the same things. I was sick - surrounded by doctors and the law - a woman would have to be nearly heartless - it was I who received his dead body.'

The president cut in. 'Dona Montez, the court appreciates that this must have been a great shock for you, but please answer Monsieur Berryer's question.

'Mon Dieu, monsieur! I opened the door of the carriage. He fell into my arms. He was dead.'

The room held its breath. Would the president suffer such contempt in silence? The old man studied her with his piercing eyes for a few moments. Then he raised one gnarled hand.

'I am sorry for your loss, madame. In view of it, I shall excuse this performance, but do not try the court's patience again. You may stand down.'

'If the matter were to be decided in accordance with the law, there is no question that Beauvallon would be found guilty of murder,' Dumas said the following week. The final arguments were due to be heard that evening.

'Then he will be convicted?' Lola asked.

Dumas shrugged. 'Everyone knows that the courts never convict in a duel if it can be proved that the code has been observed. There must be clear evidence that some unfair advantage has been taken.'

'You do not call it an unfair advantage that Beauvallon shot to kill when Alexandre was already disarmed?'

'Alexandre elected to shoot first. The rules were obeyed.'

Lola bit her lip. She was too angry to speak. Gently, Dumas took her hand.

'Even the best and holiest causes have been lost, Lola. If the worst happens, our consolation must be that a defeat will shame our opponents. If Beauvallon leaves the courtroom absolved, the fraudulent duel will have won the day, but the principle of duelling will be irreparably dishonoured.'

That evening, thousands of people besieged the Palais de Justice, angry that there was no room for them inside. Squads of soldiers and gendarmes fought to hold them back. At midnight, the jury retired to consider their verdict. In the noisy courtroom, Lola alone was silent as bitterness fought with hope. If Beauvallon escaped, she would leave Paris. It would be impossible to remain to endure his triumph.

A bare ten minutes had passed when the jury returned. Listening to the verdict, she sank into despair. Her worst fears had come true. It was as if Beauvallon had murdered her lover a second time. He was a free man.

Part Three

1846 - 1848

Lola and the King

Chapter 23

Munich

Ludwig of Bavaria wrapped the hem of his faded, green housecoat close around his skinny frame. It was the time of year when the kingdom celebrated his birthday. At the parade ground on the edge of the city, the Oktoberfest would be in full swing for days. He would have to pretend that he was enjoying it all, even though he was old and tired and did not care for parties any longer. He felt as dried up as the kitchen scraps that the servants threw out.

The fire in the grate barely took the chill from his study. It was a quarter to six in the morning but he had already been at work on his papers for an hour. He prided himself that, winter and summer, since he had ascended the throne of Bavaria twenty-one years ago, his lamp was always one of the first in the city to be lit.

He ran his eyes down the account book open on the desk before him. The sum for logs used in the palace last month seemed excessive. His thin, bloodless fingers ached as he grasped one of the quill pens that the servants sharpened in readiness for him each day. Scrawling a reproof in the margin in his spidery hand, he went on to the entry for the number of onions that had been used in the kitchen.

Finishing his scrutiny, he stood up and went to the window. Slowly, his beloved Munich was emerging in the grey, dawn light. Whatever household economies he insisted on, money spent on the city's beautification was never wasted. He thought fondly of all the works he had commissioned during his reign: spacious parks, elegant squares and fine buildings of classical grace and power.

The sky lightened and all over the city, church bells began to toll the hour. Ludwig frowned as he strained to listen. The deafness that had afflicted him all his life was becoming worse every year. With a sigh, he turned away and went back to his work. Later he would dress and breakfast with the queen before they attended the festivities.

Lola had arrived in the city a few days previously. Struggling to put Paris behind her, she was en route for Vienna, but on the way, it had occurred to her that Munich's Octoberfest might provide an opportunity to secure a guest appearance at the court theatre. As usual these days, there was never as much money in her purse as she would have liked.

The city was bursting at the seams with visitors but she charmed the owner of its best hotel into finding her a small suite overlooking the elegant Promenadenplatz.

Her next step was to visit Baron Frays, the manager of the Court Theatre. He was not impressed by her suggestion that she perform at his theatre for half the box office takings. 'In any case,' he said, 'all decisions are made by the king.'

'I'm sure he will agree when he knows I am here.'

Frays laughed. 'You are very confident, Dona Montez, but the king is a busy man. You might have to wait some time for an answer.'

'But you will ask him?'

'Perhaps, but please do not count on his agreement. In any case, I have no need of a new dancer at present.' He bowed. 'I wish you good day.'

Back at the hotel, she stood on her balcony watching the people passing by below. Perhaps she would attend the festival races that afternoon. It was a pity she knew no one in Munich; it would be more congenial to have an escort, but unless luck brought any of her friends to town, she would have to go alone.

At her feet, her lapdog Zampa pawed her skirt. She picked him up and tucked him under her arm. 'Never mind, I am sure we shall soon find new friends, shan't we my pet?' she smiled.

She was about to turn back into the room when a figure strolling across the Promenadenplatz caught her eye. She recognised the well-dressed man straight away, for they had often met in Paris. Baron von Maltzahn was a charmer, a man made for any occasion, yet under his urbane manner she recognised a kindred soul. She felt sure that he saw life as she did: a game to be played with every trick and skill at one's command if one was to win. And what else was there in life for her now but winning? Since she had lost Alexandre, love was impossible.

She leant over the balcony. 'Baron! Up here!'

He tilted his cream panama hat back from his eyes and looked up. His face broke into a grin. 'Why, Lola! What a delightful surprise.'

'My rooms are at the top of the stairs.'

He bowed. 'I shall be there directly.'

She hurried inside and after a quick glance in the mirror over the mantelpiece, arranged herself in a chair. It could not be better - thrice-widowed, and richer with every bereavement - the baron knew almost everyone who mattered. She recalled him mentioning that he had met the Bavarian king on several occasions. With his help, she might be able to side-step Frays.

'Have you been in Munich long?' he asked when he had sat down, one manicured hand resting on his gold-topped cane.

'Just a few days.'

He reached out to stroke Zampa. The little dog wagged his stumpy tail.

'I'm glad to see you still have this fellow to keep you company. But you look a little pale, Lola. I trust you are in good spirits?'

The kindness in his voice shook the defences that she had built up since Dujarier's death.

'I try to be, but it is not always easy.'

He saw a flash as she twisted the ring on her finger.

'I'm sorry,' he said quickly. 'It was foolish of me to ask. Dujarier was an exceptional man; you must feel his loss deeply.'

'Yes.'

His smile held a hint of mischief. 'But life has to go on, eh?'

Lola gave him a sharp look. The months since she had left Paris had been closely followed by the press and the public, but she shrugged off their slurs. The lovers she had chosen for consolation were no one else's business.

Maltzahn flushed. 'I meant no offence.'

Her expression softened. 'And none is taken.'

'So what are your plans? If there is anything I can do to help, you must not hesitate to ask.'

'How kind you are and you are right, life must go on. There is one thing that you could do for me. I had hoped to dance at the Court Theatre but the manager tells me that he must consult the king before he can give me an answer and that will take a long time. I wonder, may I ask for your help?'

'Why of course. Ludwig has an eye for a beautiful woman and he's a great admirer of all things Spanish. I am sure that if he knows you are here, he will be eager to see you perform. Shall I request an audience for you so that you can talk to him yourself?'

Lola beamed. 'I should be so grateful.'

Two days later, armed with von Maltzahn's letter of introduction, she rose early and dressed in her favourite black velvet. She studied her reflection with satisfaction: the dark, sensuous fabric emphasised the perfect curves of her figure and heightened the beauty of her deep-blue eyes.

The palace was close by and she could have walked there, but she ordered a carriage. 'It would never do to arrive on foot like a beggar, would it, Zampa?' she remarked, fondling the dog's silky ears.

At the massive doors on the Max Josephplatz, she handed the letter of introduction to the military adjutant on duty and watched him as he read it laboriously.

'Well,' she demanded after a few moments. 'Are you going to keep me waiting all day?' The adjutant was tempted to answer in the same vein but he was aware that von Mahltzahn was an influential man and the king's interest in beautiful women was well-known.

He bowed stiffly. 'If you would be so good as to remain here, I shall enquire whether His Majesty will receive you.'

He disappeared up the grand staircase leaving Lola to tap her foot and wait. Whilst she did so, she ran through in her mind what she knew of the king. Maltzahn had mentioned that he loved poetry as well as art and wrote a great deal himself.

'And what of the queen?' she had asked.

'Thérèse? She was a princess of Saxe-Hildburgenhausen: very pious and noted more for her good works than her wit and education. She has born the king eight children. He is devoted to her but has often found love elsewhere.'

The adjutant hurried back down the stairs, the spurs on his well-polished boots jangling.

'His Majesty will see you now Dona Montez, but he can spare no more than a few minutes.'

When she entered the room, Ludwig was looking at some papers on his desk. He raised his head and she saw a flicker of interest in his grey-blue eyes. He was not such an impressive figure as she had expected, quite short with a long, pointed nose set in a thin face marked by small-pox. A large growth stood out on his forehead.

'Dona Montez, Your Majesty.'

The king stood up and greeted her in halting Spanish. Remembering that von Maltzahn had warned her that he was becoming deaf, she took care to speak clearly.

'Your Majesty does me great honour. Baron von Maltzahn told me that I would have the pleasure of speaking with you in my native tongue, but he did not tell me that your command of it was so fluent.'

'You are very kind. Now, how can I help you?'

He listened to her politely before speaking.

'Baron Frays deals with that kind of thing. Have you seen him?'

'Yes, Your Majesty, but he was not encouraging.'

'Then why have you come to me?'

'Because I thought you might wish to overrule him.'

A wry smile came over the king's face. 'I am not in the habit of overruling my officials unless it is absolutely necessary. Why should I do so now?'

'Because you love Spain and I am an accomplished performer of her dances.'

He looked at her with amusement. 'I am sure you are and you also have a fine figure, although, if you will forgive me, I wonder whether you owe it all to nature.'

'That is easily proven.'

Snatching up a pair of scissors from his desk, she jabbed them into the neckline of her dress and began to cut.

For a moment, the king was too taken aback to speak, then he started to chuckle.

Outside the door, the adjutant sprang to attention as his monarch peered into the corridor.

'Fetch a needle and thread,' he commanded. There was laughter in his voice and he looked years younger.

'Your Majesty?'

'Are you deaf, man? I said fetch needle and thread.'

'At once, Your Majesty!'

'And tell Frays that he is to drop whatever he is doing and come to me.'

The play on the night of Lola's first performance was entitled *The Enchanted Prince.* She was impatient as the first act drew to its end and the cast took their bows. The curtain came down and workmen rushed to haul off the old scenery and replace it with a set showing a Spanish town. As the orchestra tuned up, Lola fastened her castanets and went to the centre of the stage.

When the curtain rose, her eyes swept the auditorium. In the half-light, she saw the king in the royal box. Beside him sat a dumpy woman in dark-blue silk and a diamond tiara who must be the queen. The rhythmic pulse of the *bolero* rose from the orchestra pit. In time with it, she moved with languid grace, becoming more animated as the music grew louder and more insistent.

The king leant forward. The performance outstripped all his expectations. She was magnificent, full of fire and passion. When the dance ended, there was a moment of silence then he got to his feet and began to clap. The rest of the audience followed.

Lola clasped her hands to her heart then stretched them out in a gesture of thanks before turning to face the royal box. Eyes lowered, she sank into a deep curtsey, but as she straightened again, she glanced up to judge the king's reaction. To her satisfaction, he was still clapping with gusto, a broad smile lighting his face. She dipped one last curtsey in the direction of his box then left the stage.

'You are to be congratulated, Lola,' von Maltzahn smiled as they quaffed champagne in her suite at the Goldener Hirsch Hotel a few weeks later.

'You mentioned that you had an offer of work in Augsburg but looking at all this,' he gestured to the luxurious room, 'I imagine that you are in no hurry to leave Munich?'

'The king has implored me to stay. Augsburg will have to wait.'

'I suppose that magnificent necklace is one of his gifts?'

She fingered the heavy collar of sapphires and diamonds.

'Beautiful isn't it?' She stroked the little dog in her lap. 'See, Zampa also has a jewelled collar and Ludwig has promised to buy me another dog as well. I have chosen a mastiff: I shall call him Turk after Prince Heinrich's dog in Ebersdorf.'

Von Maltzahn raised an eyebrow.

She laughed. 'Do you disapprove?'

He shook his head. 'Not at all, I rejoice for you, just be careful. By nature, Ludwig is tight with money; don't push him too far.'

Lola tossed her head. 'He says I can have whatever I want. I simply send the bills to General Heideck to be settled.'

Von Maltzahn spared a sympathetic thought for the bluff soldier, one of the king's oldest friends. He was reputed to be as frugal as his master. How he must grind his teeth at Lola's extravagances. He tossed off the rest of the champagne in his glass and stood up.

'Well, I fear I must leave you, I have an appointment.' He kissed her hand then paused.

'There is something on your mind,' Lola said. 'You may as well tell me.'

He shrugged. 'Just one more piece of advice; please understand, it is well meant.'

She squeezed his arm. 'I know it is.'

'Even though Ludwig expelled the Jesuits when he came to the throne, most of the men of influence are still of the High Catholic and reactionary stamp. They guard their privileges. If they think that your hold over the king grows too great, they will try to bring you down.'

She smiled. 'I am sure that you are right, but I think they will find that they have met their match. Anyway, the king has more power than any of them.'

Von Maltzahn shrugged. 'True, but these days with republicans everywhere plotting revolution, it would be unwise for him to wield it too bluntly. Just take care, Lola, that's all I'm saying. The Bavarians love their king but no monarch can take that love for granted any more.'

Chapter 24

It was late November and with her new friends Berthe and Mathilde Thierry, a dancer and an actress at the Court Theatre, Lola strolled through the bright, frosty streets of Munich. The air was lively with the aromas of gluhwein and spiced Christmas biscuits that wafted from the street stalls that they passed. They were on their way to see the house that the king had bought for Lola.

'I'm sure you will love it as much as I do,' she enthused. 'Old General Heideck suggested a few others, but they were far too modest. I wanted something elegant that would show how highly the king values me.'

Turk, her newly-acquired mastiff, stopped to sniff at a piece of discarded paper in the gutter and she paused. 'I have so many plans. No one will recognise the place when I have finished. The workmen have already begun.'

The mastiff finished his inspection and they continued on their way. After a few more minutes, they turned into the Barerstrasse and saw the house. The façade was pleasingly proportioned, with five tall windows on each floor that gave it lightness and elegance. A large, rather bare garden extended on either side.

'The garden needs to be improved, but I have already spoken to the king about that. I think roses would be charming at the front, don't you? I have lots of ideas for fountains and classical statues as well. In the finest marble of course.'

Berthe smiled. 'It is lovely. I am very envious.'

Lola squeezed her arm. 'You and Mathilde have been so kind to me when I needed friends. You must promise to tell me if there is anything you want and I shall talk to the king.'

They went inside the house and Lola began to show them around the spacious rooms, but the dust and the noise of sawing and hammering soon drove them out. They were halfway back to the Goldener Hirsch when a dray piled high with beer barrels came level with them. As it did so, Turk noticed a cat on the other side of the street.

His hackles rose and he tugged on his lead. Lola tried to hold him but he was too strong for her. Breaking loose, he lunged after the cat with a volley of barking.

Alarmed by the commotion, the dray horse shied and backed into the shafts. The dray lurched and two barrels rolled off. Crashing onto the cobbles, one split and a golden stream of beer gushed out.

The drayman jumped down to calm his horse then turned on Lola.

'Why don't you keep that damned dog under control?' he shouted.

She laughed. 'I could ask the same about your horse. It is not poor Turk's fault if you don't know how to handle it.'

The man reddened and shook his fist. 'When I catch him, I'll teach that dog of yours whose fault it is.'

Lola stopped laughing. 'Don't you threaten my dog, you oaf,' she snapped. She looked around for Turk who had given up hope of catching the cat and trotted off to sniff around some rubbish outside a nearby café.

'Turk, come,' she shouted. He ambled back to her side.

The man fingered his whip and took a step forward then saw her ferocious expression and hesitated.

'Mathilde, Berthe,' she said calmly, 'shall we be on our way?'

They turned to see that a small crowd had assembled behind them blocking the end of the street. Mathilde clutched Lola's arm. 'What shall we do?' she asked anxiously.

'Do? Why we shall go home as we intended. These people would not dare hurt us.'

But it soon became obvious that the crowd intended to stand their ground. A few yards in front of them, Lola halted. She would show these common people that she was not afraid.

'Let us pass,' she commanded.

A swarthy man dressed in workmen's overalls and heavy boots spoke up. 'Not until you pay Matthias for the damage done.'

'I do not carry money, you can apply to General Heideck if you wish; tell him I sent you.'

'Lola,' Berthe said nervously, 'I have some money we could give them.'

Catching her words, the man frowned. 'Lola? Lola Montez? That's who you are, is it, the Spanish doxy?'

Lola fingered the dagger at her belt. 'If you do not stand aside this minute, you will pay for that and you will have your king to answer to.'

A murmur rose from the crowd. A homely woman in a blue apron who stood beside Lola's opponent pulled on his arm. 'Leave them be, husband,' she pleaded. 'We can't afford to have any trouble.'

Glowering, the man backed down and the crowd parted to let them through.

'Walk slowly,' Lola hissed as they reached the other side. 'I won't have them thinking they have frightened us.'

Mathilde whimpered. 'I wish we were at the hotel.'

Lola squeezed her arm. 'We shall be soon. Don't worry, you are safe with me.'

Berthe cast a surreptitious glance over her shoulder. 'They are not coming after us.'

'I should think not. They know that if they did, I would have the lot of them punished.'

A few weeks later, the house in the Barerstrasse was almost ready. Lola was busy making plans for the grand balls and receptions she would hold there.

'The whole of Munich society will be fighting for invitations,' she said to von Maltzahn as they bowled along in the carriage he had brought back from Paris for her. It was light and square, with spanking navy-blue paint and canary yellow wheels. He had assured her that he had rejected ten others before he picked it.

'I can't wait to show you the house,' she went on. 'I think you will agree that it is exquisite.' She laughed. 'How people will envy me.'

Von Maltzahn frowned. Since he returned from Paris, he had heard it all over the city that Lola was not popular with many people. The gossips also said that she had spent more on the new house than many government ministers earned in a year. He adjusted the wrist of one of his fawn, kid gloves and gave her a sideways glance.

'Be careful, Lola. Don't forget what I once said to you: spend too much of the king's money and you will make enemies.'

Lola yawned. 'Oh, don't be a bore. The king loves beautiful things. He does not grudge the cost. In fact, he has promised to give me an allowance so that I shall no longer have to go to old Heideck for every trivial purchase. He has even hinted that he plans to change his will to provide for me.'

She lowered her voice. 'I have another promise from him too. He has agreed to make me a countess. I have spent hours in the royal library. It is full of the most fascinating maps and old almanacs, you know. I have chosen what my title shall be: I shall be the Countess of Landsfeld. No such place exists but it has a grand ring to it, don't you think?' She caught his expression. 'You look surprised. Am I not worthy of a title?'

'Of course,' he said hastily, 'but it would be unprecedented. The king has never raised a commoner to the rank of countess. It would be even more of an obstacle that you are not a Bavarian citizen.'

She dismissed the objection with a wave of her hand. 'Then the king can make me one.'

Von Maltzahn laughed. 'You have an answer for everything, Lola. I wish you luck and I hope you get what you desire.'

Later, when she was alone at her hotel, she went to the bureau and took out the design for her coat of arms. It featured a crowned lion, a silver dolphin, a sword, and a red rose on a red-and-white quartered ground. At the top was a nine-pointed crown. She had already ordered her dinner service from the Meissen factory.

The crest was to be emblazoned on every piece. It would also be stamped on the silver buttons of her servants' new blue and white livery.

No one would dare look down on her once she had her title. They would have to treat her with the respect she deserved. She would be the most important woman in the land: more important even than the queen. She clasped her arms around her and felt a frisson of delight. Not bad, she thought, not bad for a little girl who wasn't wanted.

At the theatre that evening, Ludwig left the royal box in the first interval and came to see her. She was deliciously aware of the jealous glances directed at her by the courtiers in the audience. Ignoring the murmurs of disapproval, she talked gaily until she noticed that the king was making odd, insistent gestures.

'What's the matter?' she asked.

'Up, Lolita, up,' he muttered. 'You must stand when I address you in public.'

'Forgive me,' she whispered back. 'I had forgotten.' Gracefully, she rose from her chair and their conversation continued. When he had gone, after warmly kissing her hand, her eyes swept the auditorium. She touched the jewel at her neck - a ruby as big as a quail's egg. The faces around her betrayed a mix of emotions: curiosity, envy, dislike and grudging admiration. She lowered her eyelashes with a satisfied smile. Why should she care what they thought? She was safe in the king's love.

A few days later, she watched from the drawing room window of her suite for his arrival. The afternoon was almost at an end and he was late. A steady rain washed the cobbled street and a few passers-by hurried along,

244

huddled under black umbrellas. At last, she saw his slight figure. He was dressed in one of the shabby coats and hats that his frugality made him unwilling to discard. He did not look like a king, she mused. It was no wonder that no one acknowledged him as he passed. In their haste to get out of the rain, they probably did not even realise who the forlorn figure was. She felt a rush of affection for him.

Going to her bureau, she took out the slim, handwritten volume of poems that he had sent her the previous day. To please him, she often wrote a poem of her own in return, but for the last few days, there had been too many other things to think about.

'You should not have walked in this weather,' she scolded when he came in. 'Give me your coat and hat. I'll call my maid and have them dried. Come and sit by the fire. You must be more careful. The thought of you becoming ill terrifies me. What would I do if we could not see each other?'

He smiled at her solicitousness and held out his cold hands to the fire. They tingled as the blood flowed back into his fingers. The comforting scent of wood smoke mingled in his nostrils with her spicy perfume.

'I have been reading your poems,' she smiled. 'They are so beautiful that I was moved to tears. Will you read some of them aloud? I should love to hear them in your voice.'

To her surprise, he did not respond with his usual enthusiasm.

She touched his arm. 'What's wrong, Luis? You seem troubled.'

'We need to talk,' he said hesitantly. 'I have promised to have no secrets from you. I want to hold to that.'

She laughed. 'I hope that the secret is not too dreadful.'

'Baron von Pechmann came to see me this morning.'

She tensed. She had never met the chief of police face to face but she did not like the sound of him. Apparently, he was a severe, unapproachable man and a stickler for formalities. On several occasions, he had demanded that she produce her papers and register as a foreign resident in Bavaria. Fortunately, she had managed to deal with that by visiting one of his junior officers who had been easily charmed into overlooking her lack of identification.

'Why are you telling me this?'

'He is concerned at the ill-feeling that is growing in Munich. People are saying that I let you take too great a part in government. Pechmann believes that is the root of the problem. Even when I do something they would normally approve, the people condemn it because they think it was done on your advice. I asked him to justify himself and he mentioned the increase in teachers' pay. Lola, did you tell anyone that you recommended it?'

She shrugged. 'I may have mentioned it to someone. Does it matter if I did?'

He shook his head. 'In a different world, it would not: we did a good thing. But people want me to take the advice of my ministers. I know I discuss many things with you, we can speak of matters that I would not even discuss with the queen, but it would be best if you and I were the only people to know that.'

Lola snorted. 'The greatest monarchs and statesmen in Europe have valued my opinion. How dare people criticise you for considering it? In the end, every decision is yours alone.'

He sighed. 'Dearest Lolita, you and I know that is true although you are a great help to me. But I beg you to be more discreet. If I was plain Mr Wittelsbach, my private life would not concern anyone else, but I am not. A king has to be seen to rule untrammelled by his affections.'

She shrugged. 'I understand. In future, I shall say nothing.'

'There is another matter.' He hesitated. 'Pechmann thinks that I would be unwise to raise you to the rank of countess. He believes that the nobles would be against it. Perhaps we should wait a little. The lesser title of baroness might be a safer one too.'

Her eyes narrowed. This was too much. What was the point of being the royal favourite if a mere functionary could thwart her at every turn? Pechmann must learn that, if it came to a contest, he could not win. Experience had taught her that reasoned argument did not always work best with the king. Often, he responded better if she heightened the mood. She jumped to her feet and the book of poems thudded to the floor.

'I don't want to hear any more,' she cried. 'Everyone is against me: even you.'

Letting her emotions carry her away, she flung herself across the room, knocking into a table and toppling a vase filled with yellow hothouse roses. It smashed and water flooded over the gilt-tooled leather and dripped onto the Persian rug beneath.

Ludwig gasped but his eyes gleamed. He seized her hands. 'That's not true. I made it clear to Pechmann that I did not accept that any of his complaints were valid. You are very precious to me, no one can change that.'

Her breathing quickened.

'Lola, calm yourself, I beg you.'

She took a step towards him, the colour draining from her face then, eyes closed, she crumpled to the floor. She heard the king's bones crack as he sank to his knees beside her, stroking her hair. His skin gave off a musky, animal smell and she felt his heart pound as he shouted for help. The door opened and from under her half-closed eyelids, she saw a maid staring at them open-mouthed.

'Don't stand there gawping you silly girl,' Ludwig shouted; 'fetch some smelling salts.'

Lola heard the girl scuttle away. A few moments later, the smell of sal volatile made her nose itch. She sneezed and let her eyelids flicker open.

'I have loved you too much,' she groaned, 'but you have betrayed me. My heart is breaking, but I no longer care. Let me die.'

Ludwig seized her hands once more and covered them in kisses. 'I have not betrayed you. I love you, I love you.'

She leaned on him as he helped her to her feet and took her to sit by the fire. The colour crept back into her cheeks. She rested her head on his shoulder and a smile lit his face.

'I shall tell Pechmann that I do not want his advice. No one shall come between us.'

She drew away from him a little, took his hand and kissed it. 'You are so good to me. Forgive me that I ever doubted you, but the cruelty of men like Pechmann makes me so sad and weary.'

'Shall I leave you, now?' he asked gently. 'Do you want to rest?'

She smiled. 'Dearest Luis, do not leave me yet. What would I do if I did not have you to care for me? Let us sit quietly and read together. That will be better medicine than anything.'

'You are a minx, Lola,' von Maltzahn chuckled on his next visit.

'What do you mean?'

'Gossip leaks out of the palace like water through a sieve. The whole of Munich knows that the king has snubbed Pechmann and you're the cause of it. Did you really faint at the king's feet?'

She laughed. 'The king adored our little pantomime and Pechmann is put in his place. What's wrong with that?'

'Just be careful. Whatever the king says, Pechmann is a clever man. I doubt you have heard the last of him.' He touched her hand. 'If you are determined to be a countess, you have a formidable task ahead. Pechmann will not be the only minister against you.'

'But surely Ludwig can overrule the lot of them?'

He frowned. 'You know that we've talked of this before, my dear. Thrones are fragile these days. The king needs the support of his ministers and his people. If he risks defying them, who knows what might happen? The Wittelsbachs have ruled in Bavaria for six hundred years but that might not protect them.'

'The people would never turn against Ludwig. That is just Pechmann's excuse. I refuse to let him beat me.'

Von Maltzahn shrugged. 'Very well.'

'That man again!' she stormed to Ludwig a few weeks later. Does Baron Pechmann have nothing to do but torment me?'

Sitting by the fireside in the drawing room of her suite, the king looked at her anxiously. It had proved harder than he had expected to control Pechmann and the other ministers. He sympathised with Lola's frustration but it had been a long day. He was not sure that he was up to a stormy scene.

'You must not agitate yourself, Lolita.'

'How can I not? Everyone shuns me. Pechmann is impossible. Not content with making difficulties over my registration, with all his pedantic demands for documents which I told him over and over again were lost when I had to escape from Spain, now he even dares to suggest that the reason I have no documents is because I am an impostor! It is iniquitous. Why will no one defend me?'

Ludwig sighed. 'I'm sorry, Lolita, I shall speak with him again.'

Her eyes flashed. 'There are so many other things. Your ministers oppose my grant of citizenship; your city authorities cavil over the planning permits for my house; the Art Association and the Museum Society throw out my applications for membership - even though they owe you so much for your patronage.'

Listening to the list of complaints, Ludwig was glad that at least she did not know about the vitriol his family poured on her. That very morning, he had received an impassioned letter from his sister, Charlotte Auguste, the Dowager Empress of Austria.

What about the example you are setting? she had written. *The world forgives this type of thing in a young man, but in old men? Think of your subjects. Brother have mercy on your soul, your country and on me for writing thus. But I want to be able to look at you with pride – release her, give her money, lots of it if necessary as long as she leaves. Use your mind, your will! I pray to God to help you. Your true friend, your loving sister. Charlotte.*

He stared out at the crystals of frost that patterned the windows. Why were people's hearts so cold? He wished they would understand and love Lola as he did. Outspoken she might be, but it was a rare gift to be able to give such joy.

He stood up feeling a sharp pain stab his knees, then went over to her and took her face in his blue-veined hands. They looked as gnarled as the bark of an ancient oak tree against her smooth, warm cheeks.

'Lolita, I still marvel that someone as young and beautiful as you and with wit and spirit enough for ten women, loves me. I had given up hope of such happiness. Can we not just enjoy our time together quietly?'

She bowed her head. When she spoke, her voice was very quiet. 'Dearest Luis, forgive me but I cannot be at peace while Pechmann humiliates me.'

Ludwig bowed his head. 'Then I must deal with him.'

Her heart leapt. 'Good, I imagine there is some small town in the provinces that needs a police director. Let him go there.'

Ludwig shook his head. 'Pechmann has served me well for many years. It will not be easy to replace him. This must be my decision alone, Lolita.'

'I hear our friend Pechmann is to be sent away,' von Maltzahn grinned when he next visited Lola.

She took a puff of her cigarillo and held the smoke in her lungs for a few moments before she exhaled.

'Yes, and a good thing too.'

'Was it your idea?'

'Only the king could make such an order.'

He gave a dry smile. How adept she was at not answering a question when it did not suit her to do so.

'Have I said something amusing?'

'My dear Lola, everything you say is amusing. I was just thinking of the new joke going around the beer halls.

'Tell me.'

'I'm not sure I should,' he teased.

'Why?'

'It is a little uncomplimentary.'

She reached out and pinched his arm. 'Now that you have whetted my curiosity, you must satisfy it.'

'Very well. What is the difference between Prussia and Bavaria?'

Lola took in another lungful of smoke and paused before she blew it out. 'I don't know.'

'In Prussia, the police kicked Lola Montez out; in Bavaria, Lola Montez kicked the police out.'

He watched her face and hoped that he had not gone too far. Then her expression cleared and she let out a peel of laughter.

Chapter 25

A new year dawned. Lola rose late each day and walked in the snowy streets of Munich with Turk and her guards. Anxious for her safety, Ludwig had ordered Pechmann's replacement, Johannes Mark, to second some of his men to the task. Crowds followed her whenever she went out; street urchins jeered and whistled and the boldest even hurled lumps of the horse dung that steamed on the streets.

She and the king often visited the house in Barerstrasse to supervise the remaining building works. One of her favourite amusements was ordering expensive furniture, ornaments, curtains and rugs, to the dismay of General Heideck, whose desk was awash with bills.

But the winter days were gloomy and often, in spite of the fun of preparing the house, her spirits were low. In the long, dark evenings, the prospect of becoming a countess was not enough to take mind off Dujarier's death. Munich's high society continued to shun her and, in spite of his assurances, Ludwig had yet to make the formal order for her title. She was irritable with him and increasingly, they quarrelled.

Maltzahn shook his head. 'I hope we are good enough friends for me to speak frankly,' he said. 'You must treat the king with more respect. However much he cares for you, he was born to rule and he cannot allow anyone to trample on his dignity – not even you.'

She scowled.

'I know it is hard for you to wait, but wait you must,' he went on. 'Patience, not anger, will bring you what you want.'

He saw a vein throb at her temple and waited for an outburst, but it did not come. Instead, she gave him a sad smile.

'You're right, I know. My temper is a great fault in me and I should try harder to curb it. It's just that I am so tired of everyone being against me.'

'Not everyone. Especially not the king.'

Her eyes clouded. 'Poor Luis. I will try harder for his sake. He deserves to be loved and I do care for him, I really do. He is my good old man. One of the best men I have ever known.'

She put her finger to her cheek. 'I already have a present for him. Something that is a special gift between us. I'll give it to him now. Thank you, baron, for your good advice.'

When Ludwig came in answer to her note, she felt a genuine contentment return. She called for wine and his favourite almond biscuits and they sat by the fire together.

'You are not angry with me any longer?' he asked.

She shook her head. 'I was never angry with you, just with your people who are against me.'

He took another sip of wine. 'Ah, if it could always be like this.'

She smiled. 'It is all I have ever desired.'

His face brightened. 'I wrote a new poem for you yesterday. Would you like to hear it?'

'Very much.'

She cupped her chin in her hands and watched his face as he read. 'Ah, so lovely,' she murmured when the last line died away. 'How few people have your gift.'

She stood up. 'I asked Johannes Leeb to make a special present for you. Will you wait here whilst I fetch it?'

Ludwig kissed her hand. 'Of course.'

She returned a few minutes later with a box wrapped in gold tissue. Ludwig smiled with a child's delight as he undid it and lifted the lid. Inside was an alabaster model of a small, exquisitely-formed foot.

'Your foot!' he exclaimed. 'What a marvellous surprise, and what pleasure it will give me to look at it – I have always said your feet have no equal, even in the finest statues of antiquity.'

She smiled. 'I am so glad you are pleased.'

'I am more than pleased. I shall keep it by me in my private apartments.' He fondled the smooth, ivory stone. 'You have given me perfection. What more could any man ask?'

February was carnival time in Munich. Lola and the Thierrys had chosen to wear dominos, the black, hooded cloaks traditional at masquerades. The three of them strolled amongst the crowds with an old friend of Lola's from Baden Baden, a former croupier called Fritzi whom she had met at the casinos there.

Lola's eyes danced behind her gold mask. In the crisp night air, thousands of white lights sparkled in the bare branches of the trees. Stallholders shouted out invitations to try their mulled wine and roasted chestnuts, and jugglers and acrobats showed off their skills to amuse the crowds.

Most people wore fancy dress and it added to the jollity of the occasion. Demure shepherdesses danced with warriors bristling with moustaches and horned helmets. Chinese mandarins, Oriental pashas, harlequins and pierrots provided bright splashes of colour. Jesters with caps and bells capered about and musicians played fiddles and flutes.

When Lola and her friends had tired of walking, they returned to the Goldener Hirsch. It was already late, but the manager, Ambros Havard, had decided to throw a party.

'I don't feel like going now,' Lola remarked as they went into the hotel.

Berthe Thierry yawned. 'I'm too tired as well. What about you, Mathilde?'

Mathilde shook her head. 'I'd rather come up with you.'

'Well, I'm not ready for bed yet,' Lola's friend Fritzi declared. He had already had a lot to drink and was in high spirits.

Lola smiled. 'Go and enjoy yourself, my dear. We might watch the fun from the gallery for a while.'

Up in the gallery, they craned over the balustrade, laughing at the antics below until suddenly, Lola grabbed Mathilde's arm.

'Look over there. Isn't that Frtzi? Why is he shouting and waving his arms like that? What a clown he is.'

They saw Havard hurry over to the group and seize the croupier by the shoulders. Fritzi shoved him away, but in a flash, Havard had spun him round and was marching him towards the door.

Lola's face darkened. 'Who does Havard think he is?'

Berthe and Mathilde watched open-mouthed as she ran down the gallery. They heard her footsteps thunder on the stairs and then saw her emerge into the chaos below. She caught up with Havard as he was about to hurl Fritzi through the door into the street.

'Stop it! How dare you treat my friend like this?' she shouted above the din.

'This man insulted my guests. I insist he leaves.'

'And I insist he stays.'

'This is my hotel,' Havard retorted. 'I say what happens here.'

'Your precious hotel would be nothing without my custom.'

'It did very well before you came. I am sure it will continue to do so.'

'We shall see about that,' Lola spat. 'You will be sorry when I leave.'

'I doubt it, in fact, the sooner the better.'

The words were hardly out of his mouth when he recoiled from her slap. Another guest rushed to help him, but for his pains, he received a blow from Lola that shattered his spectacles. Cursing at the top of his voice, he groped for her, but she pushed him away. Before he could mount another attack, her guards rushed through the crowd and surrounded her. In a few minutes, she was in her suite.

'You are safe now,' their captain, Weber, panted.

Her eyes glittered. 'Safe? I do not want to be safe. Let me go. I want that man thrown in jail for what he has done.'

He looked at her warily. 'That is not how we do things in Bavaria, Dona Montez.'

Lola took a step towards him but Berthe grabbed her arm. 'Let the captain go downstairs and see to it that Fritzi is not harmed,' she said. 'That is what matters.'

Lola snorted but she unclenched her fists. 'Oh, very well, but I will not have it said that I ran away. And I want the king told of the treatment I have suffered.'

Roused from bed by servants who knew that his infatuation would demand it, Ludwig reached the hotel to find it swarming with angry guests and police. Looking pale and tired now, Lola sat in her drawing room. When she saw him, she burst into tears.

'Havard was very drunk,' she ended her story, dabbing her eyes with the king's handkerchief. 'Otherwise I do not think that he would have tried to strike a woman.'

'I shall order Mark to deal with him,' Ludwig said angrily. He shook his head. 'The thought that you might have been harmed – it horrifies me.'

She put her hand in his.

Thank you, Luis. I knew that I could rely on you to defend me.'

But the following day, her breakfast did not arrive.

'Go and tell Havard that I do not like to be kept waiting,' she ordered her maid,

'So what does he think he is doing?' she asked when the girl returned.

The girl flushed. He says that you can wait for as long as you like, madam. He says that from now on, there will be no luncheon, nor dinner nor breakfast, not even a glass of water and I am to tell you that.'

'The king will hear about this,' Lola fumed. 'I'll make sure Havard eats his words. If necessary, I shall thrust them down his throat myself.'

'Even I cannot force one of my citizens to serve you,' Ludwig sighed when he visited her that afternoon. 'The house in the Barerstrasse will be ready soon. Until then, it might be best if we found you somewhere else to stay.'

'And give in to this man?'

'Lola, he has already withdrawn his demands for an investigation.'

'An investigation?'

'Yes, he came to Mark demanding one, but Mark talked him out of it.'

'I do not see what right he has to feel injured. He is the guilty party.'

'But he did not see it like that. Lola, he is well-liked and influential with the merchants in the city. Do not ask me to pursue the matter.'

She shrugged. Perhaps this was a battle that she should concede.

'Oh very well, I shall go, but only for your sake.'

The apartment that Ludwig found for her in the Theresienstrasse was pleasant and airy. Once a cook and servants had been hired, she was comfortable there. The move was not so bad, she decided. After all, she would need a household staff when she lived at Barerstrasse.

Although she was aware of a simmering resentment when she went out, she refused to give up her daily walks. But now, Ludwig insisted that her guards follow her everywhere.

One morning, out shopping with the Thierrys, they were crossing the Frauenplatz and had nearly reached the cathedral when Berthe looked around her and tugged at Lola's sleeve.

'So many people are watching us,' she whispered. 'I don't feel safe. Shall we go back?'

Lola stopped. Berthe was right. Knots of people stood about, looking in their direction. Their expressions were hostile and one man spat on the cobbles when he saw that she had noticed him.

'But we have come out to do our shopping and we shall do it,' she said. 'Herr Haffner sent me a message to say that he has a beautiful antique necklace just come into his shop. I want to look at it. If we don't go today, someone else might buy it. Anyway, we are almost there.'

Captain Weber frowned as he surveyed the situation. There were at least a hundred people in the square already and more coming in from the side streets.

'I would prefer it if you would allow us to escort you home, Dona Montez.'

'Nonsense, I won't let these people frighten me.'

Turk yelped. Lola swung round in time to see a boy pick up another stone and take aim. It caught Turk on the flank where a dark patch already showed on his fur. Snarling, he lunged, dragging his lead out of Lola's grasp. He reached the boy before he had time to run. The lad screamed as Turk's fangs crunched into his leg. Nearby, a man pulled a heavy stick from his belt and rushed forward.

'Get the Spanish woman!' someone shouted. 'Don't let her escape!'

Lola's guards sprang into action. One of them hauled Turk off the sobbing boy whilst Weber drew his pistol and levelled it at the crowd. The men nearest to him backed away, then for a moment, no one moved.

The captain was swift to seize his chance.

'Quickly,' he ordered, 'get the ladies out of here.'

As the guards hustled the three women across the square, the crowd started to shout abuse. A flurry of stones and horse dung narrowly missed the fugitives as they turned into the lane where the jeweller's shop was situated. Weber reached it first and grabbed the bell chain. After a moment, a mottled hand pulled the door curtain aside and Herr Haffner's alarmed face peered round it.

'Police,' Weber shouted. 'Let us in at once.'

They heard the bolts being shot back then the door opened. Just as the first of their pursuers rounded the corner, they tumbled into the dark little shop.

Haffner bolted and barred the door behind them. Lola peeped through one of the narrow, lattice windows, her eyes sparkling with excitement.

'I beg you, Dona Montez, stay out of sight,' Weber pleaded. 'These people could attack us at any moment. Do not make them even more angry.'

She shrugged. 'I'm not afraid. Let them come.'

He looked over her shoulder. The lane outside was full of people.

'There must be at least two hundred of them now. We shall have to stay here until they leave. My men are armed but I cannot order them to fire on their own countrymen.'

Lola smiled. 'At least I can look at my necklace at my leisure.'

'I'm afraid that you may have more than enough time for that, Dona Montez,' he said wryly.

Hours passed and the mob still waited outside, yelling Lola's name and shaking their fists. In the shop, Lola chose her necklace, and several other pieces of jewellery besides then she sat by the Delft-tiled stove, chatting as if she did not have a care in the world.

It grew dark in the shop and the jeweller lit the candles in the sconces around the walls. In their light, rubies, sapphires, emeralds and diamonds glowed. For the hundredth time, Weber looked up at the clock above the door. It was almost six. Outside, the last rays of the sun had turned the rooftops to rusty gold. A large crowd still filled the square.

Lola yawned. 'Do they have no homes to go to? I don't want to stay here all night.'

She went to the door and put her hand on the bolt. Mathilde grabbed her arm.

'You mustn't go out. It's not safe.'

'She's right, Lola,' Berthe said.

Lola turned to the jeweller. 'Is there some other way out where we won't be seen once it is dark?'

'There is a courtyard behind the storeroom. It's surrounded by a high wall but I have a ladder that should be long enough to reach the top. That is, of course, if the ladies will climb it.'

'It will be an adventure,' Lola smiled.

Two guards carried the ladder to the part of the wall that divided the courtyard from an alley that led away from the square. The younger of the two climbed up. The bricks at the top of the wall had crumbled with many winters of ice and snow and tufts of grass had dislodged the pointing but he managed to balance and hold the ladder steady as Lola hitched up her skirts and followed.

When she reached the top, he helped her to sit on the wall and swing her legs over to the other side. He blushed when he saw a flash of her small feet and neat ankles.

'There is no need to be shy,' she laughed. 'Now you have saved me, we are old friends.'

He grinned and jumped down the other side, then reached out his arms to catch her. Lola took a last look at Turk whining and scrabbling below.

'Take care of him for me, will you?' she called out to Haffner. 'I'll send someone for him in the morning.' She jumped into the guard's arms and Berthe, Mathilde and the rest followed. Together they slipped down the alley and back to the apartment in the Theresienstrasse.

Chapter 26

Ludwig was at breakfast with the queen the next morning when he heard the news. He left his meal unfinished and rushed to find Lola. To his relief she seemed unharmed.

'I wish you could have seen us,' she laughed. 'We had to climb out of the shop like thieves in the night. It was all over nothing. Poor Turk hardly touched the boy.' She stroked the dog's broad head. One of her footmen had just fetched him back and he seemed to be no worse for his night away.

She frowned. 'Of course if I had been made countess, people would not dare insult me so. Why is it taking so long? The council have not even approved my grant of citizenship yet.'

He hesitated. 'Perhaps it would be best if we waited. Just until things quieten down.'

'But you gave me your promise.'

She moved to sit beside him and reached out her hand to smooth his brow.

'It breaks my heart to see you unhappy,' he blurted out, grasping her other hand and pressing it to his lips. 'I would do anything to make you smile but what you ask is so much harder than you imagine.'

She got up and went to the window.

'Lola, I beg you to be patient,' he pleaded, but she remained with her back to him. 'Please talk to me, I cannot bear this silence. I assure you, I will do what I can but my hands are tied. I must not risk losing the support of my ministers.'

She turned, her eyes blazing. 'This is all a Jesuit plot. Isn't it time you showed everyone who rules Bavaria? If my ministers would not obey me, I should dismiss the lot of them and find others who would.'

'Lolita …'

She put her hands over her ears. 'I don't want to hear any more.'

His shoulders sagged. 'Forgive me, Lolita. I will do my best. Give me time. One way or the other, you will get your title.'

When he had gone, it was a long time before her anger subsided. She knew that to many people her desire might seem a mad obsession. Maltzahn would, no doubt, tell her once again that she was a fool, but no one, not even Ludwig, could fully understand what it meant to her. For so long, she had put up with scorn and dismissal; she wanted respect. A title would give her a position in society. It would show the world that she was not just some hole-in-a-corner mistress, but that she was loved and honoured by a king. And wherever she was, she hoped that her mother would hear of it.

It softened the strain of waiting that she had found new companions to amuse her. They were a band of rebellious students from Munich's prestigious university and their friendship with her soon came to the ear of their professors who made no secret of their disapproval. Their lead was followed by the rebels' peers.

'How much longer will you allow me to be abused?' Lola stormed at Ludwig one day, thrusting a large sheet of paper under his nose.

'See, my maid found this spiked on the railings this morning. I am sure my enemies at the university are behind it. The professors and students there insult me openly.'

Ludwig put on his spectacles and studied the paper with a frown. It showed a luxurious bed and through its half-closed curtains, a tantalising glimpse of Lola dressed in very little but an inviting smile. A wizened man in the foreground with spindly, short legs bore an unwelcome resemblance to himself.

He gritted his teeth and scratched the lump on his forehead. He was already weary from the latest battle with his council of ministers. Many who had served him for years had resigned over the question of Lola's citizenship and title. It had been hard to find men to take their place. Those who had accepted office had done so on condition that they should not be obliged to receive Lola in their homes or acknowledge her in public.

'I cannot banish the whole city for you, Lolita.'

She tossed her head. 'I should have thought you would be angry on your own behalf as well as mine.'

A muscle twitched in his cheek.

She leant her head against his shoulder. 'Dearest Luis, it is my love for you that forces me to speak. I hear that the university senate has even made a public expression of its gratitude to the ministers who resigned, thanking them for their support of the university whilst they were in power. Could there be a clearer mark of disrespect for you? What they mean to say is that they hold those traitors in higher regard than their king.'

266

With satisfaction, she felt him stiffen. 'You should make it clear that you will not let such insolence pass,' she went on.

Ludwig frowned. 'No more politics today. Let us talk of something else.'

Over the next few weeks, many more cartoons and posters appeared. Some were simply the products of crude humour, others demanded Lola's expulsion. On Johannes Mark's recommendation, Ludwig ordered that the guard at the Theresienstrasse be quadrupled.

It was late on a blustery March afternoon when the reinforcements marched into the Theresienstrasse to take up their positions. Dark clouds scudded across the sky and the branches of the trees that lined the street chafed and creaked.

'We'll be getting wet soon, look at that storm coming,' one of the guards grumbled to his companion, 'and all because the king is making a fool of himself over his Spanish whore,'

'Wait,' the other man cocked an ear. 'Do you hear something?'

'It's just the wind. You're getting jumpy, you are.'

But the sound grew louder and a few moments later, a large group of men spilled into the street. As they came towards the house, others appeared behind them like a fast rising tide.

'Close up ranks!' the officer shouted.

Above, in her drawing room, Lola heard the commotion and rushed to see what was happening. Seeing the jostling crowds below, she threw open the French windows and stepped out onto the balcony. At the sight of her, a huge roar broke from the mob. They surged forward.

'Shoulder to shoulder men, make a chain to drive them back,' she heard Captain Weber shout over the din. 'Use the butts of your rifles if you have to.'

Lola laughed and blew a kiss. 'Well done,' she called out.

'It would be better if she went inside,' Weber muttered. 'She won't help with that yelling.'

His men edged forward and had just succeeded in pushing the mob back a little way when a shout was heard: 'The king! The king!'

They turned as one to see him striding down the packed street towards the house. The crowd parted before him as he approached; his glance flashed from left to right.

'Hats off before your king!' he barked.

A ragged cheer of 'Vivat Ludwig' rose in the twilight, but very few men removed their hats.

Inside the house, Lola rushed to him. She held out a heavy stone. 'Look,' she cried, 'they have attacked me with these.'

Ludwig took the stone from her and put it down on a table. 'My men will disperse them soon.'

She answered him by flying back to the balcony. A detachment of soldiers had arrived and was facing the crowd, their lowered bayonets glinting in the fading light. As they marched forward, the crowd retreated, still shaking their fists and hooting as she screamed insults.

Ludwig watched her performance with horror. This was not the gentle soulmate he loved, the muse who inspired his poetry and nourished his heart. He went to the window and grasped her arm. 'Come inside, Lolita. I will not have you make a spectacle of yourself in this way.'

But she was on fire with excitement. 'Let me go,' she shouted. When he brought his face close to hers and repeated his words, she almost struck him, but then just in time, she stopped herself. The thrill of the moment died, leaving her exhausted. She let him lead her back into the room.

'I'm sorry,' she faltered, 'but they should not have provoked me.'

There was a loud knock on the door and the chief of police, Johannes Mark, hurried into the room. His usual composure had deserted him and his voice was hoarse.

'I have a division of mounted police on the way, Your Majesty, but the mob is threatening to march on the palace. I have sent some of my men to warn the queen.'

Ludwig squared his shoulders. 'I must go back there.'

'Your Majesty, I do not advise it.'

'Nonsense, these are my people. They would not dare touch me.'

'Then let me come with you.'

Ludwig shook his head. 'I want you to stay here to ensure that Dona Montez is safe.'

He turned to Lola and looked at her sorrowfully. 'Lolita, there must be an end to this.'

Without another word he was gone. Lola stood frozen for a few moments then she rushed back to the window. It had begun to hail and already the mob was thinning. She saw the king walk away through the debris of broken sticks and crumpled posters they left behind them. His face was hidden by the umbrella he sheltered under and he did not look back. What had he meant by his parting words to her? For the first time, she felt a tremor of fear. Had she gone too far?

When Ludwig did not return the next day or the one after that, she put on his favourite dress and went to the palace.

'The king is not seeing anyone,' an equerry said, barring her way.

'I am not anyone,' she snapped. 'Go and announce me.'

The equerry hesitated and she let her hand linger at her belt making sure he saw the dagger gleam there.

'Very well, I shall tell His Majesty that you are here, but if he will not see you, I shall have to ask you to leave.'

Lola laughed. 'Oh, he will see me, I'm sure of that.'

A few minutes later, she was shown into Ludwig's library. Rays of watery sun filtered through the narrow windows but the room was otherwise in darkness. He dozed in his favourite, shabby armchair, a book open in his lap. As her eyes became accustomed to the dim light, she saw his face. A mass of angry blisters disfigured it. When he stirred and saw her, he groaned. 'I must disgust you. Even the queen cannot bear to look at me.'

Contrition overwhelmed her. What if her demands had caused his illness? She came over to where he sat and touched his cheek. 'Oh my poor Luis,' she murmured, 'I am so sorry. But why did you try to keep me away?'

He looked startled.

'You do not mind this - this repulsive affliction?'

She bent down to kiss his forehead. 'You are still the dear man that I love and respect above all others.'

Tears sprang into his eyes.

'What do your doctors say?' she asked.

He sighed. 'It is a malady that has troubled me before. They say what they always say: that I must rest and let it run its course.'

'I shall speak with my own physician. Perhaps he can think of a way to help you. Meanwhile I shall come every day. We can read and talk together like we used to do, just the two of us.'

She picked up the book that had fallen on the floor and sat down in the chair beside him. 'Don Quixote,' she smiled. 'How many happy hours Cervantes has given us. Shall I read to you now?'

The tears rolled down his cheeks. Kneeling before her, he rested his head in her lap.

'My darling Lolita,' he said in a cracked voice, 'just the sight of you makes me better already. How could I ever have thought that I could live without you?'

She smoothed his grizzled hair. All was not lost; he still loved her.

Chapter 27

The house in Barerstrasse was ready at last. Even General Heideck, still tormented by the avalanches of bills that brought the cost to a total far larger than agreed, had to admit that the result was magnificent.

Through windows that reached from ceiling to floor, the spring sunshine streamed into elegant rooms frescoed in the style of ancient Rome or painted with scenes from Don Quixote. A fountain decorated with marble dolphins played in the entrance hall and a crystal staircase led up to Lola's boudoir on the upper floor. Ludwig had made her presents of a valuable Etruscan vase from the Royal Collection as well as an outstanding copy of a Raphael Madonna and a piano with exquisite silver and brass inlays.

There were few distractions to disturb them during his convalescence. The prospect of opportunities for even greater privacy now that she had her own household excited Ludwig. He kept the model of her foot close by. When he touched the smooth, cool stone, his blood quickened.

By the end of April, he felt well enough to appear in public once more. The city had returned to a semblance of normality but he was aware that trouble could flare again at any moment. Although he spent all his spare hours with Lola, he took care not to neglect his duties. Lola left him in peace on the subject of her title and contented herself that he commissioned the court artist to paint her portrait. The finished painting was hung in the palace gallery.

Summer came and the queen left Munich to take the waters at Franzenbad. On the second evening after she had gone, Ludwig and Lola spent the evening together at Barerstrasse. In the Don Quixote room, he read his poetry and she listened, occasionally praising a line or suggesting an alteration.

Midnight came, the time when he usually left her and he closed the book.

'You look tired,' she smiled. 'You should go home and sleep but promise me you will come back tomorrow?'

A muscle worked in his cheek. 'I do not have to leave.'

'What do you mean?'

He took her hands and clasped them to his chest. She felt the hard edges of the gold buttons on his coat. A faint apprehension flickered through her. Something had changed. She sensed that if she sent him away, she would regret it. She knew what she must do. Leaning forward, she kissed him tenderly. 'Then stay.'

'You are sure?'

'Yes, I am going to my room now. Come to me soon.'

When he woke the next morning, he marvelled that she was there beside him, her dark hair spread over the lace-edged pillows. Where the sheet had slipped down, he saw the curve of one breast and the dark aureole of her nipple. He put his lips to it. She stirred and he drew back.

'I hope the old fiddle played a good tune,' he asked shyly.

Her lips curved in a smile and she stroked his cheek. 'Dearest Luis,' she murmured, 'you need have no doubts about that.'

'I am not a young man. I was afraid I would not …'

She put a finger to his lips. 'No man can compare with you. You are everything to me.'

So it is done at last, she thought as her maid dressed her hair after the king had gone back to the palace. She had made him happy. Perhaps tonight would be a good time to remind him of his promise of the title.

'I shall be the Countess of Landsfeld,' she whispered. 'I shall.'

She touched the small bruise at the corner of her lips. After last night, he might want more but she would have what she desired first. She deserved it. Let people call her selfish if they wanted: she did not care. No one knew how much suffering and disappointment had brought her to where she was. If people would not be her friends, then they must take the consequences of being her enemies.

Chapter 28

It was a fine summer evening and, as the king was engaged at a state banquet, Lola invited some of her new friends from among the students to a party. The windows to the gardens stood open to cool the rooms and the scent of lavender and roses drifted in on the breeze.

Dressed in a loose, ivory silk robe, she lounged on one of the sofas in the drawing room, smoking cigarillos and laughing and talking with her guests. Halfway through the evening, two young men joined the party. She knew the shorter of the two but the other, tall with thick, dark hair and a handsome profile, was a stranger to her.

She turned to the student beside her. 'Who is that?' she asked.

'Fritz Peissner. He is in the Palatia fraternity as I am but he is far more important than me. He holds the office of senior, whilst I am a mere foot soldier.'

'Why have you not come to visit me before, Fritz Peissner?' she asked with mock annoyance when his friend brought him over to introduce him. 'I am offended.'

He flushed. 'I had no wish to offend, Dona Montez.'

'I am teasing you,' she laughed. 'Come and sit beside me and we shall make up for the time we have lost.'

'I often wish that I was a man,' she remarked after they had talked for a while. 'It must be marvellous to study at the university and belong to one of the fraternities. We poor women are denied the camaraderie that you men enjoy. It seems very unfair. Wouldn't you agree?'

'I am sure that you would be an ornament to any fraternity.'

'I insist that you join ours,' his neighbour joked. He took off his cap and gave it to her. She put it on her head at a jaunty angle.

'How do I look?' she laughed. 'What do you think, Fritz Peissner?'

He swallowed and avoided her eyes.

'Is something wrong?'

His colour deepened. 'Forgive me, I may have misled you. It is forbidden for anyone outside the Palatia to wear the cap.'

The student who had given it shrugged. 'Don't be a bore, Peissner.' Wine slurred his words.

Lola saw the other students who still had their wits about them exchange uneasy glances. So this business of fraternities was far more important than she had realised. She removed the cap and handed it back.

'There,' she said gaily. 'I have been a member of your fraternity for a whole minute. That is enough for me.'

She smiled at Peissner and took his arm. 'You are quite right; the fraternities should be respected. I'm glad that I shall be able to rely on you to pull me up when I need it. We shall be great friends. I know it already. May I call you Fritz?'

Peissner nodded and she noticed how sweet his smile was.

She tapped his arm with her fan. 'And you must call me Lola.'

She kept him beside her for the rest of the evening. When the party ended in the small hours, he was one of the last to leave. Lola walked to the drawing room door with him.

'Come again soon, Fritz Peissner,' she smiled. 'Come whenever you wish.'

It was time for the king to leave Munich and join the queen for the rest of the summer. 'Every day will seem like a year,' he sighed when he said goodbye to Lola before his departure for Bad Bruckenau.

'I shall write you a hundred letters. Parting will be agony for me as well. At least you will have the distractions of the court to amuse you.'

He grimaced. 'I doubt there will be much amusement.'

The next morning, when he had left, she sat down to pen a note to Peissner.

What harm could a little flirtation do? She could still make the king happy and she would be discreet.

Ludwig wrote every day, giving her minute details of his daily life. In one of his letters, he begged her to send him something she had worn next to her skin. She smiled at the thought that if she and Fritz had gone a little further down the path, and had he been more worldly, the choice of what to send might have proved a diverting game for the two of them, but she did not want to frighten him away. As it was, she mentioned it to no one when she ripped up her scarlet petticoat and drenched some of the pieces in Ludwig's favourite perfume.

Kiss these for me until we are together again, she wrote. *They have touched the places that I know you love the best.* She paused a moment then added: *Can it be only a year since we first met? I cannot imagine what I lived for before then.*

A week later, the letter that she received in return made her heart leap.

This morning I wrote the order to prepare your nomination as countess so that it can be ready on my birthday. Until the day of publication, until the 25th it must remain secret but after that, I will tolerate no objections for I can do without the sun above, but not without my Lolita shining in my soul.

She let out a cry of joy and clasped the letter to her. It was done: he had defied his ministers for her sake.

She skimmed over the cautious advice that the rest of the letter contained. There was no need to take much notice of that. She would conduct herself as she wished. What use was there in being a countess if one had to spend all one's days pretending to be invisible? Ludwig would soon see that he need not worry. The Bavarians loved him. Now that he had shown the way, they would love her too.

It was a Sunday and she drove to church to give thanks for her triumph. All the bells were ringing out and the city sparkled in the sunshine. Afterwards, she gave a splendid dinner for her students. There would be plenty of time to entertain Munich's elite later.

Court festivities occupied most of Ludwig's time in the weeks leading up to Christmas and Lola saw little of him.

It was not her only cause for discontent for even though he had at last openly conferred the title of countess on her the queen still refused to receive her and her invitations to Munich's aristocracy went unanswered. Nevertheless, she rallied and planned lavish festivities with the Thierrys and those of her students who had remained in Munich for the holiday.

On New Year's Eve, she gave a party. She intended it to do more than just ring in the New Year. It would also be an occasion to mark the creation of a new fraternity. That fraternity was of special interest to her, for it had been formed in her honour.

Quite a feather in my cap, she thought gleefully. She had discovered that such a step had no precedent. It showed how much her students wanted to please her. Peissner had not opposed it, although she guessed that of all of them, he was the one who had had the fiercest struggle with his conscience. The fact that he had given up his position in the Palatia to join, confirmed just how fervently he admired her.

By midnight, many toasts to the Alemania – as the fraternity was called – had been proposed and drunk. Heads were muzzy with champagne; fires blazed in every grate and the windows were closed against the freezing night air. Flushed with wine and heat, many of the students had removed their thick, woollen breeches and were sauntering about in their shirt tails.

As the chimes died away, Lola felt weariness overcome her. She looked around for Fritz, but could not see him in the smoky drawing room. He had been drinking heavily earlier in the evening. Perhaps he had gone outside for some air. A tremor of guilt went through her. She had paid him very little attention that night although at the outset she had intended something very different. After the sacrifice he had made, he must claim his reward. She smiled to herself and thought that he could have done so weeks ago if he had not been so diffident.

With a murmured excuse, she left the group she was with and went to the doors that led out to the balcony. Through the frost that filigreed the window panes, she saw him standing in the freezing night air, his back to her and his shoulders hunched. She went out and joined him at the balustrade. Above them, a million stars twinkled.

'I think you are angry with me.'

'Angry? Why should I be angry?'

'You have ignored me all evening.'

He grunted. 'You seem to have found plenty of other people to talk with.'

Reaching across, she stroked his cheek. She felt him tremble as she ran her fingers down to touch his lips. 'I don't care about any of them. All I want is to be with you.'

His shoulders went down and she heard the note of longing in his voice. 'Ach Lola, is that true?'

She put her lips to his ear to whisper her answer but before she could do so, the doors behind them crashed open. A shout went up, 'Lola! Lola! Here she is!'

Swinging round, she found herself in the arms of two burly students. She felt like a feather as they hoisted her onto their shoulders and carried her back into the lighted room. The other students formed a procession behind them, some banging gold plates together like cymbals, others blowing across the lips of empty champagne bottles to make a rhythmic drone.

The rest flourished their red caps and sang their new fraternity song.

Giddy, she looked down at the expensive furniture and priceless ornaments yards below her. 'Take care,' she shouted, 'you will break everything.' But the excitement was infectious and she was soon laughing and singing herself. Then suddenly, she saw flames dance before her eyes and felt the sting of their heat on her face. Her head struck the heavy, crystal pendants of the chandelier that hung from the centre of the ceiling. She smelt singeing hair and realised that it was her own. She screamed but the students were too drunk to see the danger, then there was darkness.

When she regained consciousness, she found that she lay on a sofa. Anxious faces loomed over her. Half-afraid, she put her hand up to her head and felt the stickiness of blood.

'Lola, for God's sake, speak,' the voice belonged to Fritz. With difficulty, she opened her eyes. His face was very close to hers, the fear in his expression was palpable.

She tried to smile. 'Dear Fritz,' she murmured. 'I shall be all right in a moment but promise that you won't leave me?'

He smothered her hands in kisses. She saw that he was on the verge of tears. 'Thank God,' he mumbled.

Rousing himself, he turned to the others. 'Get a doctor, you fools. Hurry.'

By the time the doctor arrived, the students had collected their discarded clothes and dressed themselves. Fully conscious now, Lola lay propped up on a bank of cushions. Fritz held a pack of ice to her head.

The doctor examined the wound with practised fingers then opened his bag. 'It is a clean cut, a few stitches and you will be as good as new.'

She gave him a mischievous smile as he threaded his needle. 'Then I must bang my head more often.' She did not complain as the needle pierced her flesh. Fritz watched her with adoration in his eyes.

A few days later, she made a place for him beside her at her evening gathering.

'You were so kind to me the other night,' she whispered, touching his hand. 'I should like to thank you properly. When I send the others away, make some excuse to stay.'

'Lola, I…'

'What's the matter? Don't you want to?' She leaned closer. 'I thought that you loved me, Fritz.'

'I do,' he stammered,' I worship you.'

'Then what is the problem?'

He avoided her eyes. 'I've never…'

Seeing the flush on his cheeks, she squeezed his hand. How attractive his confusion was.

'Then I shall show you how,' she murmured. 'And I promise it will be all you have dreamt of and more.'

Chapter 29

That year, the short days of January did not oppress
Lola's spirits. She was happy with Fritz and her
happiness spilled over into her time with Ludwig. There
were no more raised voices or broken vases; the hours
they spent together were some of the best they had ever
enjoyed. Ludwig's contentment convinced her that she
had no need to reproach herself and with a clear
conscience, she dismissed Fritz's own doubts.

Then an unwelcome letter arrived. It was brought to
her one February afternoon as she and Berthe Thierry
sat in the parlour at the back of the Barerstrasse house.
Outside, a thrush pecked ruthlessly at the crimson
berries on a holly bush and a light fall of fresh snow
covered the grass.

'How dare that man presume to lecture me,' Lola
raged after she had read the message.

Berthe looked anxious. 'Who is it from, Lola?'

'Prince Wallerstein, the king's new chief minister.
He had better leave me be if he expects to keep his job.
Fritz told me that the Alemania asked him to give the
speech for their first annual dinner - it is customary for
the chief minister to honour the fraternities in that way
– but he would not. His refusal alone is an insult, but
now that is not enough for him. He dares to accuse me

of endangering the king by encouraging the Alemania. He says that it will cause a revolt in the university.'

She tore up the letter and threw it into the fire. The flames licked at the scraps of paper for a moment then flared up and reduced them to ashes.

'Pompous old fool,' Lola muttered, 'these people are all the same, they do not want anything to change. Well to Hell with them. I won't let any of them stand in my way.'

'Perhaps it would be better not to make an enemy of Prince Wallerstein, Lola,' Berthe said. 'He is very grand.'

Lola scowled. 'I will not crawl to a bully.'

They heard footsteps outside the door then a knock. Instantly, Lola forgot her anger. Her face brightened and she smoothed her hair. 'It will be Fritz. He promised to come this afternoon.'

She ran across to the door and opened it to find him outside. Berthe got up from her chair and smiled at him as he came into the room.

'Good afternoon Herr Peissner, I hope you will excuse me, I have some letters to write.'

Fritz bowed. 'Of course.'

As soon as Berthe had gone, Lola flew into his arms. 'I have missed you so.'

He winced as she hugged him and noticing it, she frowned. 'What's the matter?'

Gently, he detached himself. 'I took a tumble from my horse, that's all. He slipped on a patch of ice. It is nothing serious, just a few bruises.'

'Oh Fritz,' she laughed, 'you are so careless. I expect you were dreaming of some philosophical theory or other. Where did it happen?'

'In the Ludwigstrasse.'

'But I was there this morning, I'm sure there was no ice.'

He coloured. 'Did I say the Ludwigstrasse? I meant the Feldstrasse.'

'You're lying to me. What are you hiding?'

Before he could protest, she undid the buttons of his jacket and pulled his shirt out from his soft leather breeches. Over his left side, she saw a mass of bruises.

Her eyes flashed. 'Who did this? You did not fall from your horse, did you?'

He hung his head. 'I'm sorry I lied to you. I got into a fight.'

'Come and sit down. I'll send for some ointment and ice.'

'No please, I don't want a fuss,' he protested, but he let her take his hand and lead him to the sofa by the window.

'You must tell me everything. I shall know if you are hiding the truth,' she said.

He sighed. 'Very well. We have been barred from lectures. When we went to complain to the rector, he said he could do nothing. Apparently, if any member of the Alemania is seen in a lecture hall, the other students will walk out.'

'That is bad, but words do not cause bruises. What else?

'We left the rector's lodgings intending to go to Rottmann's Café and hold a meeting, but on the way there, a gang of students set on us.'

He grimaced. 'I used to think most of them were my friends. Still, we gave a good account of ourselves, even though we were outnumbered three to one.'

'I shall speak to the king.'

'No, I don't want that.'

She frowned. 'Not this silly notion again that you and I are doing something wrong? I've told you more than once, the king and I are very close but we are simply dear friends, we have never been lovers.'

That was not really a lie, she reflected, for ever since that first night she had pleaded ill-health or fear of pregnancy to avoid any more intimacy and it had not seemed to trouble Ludwig.

She stroked Fritz's cheek. 'Ludwig would not grudge me happiness. It is only out of delicacy that I do not want anyone to know what you and I are to each other, but if you do not trust my judgment, I am not afraid to confide in him. Then you will see for yourself.'

He took her hand and kissed it. 'My darling, of course I trust you, but I should still prefer it if you did not speak to him. I must deal with this.'

'If you insist, then I shall do as you say.'

One morning soon afterwards, accompanied by the guards, Turk and her maid, Lola set off for her usual walk. The crisp, cold air made her cheeks glow but she felt snug in the white, fox-fur cloak that the king had given her as a Christmas gift. At the corner of the Barerstrasse, a group of students stood talking on the pavement.

'You are in my way,' she called out. None of them looked at her. She raised her voice. 'I said you are in my way.'

One of the students cast a glance over his shoulder and shrugged before turning back to his friends.

'Do you expect me to walk by in the gutter?' she shouted.

Another student sniggered and nudged his neighbour. Turk growled and strained at his lead. The students closest to him backed away.

'Cowards,' she spat, 'you insult a defenceless woman but you are afraid of a harmless dog. Just wait until the king hears of this. He will punish you all.' She flounced away down the street, leaving them glowering after her.

That evening, when she went to the theatre, she wore her most magnificent diamonds. Across the auditorium, she saw Prince Wallerstein sitting with his wife. In the stalls below, the red caps of the Alemanen bobbed like poppies in a windy meadow. She raised her lorgnette and fixed her gaze on Wallerstein. He returned the look, his patrician face a mask of disapproval as his wife whispered to him behind her fan. Lola chuckled. The elderly princess was obviously giving her opinion in the most emphatic terms. The black feathers of her headdress bobbed above her grey locks as she jerked her head about, for all the world like a hen deprived of her chicks. Well, the Wallersteins could stare all they liked. She, Lola, would not be the one to look away first.

But in the days that followed, it became increasingly hard to dismiss the hostility that crackled in the very air of Munich. On every excursion from the Barerstrasse, catcalls and whistles pursued her.

'Stay in the house, Lolita,' Ludwig begged.

Her brow furrowed. 'Must I be a prisoner then?'

'It is for your safety. It will not be for long. This will pass, I'm sure of it.'

She nodded. 'Perhaps you are right.'

But after he had gone, she let out a snort of anger. She would not allow anyone to curb her freedom. She had not exactly promised the king. If she wanted to go out, what harm was there in it?

The following morning, she had planned to visit Fritz. Unwilling to abandon the idea, she slipped out through a back door whilst the day's deliveries were arriving. On guard at the front of the house, Captain Weber and his men did not notice that she had gone. Ten minutes from home, she met Ludwig hurrying towards the Barerstrasse, his old green hunting coat thrown over his dark suit. His face was flushed and the veins stood out on like ropes on his neck.

'Lolita, what are you doing here?' Where are Weber and his men?'

She smiled. 'You see I have come this far and no one has molested me. You worry too much, Luis.'

He grimaced. 'I warned you that it is not safe for you on the streets. Today is worse than ever. Lola, you must not defy me like this.'

She ignored his anger.

'Why? What has happened?'

'The Alemania are hiding in Rottmann's Café. A mob of students is baying for their blood. I have called out the police but I must go back to the palace,' - he indicated his suit - 'when I heard the news, I was in the middle of a meeting of my ministers.'

Lola felt a stab of alarm. 'I must go to my friends at once.'

He grasped her shoulder and brought his face close to hers. 'No! I forbid it. I promise that you will be the first to be told when they are safe, but you must go home.'

She touched his cheek. 'You are so good the way you care about me, my dearest,' she said. 'If you want me to go home then I shall.' Her sudden pliancy reassured him and with a swift goodbye, he left her to return to the palace.

In the Barerstrasse, Weber's jaw dropped as she hurried past him and into the house. She flew up the crystal staircase to her boudoir. There, she changed her plumed hat for a plain, dark-blue bonnet and wrapped herself in a dark cloak. Then she ordered her maid to call for her carriage.

The girl hesitated.

'Do as you are told,' Lola snapped.

A few moments later she swept past Weber once again. Humpelmeyer, her coachman, hovered by the carriage. 'Quickly, help me in,' she ordered. 'We are going to Rottmann's Café.'

Nearing the café, Humpelmeyer saw a large crowd outside it. The noise they made alarmed the horses and they jibbed at moving on. He got down from his box and tried to calm them but they continued to toss their heads and flecks of spittle frothed around their nostrils.

Lola leaned out of the carriage window.

'What's the matter?'

'They won't move, countess. We shall have to turn back.'

'I'll walk the last part of the way. Oh, don't look so scared man, nothing will happen to me. Take the horses home and see to it that they are rubbed down and fed.'

The firmness in her voice silenced his protest. He watched as she strode off into the throng, then got back on his box and turned the carriage around. He hoped that he would not have to answer to the king for what he had done.

Outside Rottmann's, the crowd was even denser than before and in spite of the cold, the heat of packed bodies was tremendous. A thin rain had begun to fall and the smell of sweat and damp wool made Lola gag, but she pressed on. A roar went up as people recognised her. At first, she managed to shake off the hands that reached out to grab her, but step by step, her progress slowed until she was hemmed in by a heaving mass of men brandishing sticks and hurling abuse.

They are like gargoyles, she thought, so vicious that they seem inhuman. All at once she knew that there would be no reasoning with them, no chance of holding them back with the force of her scorn. She looked around for someone to help her. She wished now that she had not left Weber and his men behind.

Some of the men beat the ends of their sticks on the cobbles, chanting her name as if they were performing some sacrificial rite. *Lola, Lola, Lola.*

'I am the Countess of Landsfeld,' she screamed, trying to keep the panic out of her voice, 'let me pass.'

All at once, she heard a familiar voice at her side. She turned and saw that it was an upholsterer named Wegner who had done a great deal of work on the house in the Barerstrasse. She had recommended his son-in-law to the king and obtained him a well-paid government post. With a surge of relief, she thought that he was probably one of the few men in Munich who would still help her.

'Herr Wegner! Thank goodness you are here, but where can we go?'

'The Theatriner Church is nearby. They will not dare to follow us there.'

He stumbled as a swarthy man the size of an ox tried to push him aside but quickly regained his balance and drew a dagger from his belt.

'I'll use this on any man who tries to stop us,' he growled. 'The king has commanded me to keep the countess safe.'

The front rank of the mob hesitated. Wegner lowered his voice. 'Walk slowly, countess. Do not meet their eyes.'

Shaking, Lola stayed close to his side as they stepped through the mob. The angry roar had turned to a low grumble.

'Good, that's good,' Wegner whispered, 'just a few more paces and we shall be safe.'

But the walk seemed to take a very long time. The rain was heavy now and her thin shoes skidded on the wet cobbles. She was soaked by the time the imposing, Baroque façade of the Theatriner reared up in front of them. The broad, stone steps looked reassuringly solid as, clinging to Wegner's arm, she mounted them.

Then they were inside. But she soon realised that it would not be so easy to escape. The sound of hundreds of heavy boots ringing on the steps followed them. She froze as she heard it.

An elderly priest in his black soutane rushed down the nave.

'This is a house of God, not a beer hall,' he thundered as the leaders of the mob reached the threshold.

Overawed by the solemnity of the vast church, the invaders halted. Other priests appeared from the shadows. Together, they faced down the attackers and drove them out then swung the great doors shut.

Lola let go of Wegner's arm and stumbled down the aisle. She shivered in her wet clothes and shoes. Reaching the altar rail, she threw herself on her knees, buried her head in her hands and began to pray. It was some time before her composure returned.

Standing up, she made the sign of the cross then walked back to where Wegner sat slumped in a pew, overcome with exhaustion.

She gave him a shaky smile. 'The king will reward you for this.'

'I fear it is not over yet, countess.'

'If it had not been for you, it might have been.'

The sound of one of the great doors scraping open made them both start. Wegner jumped to his feet and drew his dagger again, but it was a group of uniformed men who came in. Lola put a reassuring hand on Wegner's wrist. 'We shall not need that,' she said. 'Those are my guards.'

Weber hurried over to her and saluted. 'I have orders to escort you to home, countess.' His voice was impassive but she saw the anger in his eyes. For once, she felt a measure of contrition.

'Thank you, Captain Weber,' she said. 'I am sorry to have caused you so much trouble.'

Surrounded by Weber and his men, they left the church and walked to a waiting carriage. Moments later, they were inside it and on the way to safety.

A week later, she sat alone in the small parlour at the Barerstrasse. The room was very warm and the pungent smell of oil of eucalyptus sharpened the scent of the beech logs burning in the grate.

After the incident at the Theatriner Church, she had caught a chill that had rapidly turned to a feverish cold which confined her to bed for five days. When she felt well enough to get up, the king had insisted that she follow her doctor's orders and remain indoors until she was completely recovered.

Ludwig had come to visit her every day to ask after her health but there had been no sign of Fritz. She sent messages to his lodgings but there was no reply. Anxiety and longing troubled her sleep and often, when she woke, fear clutched at her heart. Had he tired of her, or was he afraid of meeting the king if he came to her house?

When Mathilde Thierry arrived, her friend's worried expression made her heart miss a beat.

'What is the matter? He is not hurt or in trouble is he?'

'I don't think so, but he may have left Munich.'

'What, without seeing me first?'

'Lola, the king has closed the university. Any student whose family does not live in Munich has been ordered to leave. Most of them have already gone. The theatres are all shut up and Captain Weber told me that all army leave has been cancelled.'

Lola bit her lip. So Wallerstein had been right that unrest was coming, but she would not take the blame for it. Unless it was a crime to be Ludwig's confidante, the one who tried to help him to rule his people wisely and well, she had done nothing wrong.

She pressed Mathilde's hand. 'If Fritz is still in Munich, will you try and find him for me? I must see him.'

'I could go to his lodgings I suppose, but I am afraid to walk far on my own.'

Lola reached for the bell pull.

'I shall send for Humpelmeyer,' she said. 'He can drive you there.'

The daylight had faded by the time Mathilde returned. Her teeth chattered and Lola took her to sit by the fire.

'Warm yourself, then tell me what happened.'

Mathilde shivered and stretched out her hands to the flames. 'He wasn't at his lodgings. The landlady says he's paid his bills and left. She doesn't know where he's gone. When I pressed her, she slammed the door in my face.'

Lola bit her lip.

'I didn't know what else I could do,' Mathilde went on, 'so I thought I had better come back here. I'm sorry, Lola.'

Lola squeezed her hand. 'It's all right, Mathilde. It was brave of you to try. I'm very grateful. Go home now and rest. Humpelmeyer will drive you, but you will come again soon, won't you?'

Mathilde stood up and kissed her cheek. 'Of course. Try not to worry. I'm sure Fritz will send a message when he can.'

It was raining heavily as she left the house. Captain Weber saluted smartly but she noticed that the rest of the guards looked surly and disconsolate.

'I wouldn't be out in this weather if I didn't have to be,' one of them muttered, loudly enough for her to hear, 'but we've got our orders. Even if the swans from the palace lake swim down the street, we're stuck here, catching our deaths for the sake of the Spanish whore.'

Mathilde bridled. 'You had better not let your captain hear you say that.'

The man scowled. 'Friend of hers are you?'

Mathilde held her head high. 'Yes, and proud to be.'

Chapter 30

Ludwig was determined that Lola should hear no bad news whilst she was convalescing, but the week of disasters exhausted him. It was an additional strain that, out of concern for her, he bore his doubts alone.

Had it been a step too far to close the university? So much of Munich's prosperity depended on it. The result had been rioting in the streets every day, police headquarters attacked, window smashed and the Town Hall invaded by a mob. The Minister of War had refused to intervene and announced that if he was ordered to use his troops to defend Lola, he would take his pistol and blow out his own brains.

Ludwig groaned. Wallerstein would be arriving at any moment for a meeting; no doubt the bad news was not over.

'Well, what have you to tell me now?' he snapped when the prince sat before him, his face a picture of gravity.

'Your Majesty, my agents say that there are factions all over Munich plotting to burn down the countess's house, some threaten that they will kidnap her if she will not go of her own accord. I cannot advise too strongly that she leaves Munich immediately. It is not only for her safety. If she insists on remaining, it will be impossible to restore order. I fear there will be bloodshed.'

Ludwig bent his head and rubbed his tired eyes. 'As soon as she is well enough, I shall suggest she goes to my hunting lodge at Starnberg for a few days. She will be safe there. Perhaps I can follow her when everything has quietened down.'

Wallerstein raised his eyebrows and Ludwig felt his irritation rise. 'You have something to say about that?'

'Sir, it is my duty to tell you that the Reichstadt proposed this morning that you should abdicate in favour of the Crown Prince. In my view, if you will not break with the countess, they will not withdraw their demand. You will have no support left.'

For a moment, Ludwig froze then he recovered his voice. 'How dare they? I am their king. I shall be until the day I die.'

Wallerstein drew a deep breath. 'I devoutly hope so, Your Majesty, but I truly believe that if disaster is to be averted, there is just one choice open to you. The countess must go.'

'I cannot desert her, Wallerstein; she is too dear to me.'

'Then I cannot answer for the consequences.'

'The city is calm now,' Lola insisted, fully recovered a few days later. 'No one has come near us since that day at the Theatriner. Even then I am sure that it was just a small group of troublemakers involved. I have told the king I shall not leave Munich on their account.'

Tea had just been brought in and a good fire warmed the room. Berthe and Mathilde Thierry looked at her with anxiety in their eyes.

'I told the king that he should reopen the university too. Wallerstein's talk of revolution has been so much nonsense. The people love their king. If he shows magnanimity, all will be well. Anyway, I long to see Fritz. I think when he and the others come back I shall hold a grand party for them.'

Berthe crumbled the piece of seed cake on her plate. She has not been out in the streets as I have, she thought. There are posters everywhere calling for her to be banished and the mood is still ugly.

The sound of shouting and hurrying feet made her get up and hurry to the window.

'What is it?' Lola asked.

'I can't see much, these windows are so steamed up, but something must be wrong.'

Lola shrugged. 'It's probably nothing, just the guard changing.'

'No, there is too much noise for it to be that.'

Mathilde joined her and peered out.

'That's odd I don't think there are any guards outside. Perhaps we should send one of the servants to find out what is happening.'

Lola frowned. 'Ring the bell.'

Several minutes passed and no one came. The noise of shouting in the street was unmistakeable now. Lola marched to the doors that led to the balcony. As she flung them open, a blast of icy air rushed into the room accompanied by a roar of voices.

Berthe rushed to her side and looking over her shoulder saw scores of faces below.

She gasped. 'Come back inside, Lola. We must shut the doors. Oh, where is Captain Weber? Surely he hasn't deserted us?'

Lola gave a scornful laugh. 'If he has, I shall have him whipped, but I'll show these people I'm not afraid.'

'Lola don't, you will make matters worse.'

She tried to grab Lola's arm and pull her back but it was too late. Ignoring her, Lola was already on the balcony. A feral roar broke from the crowd and a volley of stones thudded against the railing. The blood pounded in Lola's ears as excitement surged through her. Snatching her jewelled pistol from her garter, she took aim.

'If you don't leave, I shall fire,' she shouted. A chorus of jeers and curses answered her.

She raised the barrel of the pistol and was about to fire a shot over the heads of the mob when she felt strong arms grab her elbows. Surprised, she let the pistol clatter to the floor and struggled to get free.

Captain Weber's voice hissed in her ear. 'You must come inside, countess. My men are overwhelmed. I can no longer guard you here. All the windows of the kitchens are smashed and the stores looted. The house will be next.'

Lola looked down at the street again and saw that what she had thought were clubs and knives were in fact her own gold candlesticks, kitchen irons and carving knives. Whooping and yelling, one man brandished a half-gnawed leg of mutton above his head. Another hurled a bottle of champagne that splintered against the edge of the balcony in a shower of green glass.

Suddenly, she felt a chill. These people really hated her. It was no longer a game.

Weber seized his chance and pulled her inside. He kicked the doors shut.

'I've ordered your coachman to bring the carriage to the side entrance. The mob has not found that yet, but we must lose no time, they soon might.'

Berthe was at her side. 'Please, Lola,' she begged. 'We cannot stay here. Let's do as he says.'

Lola felt her heart pound. If the mob managed to break into the rest of the house, they would all be trapped. The noise from outside reached a deafening pitch. She put her head in her hands. 'All right, I'll go,' she muttered.

'Weber breathed a sigh of relief. A few minutes later, he led the women down the grand staircase and out to where the carriage waited. Bundling them, he jumped up on the box beside Humpelmeyer.

'Get us out of here as fast as you can,' he ordered. 'All our lives depend on it.'

Chapter 31

The village of Grosshesselohe slept under a starlit sky. A week had passed since Lola had reached the inn there and Berthe and Mathilde had returned to their homes.

She had decided to go no further towards Starnberg where Ludwig had wanted her to take refuge. In Grosshesselohe, she was still close to Munich and not far from the village of Blutenberg where she had now had reports that Fritz was hiding. It still hurt that he had gone without a word, but she was sure he would explain everything when they were together again. In the meantime, she needed to speak with the king.

The clock on the tower of the village church struck five as she slipped downstairs. She found the servants asleep near the remains of the fire, huddled on pallets under piles of coarse blankets and animal pelts.

The room smelled of stale beer and sweat. Picking her way over to Humpelmeyer, she shook him awake. He grunted and sat up with a jolt, fumbling for the stout stick beside him.

His eyes rolled. Have they come for us? Just let 'em try. I'll break all their heads.'

Lola put her finger to her lips. 'Hush, no need to wake everyone. I want you to go to Munich with a message for the king. If the city is peaceful, come back and take me to him.'

'Countess, I'm not sure that is wise.'

'Let me be the judge of that. Tell the innkeeper I want him to lend you some clothes. Don't take my carriage. It's bound to be recognised. You'll have to walk.'

Half an hour later, she watched him disappear down the road to the city, dressed in one of the innkeeper's jackets and breeches. It would be past dawn by the time he got there but she doubted that anyone would recognise him. So many workmen came into Munich in the early morning.

The rest of the day passed with no news and then the night. In the morning, Lola paced up and down her rooms. What could be keeping the wretch?

When at last he came, she hurried out to meet him. She turned pale when she saw that one sleeve of his jacket was almost torn off and a livid bruise disfigured his face.

'Who did this?' she demanded.

'A coachman from the Goldener Hirsch recognised me. He and his mates set about me with their fists. It would have been worse but a couple of policemen came to my rescue.' He grimaced. 'I'm afraid they were not much gentler with me. I spent the night in the cells.'

'I'm sorry. I'll make sure you have your reward when this is over. Did you deliver the message?'

He nodded. 'I'd already managed to get to the palace when they spotted me.'

'Was the king there?'

He looked down at his feet.

'What is it? He is not in danger, is he?'

'There is talk that the king will abdicate in favour of Crown Prince Maximilian, countess.'

Lola's head reeled.

Maximilian? He detested her. If Luis abdicated, her position would be desperate.

She passed an anxious week waiting. No message came from Ludwig or from Fritz. It was too dangerous to go to Munich, she decided, but she could try and find Fritz. Her maid packed a few clothes for her and they set out for Blutenburg.

He was, as she had hoped, at the ancient hunting lodge there. He looked tired and careworn. It saddened her that he did not seem overjoyed that she had come but she held her tongue.

A week after her arrival, she sat alone in the bedroom that they shared. It was a comfortless room with damp, roughly-dressed stone walls and bare floors. The fire in the small grate belched smoke that made her eyes sting.

At least, she consoled herself, the place was cleaner than it had been when she arrived. On her orders, her maid and the few servants the Alemania had brought with them had scoured all the floors and swept out the spiders and cockroaches that lurked in the corners of the rooms and behind the dilapidated furniture. She had also made the servants tear up old sheets for rags to clean the windows and take down and beat the curtains before re-hanging them – an operation that had choked them all with clouds of dust.

She stretched and stood up then went to open the door. The draught caused another balloon of smoke from the fire as she stood and listened to the voices drifting up from the great hall below. No doubt Fritz and his friends were polishing off some more of the wine that they had found in the mouse-infested cellar.

She banged the door shut and went back to the armchair by the fire. It was no use pretending that all was well between her and Fritz. When they talked of their future together, she heard the reluctance in his voice. She was not sure that she cared any longer. She had already lost so much.

Deep in thought, she did not even notice that he had come until she heard him speak.

'I'm sorry. I hope I haven't woken you.' His voice was slurred and he swayed a little.

'I was not asleep.'

He came over to the fire and spread his hands to the flames. 'It is no warmer here than in the hall,' he remarked with a shiver.

'But you appear to have found the company more diverting,' she said dryly. He turned to face her, his brown eyes wary behind his round spectacles. He pushed a lock of dark, wavy hair off his forehead. She saw beads of perspiration there.

'Lola...'

'You think it is time we talked frankly? Did you need to drink so much wine to give you courage to tell me so?'

He reddened to his ears. Before he could say anything more, she put up her hand to silence him. 'Poor Fritz, you had a great deal to give up, didn't you? You were clever and respected. You had a bright future in Munich. I think you still do. You should go back when the university re-opens; make your peace with the fraternities and the officials. I understand the king well enough to know that he will not bear any grudges.'

He hung his head, 'But I love you.'

'And I you, but it is not enough. You would not be happy living as an exile. I shall not ask it of you.'

303

The look of ill-concealed relief on his face almost made her smile.

'I would - if you asked,' he said awkwardly.

She put her finger to his lips. 'Just kiss me. Let us have one more night for old time's sake. Then tomorrow we shall go our own ways.'

Chapter 32

Dressed in a dark coat and a soft hat pulled low over her face, Lola arrived in Munich late one snowy night. It was too cold for there to be many people about and she felt safe enough in her disguise.

The carriage stopped outside the house of the Wegner family and Humpelmeyer jumped down from his box and came to the window.

'Perhaps I should go in first, countess.'

'Nonsense, there is nothing to be afraid of. Help me down.'

At the front door, they rang the Wegners' bell and waited but no one came. She tried again.

On the fourth attempt, they heard the rasp of bolts drawing back. The door opened a crack and a maid peered out. She goggled at the sight of them.

'We wish to see Herr Wegner,' Lola snapped. 'Let us in at once.'

'What is it, Lisle?' a woman's voice called. 'Who is calling at this hour?'

Wegner's daughter, Caroline, stood at the top of the stairs. She wore her night clothes and carried an oil lamp in her hand. When she was halfway down to the hall, her hand flew to her mouth. 'Countess, is it you?'

Lola pulled off her cap. 'Yes. I need your help, Caroline. Can I come in?'

Humpelmeyer left them and drove the carriage away to a side street for safety. As Lola followed Caroline up the stairs, she did not notice the light under one of the doors on the ground floor. The policeman who lived in the apartment closed it softly and went back to his bedroom. He started to pull on his clothes.

His wife sat up in bed. 'What on earth are you doing?'

'Funny time of night for the Wegners to have a visitor. There's something not quite right about it.'

'Why should it be our business? Come back to bed.'

He shook his head and fastened his boots. 'There've been rumours that agitators plan to torch the grain store in the Wurtzerstrasse. I'm going to go down to the station to get some help'

'You're crazy. The Wegners are respectable people.'

Her husband shrugged. 'These days, who knows?'

Upstairs, Lola and Caroline hugged each other.

'Wait while I wake father,' Caroline said. 'Then you must tell us everything.'

She hurried out of the room.

'We've been so worried about you,' she said when she returned with Wegner. 'Where have you been?'

'Ludwig arranged for me to go to Switzerland. He wanted me to stay there for safety but I could not bear to be so far away. I went to Grosshesselohe and then Blutenberg. But I must see him. That's why I've come back. Will you take a message for me?'

Wegner flushed and would not meet her eyes. 'Countess, we dare not. Suppose you are found out? The city is like a powder keg. The king struggles to restore peace and respect for the monarchy. The army is on alert.'

Lola bit her lip. 'Herr Wegner, you could not blame me any more than I blame myself but I beg you, help me.'

Suddenly, they heard footsteps on the stairs.

Caroline started. 'Who can that be so late?'

'Whoever it is, we won't let them in,' her father said firmly.

But a few moments later, a fist hammered on the door.

'Open up,' a voice shouted, 'or we break it down.'

'Quickly,' Lola hissed. 'Hide me.'

Caroline hurried her to another room and helped her climb into the big, oak cupboard that stood in one corner. Through the door, she could hear Wegner's voice. It sounded as if he was talking with several men. Then she heard a scuffle and Caroline's scream. Her head sank to her knees and her arms tightened around them. Her blood froze. There was no way she could escape now.

A few moments later, the door of the cupboard swung open and hands reached in to pull her out. She blinked as she emerged into the light to see three policemen in front of her. One of them took hold of her cap and pulled it off. The shock on his face might have made her laugh if her plight had not been so desperate.

He let out a long whistle. 'My God, it is the Countess of Landsfeld.'

Pretending a confidence that she did not feel, she faced him defiantly.

'I refuse to speak with anyone but King Ludwig, do you understand? Take me to him.'

She waited for him in Police Director Mark's office. Mark, roused from bed, sat at his desk scowling. Lola had kept her silence. She refused to let him intimidate her.

When Ludwig came into the room, she rushed into his arms.

'Leave us, Mark,' he said in a muffled voice.

Alone together, she saw that his cheeks were wet with tears.

'You have come back to me,' he said in a broken voice. 'You should not have taken the risk.'

'How could I not? My heart was ripped in pieces. Do not tell me to leave you again.'

'I must, for your safety and my own.'

Lola slipped out of his arms and gave him a searching look. 'If we are not safe in Munich, come away with me. We shall talk of art and books. You can write your poetry and we shall read it together.' She stroked his cheek with her fingertips. 'We shall forget the rest of the world.'

'It is not so easy. I have a duty to my family and my country.'

She saw the sad resolution in his eyes and felt a lump rise in her throat.

'But what of us?'

'Your love will always be the most precious thing I have. I shall think of you every moment of the day. When I can, I shall come to you.'

His voice faltered. He looked grey and tired.

She took his hand and led him to a seat by the fire. For an hour they talked of the past and her heart ached for him. He had risked so much for her sake. But noting to the feelings that underlay his reassuring words, her instinct told her that it was over. They could not go back. She understood him better than he did himself. He would never desert his duty.

'After all that has been between us,' she said at last, 'let us part friends.'

He frowned. 'You speak as if it will be forever.'

She gave him a sad smile. 'Perhaps it will. Will you promise me one thing?'

'Anything.'

'Whatever people say about me, whatever happens, you'll never believe that I am all bad.'

'How could you think that?'

'We may be far apart. It is easy to believe things then.'

'Never: you and I will always be one soul. I only live to be with you.'

'But if you cannot? Promise me Luis: that is all I ask.'

He bowed his head. 'Very well, but we shall be together again, I know we shall.'

There was a rap at the door. Director Mark came in.

'Forgive me, Your Majesty, but for her safety, I must advise the countess to leave now. We do not know who else may have recognised her.

Ludwig nodded reluctantly.

'He's right, Lola. You must not endanger yourself. Mark will arrange an escort to take you to safety.'

'Very well, if you think it best.'

He nodded and kissed her forehead then turned to go.

When the door had closed, Mark bowed.

'Are you ready, countess?'

'I should like a few moments alone, please.'

He gave her a suspicious look.

She gestured around the room. 'For the love of God man, where do you think I shall escape to?'

He cleared his throat. 'I'll leave you,' he said; but she noticed that he did not close the door and remained outside.

Going to the window, she watched Ludwig walk away down the street. I am seeing him for the last time, she thought sadly.

She lifted her chin. 'Brava, Lola, brava,' she whispered. It was time to face the world alone once more; she would not be afraid.

'Director!' she called out. 'You may come back. I am ready.'

Epilogue

After her dramatic departure from Bavaria, Lola Montez became 'Lola', an early leader of the select number of celebrities whose first name alone is enough to identify them. She would spend the rest of her life in the glare of the public's curiosity and its often capricious judgments.

For a while, she resumed her affair with Peissner who still could not quite do without her, but the chaotic life they led and her wild extravagance eventually defeated him.

She spent some time in Switzerland waiting for Ludwig, but her instinct at their parting proved correct. Even though he abdicated, his fear of de-stabilising Bavaria any further prevented him from joining her.

Separation weakened his ardour and with his revenues drastically reduced, he could not afford to be too generous. Lola's dissatisfaction grew. She wanted more than the life of a rusticated mistress.

As winter approached, she left for London. She had not been there long when she met George Heald, a wealthy and impressionable young army officer who proposed marriage. She accepted but was soon disenchanted with his insipid character.

Worse still, enough people remained in London who remembered the Eliza James scandal. Heald's aunt, horrified by her nephew's plans, did not have much trouble finding them.

She launched a private prosecution for bigamy on the grounds that Thomas James was still alive in India and Lola was only legally separated from him, not entitled to remarry. This was something that Lola had chosen to overlook.

To a packed courtroom, her counsel argued that Miss Heald's proof was out of date and the court adjourned for fresh enquiries to be made in India. Fearing imprisonment, Lola fled to the Continent with Heald.

The prosecution collapsed, and the 'marriage' followed. The stress of the previous year had finally unhinged Lola. Her behaviour was increasingly erratic. After a violent quarrel, she stabbed Heald who fled for good.

Alone again, she decided to revive her career and toured America and Australia. After sacking several managers, she organised her own company and bookings. The critics were not always flattering but the public flocked to see her and the titillating *Spider Dance* became her trademark.

As she grew older, however, dancing wearied her. She turned to acting where, in spite of Fanny Kelly's prediction, she was a great success, particularly in the role of Lady Teasle in Sheridan's *School for Scandal*.

Many more lovers came and went as well as another 'marriage' to a San Franciscan journalist named Patrick Hull. Her volatile nature also involved her in further court cases where she frequently pleaded her own defence.

In her final years, she developed a fascination with the occult and studied the teachings of Thomas Harris who claimed to speak with spirits who told him the secrets of the universe and stories of the civilisations on the moon and the planets.

It was his friend Chauncey Burr, however, who became Lola's guiding light and when she decided to leave the stage and begin a career as a lecturer and author, he helped her to prepare.

Her autobiography, well-laced with fiction, sold splendidly and she was hailed as the queen of the lecture rooms. Records indicate that she made more money than that other popular lecturer, Charles Dickens, but as usual, it slipped through her fingers.

It was a broiling June morning in New York when she felt giddy soon after waking. Moments later, she suffered a stroke that left her paralysed and speechless. Helped by kind friends, she fought her disability with the same determination that she applied to every aspect of her life.

In the autumn of the same year, 1860, she received an unexpected visit from her mother, by then a widow, but it seems that there was no reconciliation. One observer described Elizabeth Gilbert as a cold and passionless woman, who greeted and said her adieu to her daughter much as she might have made a fashionable call. She seemed greatly disappointed at finding her without worldly wealth and visited her only twice in a stay of two or three weeks.

On Christmas Day, Lola felt better and went outside for a walk, but it was ill-advised. The chill she contracted developed into pneumonia. She died two weeks later, a month short of her fortieth birthday.

Eerie reminders of the cruel jibe made after Alexandre Dujarier's death that Lola's love was a curse echoed through the years.

Aged twenty-three, George Lennox died of fever shortly after his return to India.

The remainder of Ludwig's life was marred by sorrow and ill-health. His son, King Maximilian died young and was succeeded by Ludwig's eighteen-year-old grandson, another Ludwig, who earned himself the soubriquet 'the Mad'. Alienating the Bavarian people with his eccentricities, he withdrew into a dream world and spent the royal fortune building castles, including the famous Neuschwanstein, before drowning in suspicious circumstances.

Fritz Peissner went to America to become a professor of languages. He commanded a German volunteer brigade in the Civil War and was shot from his horse whilst riding up the line to encourage his troops. He was thirty-seven and left a wife and three young children.

Aged twenty-eight, George Heald met a slow and agonising end from tuberculosis and chronic ulceration of the bowel.

Patrick Hull suffered a fatal stroke not long after he and Lola parted.

Another lover, a handsome actor named Folland, who toured with her in Australia drowned on their voyage back to America after a violent quarrel. Many believed that he had committed suicide.

Only Thomas James lived into old age. In his mid-fifties, he met a young woman with whom he had several children and he eventually married her.

It is not clear whether Lola could have children herself. Possibly malaria or the methods advocated in Victorian times to avoid unwanted pregnancy affected her fertility. After her death, numerous young women came forward claiming to be her daughter, but their claims were never validated. In the end, it seems that all that Lola left behind her was her legend.

Lightning Source UK Ltd.
Milton Keynes UK
171117UK00001B/3/P